That Summer

Janis Crockett

TRILOGY CHRISTIAN PUBLISHERS

TUSTIN, CA

Trilogy Christian Publishers
A Wholly Owned Subsidiary of Trinity Broadcasting Network
2442 Michelle Drive
Tustin, CA 92780

That Summer

Trilogy Christian Publishers A Wholly Owned Subsidiary of Trinity Broadcasting Network

2442 Michelle Drive Tustin, CA 92780

Rights Department, 2442 Michelle Drive, Tustin, CA 92780.

Trilogy Christian Publishing/TBN and colophon are trademarks of Trinity Broadcasting Network.

For information about special discounts for bulk purchases, please contact Trilogy Christian Publishing.

Trilogy Disclaimer: The views and content expressed in this book are those of the author and may not necessarily reflect the views and doctrine of Trilogy Christian Publishing or the Trinity Broadcasting Network.

Manufactured in the United States of America

10 9 8 7 6 5 4 3 2 1

Library of Congress Cataloging-in-Publication Data is available.

ISBN: 978-1-68556-334-9

E-ISBN: 978-1-68556-335-6

Dedication

To my husband, Willie, who has taught me that when your heart is full of the joy of the Lord, there is no room left for hate.

Contents

Chapter 1:
New Discoveries

The freshness of the early morning air and the exuberantly cheerful birds are what lured me outdoors that morning. I made my way to the end of the porch with a thick spiral notebook tucked firmly under my arm. Once I settled myself gingerly on the porch swing, I was suddenly flooded with so many old memories, all hitting me at once. I closed my eyes and took a deep breath of the fresh country air to calm the rush of images that were overwhelming me. When I finally felt settled enough, I carefully placed the notebook in my lap, and a large teardrop plopped with a big splat on top of the notebook cover.

Earlier that morning, I had discovered my treasured notebook in an old trunk I was planning to give to the second-hand store. Just as the two teenage boys were walking away, holding a strap on each end of the trunk, I was suddenly struck with the realization that I had failed to look inside the trunk before letting them haul it off. They stopped abruptly when I hollered out to them, and then they gently rested the trunk on the floor. Seeing my struggle, they helped open the heavy lid for me. It appeared the trunk was full of old worthless papers, but I felt the need to check them all and then toss them in the trash. The sweet young boys waited patiently. At the very bottom of the stack of papers sat the crumpled edges of the old spiral notebook. The thought that I had almost sent the trunk off without checking the contents gave me a fright, the kind of fright you get when you realize you could have lost something valuable and you would have no one to blame but yourself.

It had taken me over a year to finally decide to let go of many things I had been holding onto so tightly. Memories were all I had left, and each day, those memories were harder to recall. Sometimes people would look at me with sadness in their eyes, in a pitying sort of way. When I saw that look, it made me smile. They had no way of knowing I didn't need their pity. I would tell them about a scene in the musical *The King and I* when the young ladies in the king's court were feeling pity for the new teacher, who was a single mom. She sang the pretty love song called "Hello Young Lovers," in which she shared that she once had a love of her own. The memory of her love was enough for her. I'm sure by now, people were tired of hearing me repeat that same old story.

I lifted the cover of the notebook, and excitement began to course through my veins as I rested my eyes on the familiar handwriting in the title, *That Summer*, and embarked on my journey to discover the innermost thoughts written in this precious journal. I already knew the story because I had lived part of it. The excitement was reading it for the first time from his eyes, from his heart. I automatically reached up and gently stroked my pearls around my neck out of habit before turning over to the first chapter of his side of our story.

Chapter 2:
Brent's Journey

The early summer breeze brushed our faces as we rode in the back of the large open-backed farm truck hauling us to where we would be working that summer. Now and then, a bug would slash against our skin, creating laughter or disgust from the other boys on the truck. School had just ended, and we had big plans to make money over the summer. It was my first year on the farm crew, so I was the one most chided. Many were bragging about all the cash they planned to make over the summer and all the girls they planned to snag while out from under the watchful eyes of their parents. I didn't have a choice about my work location, being my first year, so they liked to poke fun at me for getting the old widow lady at the small farm. It was readily deemed the worst job of the summer. There wasn't the opportunity to earn as much money on her small farm, and there were no young girls to flirt with all summer. There wouldn't even be other guys my age to hang out with after a hard day of work. It looked to be a very boring summer, but I was happy to be chosen for the crew nonetheless. It would be more money to send home.

"Hey, Butch," Ralph yelled in my direction. "We're coming up on your little farm." All the other guys laughed, enjoying one last poke at me before dumping me off for my long assignment away from any kind of normal summer activities. All the guys liked to call me Butch, even though my real name was Brent. They thought Butch sounded more like a farmer.

I gathered my little bag of belongings and held on tight as thoughts of this new chapter played out before me. I was fortunate to be on the crew, as good-paying jobs for young Black kids were hard to come by. With the civil rights movement spreading all across the country in the sixties, new doors were being opened, and I planned to walk through as many as I could. I guess hard labor wouldn't seem much like an open door to some people, but it beat picking cotton like I did when I was younger. The state was contributing to our salary, so that gave us an opportunity to earn more money than straight pay from the farmer, which was way below minimum wage most times. I said a little prayer when we got down the long dirt road to the farm. I hoped I would find my old widow lady to be kind and I wouldn't get too lonely over the summer.

I noticed on the drive up to the farm that her place was run-down, and the grounds were overgrown. I had worked with my dad at a landscaping nursery, so I knew how things were supposed to look when they were well-manicured and taken care of. I could see right away that my hands were going to be full at this place.

When we got to the end of the drive, we pulled to a slow stop. I hopped off the end of the truck and grabbed my bag. I followed behind the driver as we walked toward the house.

"Miss La' Shore," Mr. Turner yelled out in a booming voice.

I pointed toward the back of the house, where I noticed a woman hanging clothes out on the line while the sheets blew in the strong gusts, wrapping around her arms and legs. I looked back at the truck and saw the guys holding their sides, rocking with laughter while pointing at the lady all tangled up in the sheets. More embarrassment for me. I could hear them in my head making jokes at my expense.

Mr. Turner yelled out again, a little louder, this time waving his arm. The lady peeked her face around the end of the line of clothes and then returned his wave before pinching the last clothespin to the side of the sheet on the line. There were more howls of laughter from the truck as she picked up her empty basket off the ground and headed in our direction. She was wearing a baggy house dress, much like what my grandmother often wore. But unlike grandma, Miss La' Shore was wearing black Converse tennis shoes on her feet, and her hair was twisted in braids that hung down over each shoulder.

I looked down and shuffled my feet when she approached. "Miss La' Shore, I have your summer worker. This here's Reginald Lake, but he likes to go by his middle name for some reason, which is Brent. The guys call him Butch. I guess he will let you know which he prefers. Let me know if it doesn't work out for any reason."

"Thanks, Mr. Turner. I appreciate you bringing him all the way out here. I was still hoping for two guys, though, since I don't have my dad helping out this year. You know how lazy teenagers can be these days. All they want to do is sleep half the day."

"Sorry about that, Miss La' Shore, but you know the rules. With this small size farm, you were lucky to get this one worker, and that was only because of your dad's influence around here. You'll just have to rule with an iron fist. Maybe Butch won't be a lazy teenager. He's almost a full-grown man. He turns eighteen in a few weeks. He's lucky to be on the crew at his age. Usually, only teenagers are allowed on the crew, but since he is still in high school, he qualified."

"What's the matter?" she barked. "Did he flunk?"

"No," I said abruptly, raising my head to answer for myself. "I stayed back in first grade and repeated that year so I could be bigger and stronger to play sports."

"Oh. I never heard of that before. How'd that work out for you?"

"Great. I'm smarter than the kids in my grade, and I'm a starter on the varsity football, basketball, and baseball teams." I felt anger all over me as I stood up to her snide remark.

Ignoring our exchange, Mr. Turner interrupted while peering over Miss La' Shore's shoulder with searching eyes. "By the way, where's the man of the house?"

"Oh, my dad is in town at the doctor's office. You know he tore up his knee, and that's why I desperately needed two workers this year. Besides, he's back at his farm now that the repairs are finished over here from last year's tornado."

"You know I heard that Cleon Jarvis was interested in your place," Mr. Turner casually remarked as he flipped through the papers on his clipboard. "He says he could make a good farm out of this dump in no time."

"I beg your pardon," Miss La' Shore said, getting her feathers all ruffled. "This place is no dump, and I'm sick and tired of people telling me I should sell it and move on with my life. I'm going to make a working farm out of this place one way or another."

Apologizing, Mr. Turner replied, "Sorry about that remark. No offense. I'm sorry to hear about your dad's injury too. I just wanted him to sign off on this form so I can drop off Butch."

"I'll do it," she said sharply, snatching the clipboard from Mr. Turner's hands and quickly signing at the bottom of the form. She handed it back to him in one fluid motion, as if in defiance to the thought that only the man of the house could sign the dumb form. I could sense this lady was no pushover.

Mr. Turner turned on his heels and headed back to the truck in a huff, leaving me alone for the first time with the person I would be spending the entire summer with. Finally remembering my manners, I looked up to speak. Miss La' Shore was standing there with the clothes basket cocked on one hip.

"Good day, Miss La' Shore," I said, trying to make a good impression.

"Hi there, Reginald...or is it Brent...or maybe Butch?" she asked, shrugging her shoulders.

"I prefer Brent," I answered. "That's what my family and friends call me."

"So your whole name is Reginald Brent Lake, is that correct?"

"Yes," I responded, not appreciating what sounded like a condescending tone.

She motioned with a sideways nod of her head for me to follow her. "I'll show you where you'll be staying. I have a small garage apartment that should be okay for you." She started up the stairs that led to the apartment, with me following behind her, staring at her funny-looking shoes. When we got to the top, she opened the door, and we walked into a big open room, larger than my bedroom at home that I shared with my two brothers. It had a full-size bed, a small couch, and a little kitchen with a small table and a chair. Then, she opened the door to a small bathroom with a shower, toilet, and sink. There was an open cabinet stocked with clean towels. I stashed my bag on the floor in the corner of the room, and we went back downstairs to discuss the plan for my work schedule.

As we approached the backdoor of the old rock farmhouse, Miss La' Shore said, "Let's go in the kitchen and sit down." She opened the screen door off the porch. "I'll fill you in on what I need done this summer."

I hesitated just short of the threshold.

"What's wrong? Come on in," she said again, gesturing toward the screen door.

I looked up into the face of my employer and still hesitated. She stared back at me with a frustrated look while holding the door open wide for me to enter.

Finally, I spoke up, saying, "I'm sorry. I've never been in a White lady's house before. It's just an unspoken rule with deep-seated roots."

She tilted her head sideways, looking a little baffled as she slowly let go of the screen door and placed her hands on her hips. "I'm sorry. You'll have to excuse me. I never thought about it being a problem. You did realize that you would be working for a White woman, didn't you?"

"Yes, of course, but I didn't give any thought about going inside your house."

"Well," she sighed, "we can sit on the porch if it bothers you that much."

We sat down in the John-Deere-green-colored metal lawn chairs on the porch, and she began describing the work necessary for her to make it through the summer. "I have a large garden on the south side of the house," she said, pointing in that direction, "and I will need to have it weeded each day and have the vegetables picked when they're ready. I will keep busy most of the summer, canning and freezing whatever is ready to be put up for the winter. On the north side of the house is a large orchard, and I need it tended to and the fruit picked when they're ready. The cows pretty much take care of themselves this time of year. In your spare time, I would like you to keep the weeds away from the fence line and have the lawn cut and trimmed each week. With all the rain we've had this spring, it's been hard to keep on top of all the new growth. We will play it by ear, and I'll direct you with other duties as they come up. Of course, in due time, you'll need to cut and bale the hay and store it away in the barn for the winter. To be honest, I'm disappointed that I only got one worker this summer. With my dad unavailable, I could sure use more help." Then, abruptly, she sighed before asking, "Do you have any questions?"

"No, ma'am. I'll do my best to make up for the lack of workers. It sounds much like what I do at home. When do you want me to start?"

"Why don't you check out the garden and orchard and bring me anything you think is ready to eat and just roam around the property and see what you think of the place? That will give you a good idea of what needs to be done. I'm sorry things are not as neat as they should be. My husband is gone, and as I already stated, my dad helped me last year, but he had an accident and is not able to help out this year."

"One last thing," Miss La' Shore added as I stood up from the lawn chair to start my tour, "I usually have supper ready about five or six. You can come down and eat. I always have plenty. I want to keep you strong and healthy so you can have the energy to do all the work I need done. As you heard from Mr. Turner, no one around here thinks I can take care of this place, and I'm determined to prove them wrong."

I looked down, feeling embarrassed and a little intimidated after her earlier actions towards Mr. Turner and me. "Thanks. I'll be here. I'm not one to turn down a meal." I left feeling like a farm animal in her eyes, one she wanted to keep in good working condition, not out of concern for me but to benefit her needs.

I was anxious to start my work. I wanted to put forth a good impression and keep my job. Miss La' Shore had made it perfectly clear she was unhappy with her arrangement being stuck with just me for the summer, and I wanted to prove myself to her, much like she wanted to prove she was capable of managing the farm on her own. I also knew, being a minority, I would have to work extra hard to appear to be a good worker, but that was how I was raised by my parents. We were always taught to do our best in all that we attempted. I just hoped my best would be good enough. I knew she didn't exactly trust me, and I would have to earn her trust.

I could tell right away after surveying the property that things had been neglected around there, and it was way past time to mow. I looked in the shed and found where the riding mower was located. I checked to see if it needed oil or gas and got it ready to use. However, I decided against mowing while the freshly washed clothes were on the line. Instead, I grabbed the hoe and started my work in the garden getting out the weeds, row by row. She had not exaggerated when she said it was a large garden. My goal was to have it completely weed-free before supper. I knew the weeds would grow back as fast as I could dig them out, but I planned to stay on top of them. The job took most of the day. When I looked back over my work, I was pleased. Whenever I put in a hard day of work, I was re-minded of the Lord when He worked on His creation, and He looked it over and was well pleased.

It was getting close to the time Miss La' Shore mentioned she would be serving supper. I put away the hoe and made my way upstairs to my new home away from home. I took a shower and changed out of my dirty clothes that were soaked in sweat. I didn't have a lot of clothes in my bag, but I hoped Miss La' Shore would allow me to wash them each week and hang them out on her line.

All clean and ready for supper, I tapped on the screen door of the main house. Miss La' Shore came to the door and handed me a plate piled high with good home cooking. She must have remembered my rule, or she didn't want me in her house any more than I wanted to go inside. On the plate, there was a big pile of mashed potatoes, two big pieces of fried chicken, green beans, and a big, mouthwatering biscuit. After the hard work and the heat of the day, I thought my knees were going to buckle when the aroma of the fine food hit my nose. I started to go back upstairs to my room, but I was so hungry I sat right down in one of the lawn chairs there on the porch and started devouring the chicken leg. Miss La' Shore came out on the porch with a large glass of ice tea in her hand and placed it on the little table in front of my chair. She asked me if I needed anything before turning to go back in to eat at the kitchen table. It seemed odd but also comfortable to eat separately. I was so tired and didn't want forced conversation or, worse yet, uneasy silence. My only concern was to fuel my body. I was thinking of myself as the farm animal who needed to keep in good condition, similar to Miss La' Shore's remark earlier. Each bite of food gave me a surge of much-needed energy. In no time, I was scraping my fork across the plate, cleaning every last bite of those luscious potatoes I could scrape up.

When there was nothing left, I picked up my empty glass and plate and headed to the screen door, tapping lightly. Miss La' Shore hollered for me to come on in. Again, I was hesitant. She begrudgingly pushed back from the table and walked to the door, opening it ajar for me to hand her the plate and glass.

"Wow, you cleaned that plate good. Do you want some more? I have plenty."

"Would it be a problem?" I asked.

"No, of course not. Here, let me fill your plate again. I know how growing boys can put away food."

"Yeah, you're right. If I eat too much, you'll need to take it out of my paycheck."

For the first time that day, I heard a chuckle come out of my employer's mouth. I was glad I didn't offend her. It was good to see she had a slight sense of humor. She handed me my plate back and a full glass of tea. Once again, I devoured each bite, savoring the flavor to the fullest. When I finished the second time, I thanked Miss La' Shore for the delicious meal. She smiled in appreciation of my kind words about her cooking skills. I then left to go to my quarters up the stairs over the garage.

It was still daylight, but my body was more than ready to go to bed. It had been a long day, and I wanted to get up early the next morning and do some work before it got too hot. Before falling asleep, thoughts of my family and friends kept going through my head. I felt more homesick than I had ever felt before. I wondered if I would be able to last the entire summer away from everyone I knew. It was not like going off to summer camp for a week like I had heard the rich kids talk about before. It was going to be a long hot summer and a very lonely one. It looked like the only person I would see all summer was a woman who I had nothing in common with and who I didn't even know or like, for that matter. That gave me an uneasy feeling. The thought of actually sitting in her kitchen sharing a meal made me feel extreme discomfort. I suddenly longed for the closeness I felt at home and how casual it was to sit with family and share a meal, along with laughter and conversation about our day. How could I endure three months with no contact with what was familiar to me? It wasn't like I felt I was in prison, but it was almost worse. At least in prison, the inmates were your peers. I was in solitary confinement, and the only person I could talk to was the guard.

The next morning, I rose early just as the sun was peeking over the horizon. I quickly washed the sleep out of my eyes and got dressed for my day. I was startled by a tap on the door. When I opened it, Miss La' Shore had left a covered plate on a tray for me outside the door. She was heading back down the stairs, still in her bathrobe. Looking over her shoulder, she yelled out, "I just wanted you to have a good full breakfast to get you started on your day." Then, she quickly slipped on down the stairs. Well, at least the guard was friendly this morning.

I picked up the tray and came back inside and sat it down on the small table in my room. Upon opening the lid, I saw a plate of scrambled eggs, sausage, biscuits covered with gravy, and some orange juice. My stomach started gurgling at first sight, and I grabbed a fork out of the drawer and started in on the food before it had a chance to get cold. Every mouthful was scrumptious. I was very grateful to have the energy-fueling meal because I planned to get a lot done during the day.

My first project was to fire up the lawnmower and mow the grass. It was a big yard, and it took a while, but with the riding lawnmower, it went much faster than it would have with just a push mower. I was very careful to not run over any plants or flowers. My momma had gotten after me for mowing over a new plant she had started when I first started doing our yard at home. To me, it looked like a weed, but to her, it was the beginning of something beautiful.

After I finished mowing, I raked up the excess grass and picked it up in a bag. After disposing of the debris, I then headed to the garden. I wanted to pick the vegetables that were ready to be eaten or canned. I picked a bucket of green beans, some corn, and some nice fat ripe tomatoes. I took them all to the back porch and left them there in buckets.

I was hot by then, so I took a break and drank from the hose in the yard. I let the water pour over my head to wash away the grit and grime that had stuck to the sweat on my face. I sat for a minute in the shade of the big oak tree in the yard. Even though it was still rather early in the morning, the southern humidity made it feel hot and sticky. After I caught my breath, I got up off the ground and made my way to the orchard on the other side of the house. With my hoe, I started digging out all the weeds that had been neglected. As with the day before in the garden, I knew I would have to daily tend to weeding both places to keep on top of it all.

When I was about halfway finished with the weeds in the orchard, I had to take a lunch break. I went upstairs to my room and got out the bread and baloney Miss La' Shore had given me to have for when I needed to eat on my own. I slapped on the mayonnaise, added the meat, and poured myself a big glass of cold milk. I had never tasted such a good baloney sandwich before. It was so good I made another one, enjoying each bite slowly. After a brief rest, I felt I was able to get back to my weeding in the orchard.

As I was going down the stairs, I saw Miss La' Shore out of the corner of my eye on the porch, shucking the corn I had brought up earlier that morning. I stopped and asked if she needed any help. She invited me to join her in her work. We both sat quietly, pulling the corn husks and silks off the cobs. She had a bucket of water off to one side to toss the cleaned corncobs. I noticed how quickly her hands moved as she shucked, and I tried to keep pace with her. I kept remembering her remark about lazy teenagers. She seemed lost in thought as she quickly pulled all the debris off the corncobs. I couldn't help but observe her outfit for the day. As with the day before, she was wearing clothes that I didn't usually see on other women. She had on a pair of men's overalls with a creamy pink T-shirt underneath that looked like it started out white but had gotten mixed in with something red in the wash. Around her neck, she wore a short strand of pearls, which looked oddly out of place with the rest of her outfit. Again, she was wearing the black Converse tennis shoes. If any of the girls in my neighborhood or at school were ever seen wearing clothes like that, they would have been teased for years. They would run to avoid letting anyone see them like that. But here, Miss La' Shore was wearing them with pride, it seemed. I guess she felt she could wear whatever she wanted at home.

Miss La' Shore looked over at me watching her and shrugged her shoulders and said, "What?"

"Nothing," I said, trying to deflect from my staring. "I was just admiring your shoes. We wear those shoes on the basketball court. They're our official team shoes. I didn't know normal people wore them, especially women."

She laughed at my comment. "Well, young man, I happen to have played basketball too just a couple of years ago when I was in high school, and I wasn't about to let perfectly good shoes go to waste."

"Sounds like a good plan."

"How old do you think I am anyway?" she asked.

"I guess about thirty."

"Really," she said laughingly. "Well, I just turned twenty."

"Wow, you're not that much older than me. I'm sorry about the thirty answer. I think I figured anyone who was married and had a farm had to be much older than me. I'm still trying to grasp life after high school, so I don't have much perspective on time...or age."

"I know what you mean. When I was your age, I thought I knew it all. You couldn't tell me anything. I also thought anyone a few years older than me was ancient. I think it's pretty typical not to grasp anything beyond yourself and your normal surroundings at your age."

"I like your pearls," I said, changing the subject.

"Thanks. My grandmother gave them to me, and I wear them all the time to remind me of her. We had a special bond."

I continued to observe Miss La' Shore as she chatted while working on the corn. She was not the old lady I had imagined she would be, and she was especially not the clownish old lady that the other farm crew members thought they saw fighting with the sheets on the clotheslines. Her outfit, however, did fall into that clownish category. It was hard to get a handle on what her figure looked like in those baggy overalls, but she looked to have a thin but firm build. Her hair was unbraided today but was pulled back in a ponytail. It looked to be rather long if it were let free to flow down her back. The color of her hair was ordinary. It was a very plain brown color with golden highlights here and there from the sun. Just looking at it, I imagined it to be soft to the touch and without much natural curl, but full of body judging from the bounce in her bobbing ponytail. She had a radiant complexion that was flawless. Her skin color was a pretty golden tan with just a sprinkle of freckles on her nose and cheeks. Her eyes were what caught my attention most. They were light blue but more like an icy aquamarine blue. They looked like the color in pictures you see in magazines of a beautiful coral sea. The light blue eyes were outlined with a dark rim encircling them, which made their brilliance more spectacular. They were crystal clear, and when you looked in them, they drew you in for a closer view to seek more undiscovered qualities. There you could find hints of gray and gold. Her eyes were large and expressive, with dark full lashes. Her overall look was totally foreign to me. I don't think I had ever seen anyone who looked like her before in my life. Her dark hair and olive complexion combined with her light crystal eyes gave her an appearance sort of like the odd but captivating look the husky has. Not a very flattering comparison, but the best I could come up with.

When we finished shucking all the corn, Miss La' Shore asked me to drain the water off the corncobs and bring the bucket into the kitchen for her. For the first time in my life, I broke the rule and went inside a White lady's house. When I got inside, I nervously said, "Where do you want me to put this bucket, Miss La' Shore?"

"Just over by the sink. And you might as well start calling me by my first name. I keep thinking my mother is in the house when you call me Miss La' Shore. My name is Astana."

I felt uncomfortable, as I had always been taught to address people, especially those older than me, by their last name. "I will try, Miss La' Shore...I mean Astana...but you will probably have to keep reminding me on that one."

"Okay, I will keep working on you...unless you want me to start calling you Mr. Lake."

I laughed at the thought of her calling me Mr. Lake. "Your name is rather unusual," I remarked. "How did you come by Astana?"

"Well, my mom wanted me to be a boy. I guess she thought boys would grow up and be handier on our farm. She wanted to name me after my dad, Stanley. When I turned out to be a girl, she couldn't let go of naming me after my dad, so she came up with the name Astana. Pretty lame, don't you think?"

"No, I think Astana is a very pretty name," I responded. "It fits you perfectly. You have such unusual features, so it is only fitting that you should have an unusual name to go along with your looks."

She laughed softly, "So you think I'm rather odd, do you? I guess you're right."

"No, no," I said nervously, fearing I had been too bold with my words. After spending time studying her features, it had just popped out of my mouth. "I'm so sorry. You are definitely not odd, more like exotic."

"Hmm. I like that," she replied with a smile on her face.

I left the kitchen and breathed a sigh of relief once I got out of her house, realizing all too well that I had stepped all over myself by describing her looks as odd. Heck, even describing her looks at all was kind of taboo. I didn't want her to think I was some kind of gawking pervert. White women didn't like the idea of Black men staring at them. I was kicking myself for being so stupid. I was seeing the wisdom of keeping my distance from her because I so easily fell into a trap by describing her looks openly like that.

I immediately went back to the orchard and continued digging out the weeds. I could have sworn more weeds sprouted while I was working on the corn. For some reason, a patch of weeds was always the fastest growing crop you would ever see on a farm.

When I finished weeding, I picked a bucket of the ripe fruit and took it up to the porch for Miss La' Shore.

When I had been mowing earlier in the morning, I noticed the plush grass that grew in most of the yard. It was a strong, thick Saint Augustine type of grass, or carpet grass, as we called it. But on the side of the house, the grass was a beaten-down, thin-bladed kind, and it really took away from the overall look of the lawn. I had pulled a bunch of Saint Augustine runners all along the edge of the yard before I trimmed it, and I sat them in a bucket of water. I got out the tiller and dug up a small patch of the ugly grass, and then I raked it all down nice and smooth. Finally, I took the runners and placed the roots under the soil and then mashed them firmly with the palm of my hand. After I had placed several sprigs around the patch of ground, I got out the hose and watered the area down. I planned to wet it down every morning and evening for a while until the roots took hold. I hoped to see a nice stand of grass before I left at the end of the summer.

On my tour around the yard earlier, I noticed some sapling plants underneath the Rose of Sharon tree. There were twenty to thirty baby Rose of Sharon plants that pulled up easily by the roots. I rummaged around in the shed and found some small buckets and some potting soil. I filled the buckets up with the rich soil and put each plant in its own bucket and then sat them all out to sun on the rock wall. If they took hold good and strong, I planned to ask Miss La' Shore if I could plant them for her somewhere in her yard. They made good shade trees and had beautiful blossoms all summer and into the fall. I always loved recycling plants that were already growing freely rather than buying new plants at the nursery.

By the time I finished my gardening work, it was getting close to time to get cleaned up for the nice supper I had already imagined in my mind. My stomach was growling violently, which was rather normal for me all the time. It seemed to me my stomach was an empty pot with a hole in the bottom because I never seemed to be able to get full.

I took a shower and got into my clean clothes. Before long, I could smell the aroma of cooking coming up the stairs. I quickly took off to see what Miss La' Shore had for supper.

I could see her through the screen door moving around the kitchen, first to the stove and then back to the cabinet, preparing her food. The smell went straight to my stomach and caused me to ache with hunger. I tapped on the screen, and Miss La' Shore turned and noticed me standing outside the door. "I'll be there in just a minute." She hollered over her shoulder. A little more rustling around in the kitchen, and then the screen door opened, and she handed me out a plate full of food. It took a lot of restraint on my part to keep from grabbing that plate and shoving the food in my mouth while still standing upright, but I politely took it from her hand and went over to my chair on the porch. Ms. La' Shore came back a minute later with a big glass of sweet tea. She stopped and stared at me with her hands on what I assume were her hips hidden inside those baggy overalls.

"You hungry?" she asked.

"You bet. It smells delicious."

"I hope you like it. I made a peach cobbler for dessert from the peaches you brought up on the porch. They were getting ripe, so they were perfect for a pie."

"Oh, wow. I wasn't expecting that. I can't wait."

Miss La' Shore slowly turned back around and opened the creaking screen door to return to the kitchen table, where I heard her pull out a chair to sit down. I quickly began taking in bite after bite of the delicious meal that had been prepared, thanking the good Lord for such a treat. As my fork was scraping the last bit of food off my plate, the screen opened again, and Miss La' Shore came out with another full plate of food. "I assumed you are just as hungry today as you were yesterday," she said, half-smiling as she handed me the new plate.

"Oh, I hate for you to dirty up another plate. I could have just gotten a refill."

"It's fine. I don't mind one more plate to wash. I'm just glad you have a hearty appetite."

She took my empty plate back inside and continued working on her meal as I started in on my second helping. I was finally beginning to feel my stomach getting comfortable with the new supply of nourishment inside. When I finished every last bite of food, I stood up to take the plate to the back door. Just as I started to tap on the door, I saw Miss La' Shore coming my way with her hands full. I opened the door for her, and she came on out. She walked over to the little table by my chair and set down a small bowl with a large portion of peach cobbler with vanilla ice cream on top and another glass of tea. She then turned back toward the door, taking my soiled plate and tea glass from me as she went by. It didn't take me a second to start diving into the yummy peach cobbler. The thick gel-like juice dripped a little down my chin, still warm from the oven. My tongue stretched to lick it off. Just then, Miss La' Shore came back outside with a piece of pie for herself and a glass of tea. She sat down beside me in the other lawn chair where she sat the first day I arrived when she gave me instructions on the kind of work she needed. She had not said one word about my work or what she thought about it since I started. I couldn't help but worry about what she might think, especially since she had a prejudice against teenagers. But I stopped worrying and continued eating my delicious treat. She didn't talk as she ate, only stopping to sigh now and then, obviously enjoying her pie as much as I was.

After we finished eating, we sat back and relaxed, feeling stuffed, and we sipped slowly on our ice tea. It was a cool evening, and we had both been busy the entire day. We were comfortably full and also tired from our labor. It was a good feeling. Despite the dread I had experienced upon my arrival, I was not as miserable as I figured I would be. I was too busy to be miserable. I didn't have time to dwell on my loneliness. I knew later in the evening, though, it would be harder on me as I tried to unwind and then the thoughts of family and friends would pop in my head. But for now, I was just resting peacefully.

Miss La' Shore broke the silence. "How are things going, Brent?"

Surprised by her question, I responded, "I should be the one asking you. How do you think things are going? Am I making a dent in the work you had planned?"

"Well," she said, making me nervous to hear her answer, "you have actually surprised me. With very little direction on my part, you have stepped in and taken up the slack like a grown man would do. In fact, better than a lot of grown men I know."

"Thanks," I responded with a sigh of relief. "I was worried about what you might be thinking about my work. I gather you don't like teenagers."

She laughed, and I saw a sparkle in her crystal blue eyes that I had not seen before. "I'm sorry for that remark. My dad was always hard on us as teenagers, and he had every right to be because we did as little as possible to help out. I guess I remember those days all too well. You know it was not that long ago that I was a teenager myself, so don't take it personally."

"Is this your dad's farm, Miss La' Shore?"

"Ah...remember? Astana?"

"Oh, yeah...Astana."

"No, this is my husband's farm," she stated with no further explanation.

"Oh," I said, nodding as if I totally understood the situation. We sat quietly for a while, enjoying the coolness of the evening and watching the fireflies start to dance around the yard. Then, the mosquitoes decided to join us, and we picked up our dirty dishes and headed inside to the kitchen sink. That was the second time I had been in her house that day. So far, nothing negative had happened, but I still had a sick feeling in the pit of my stomach. It was uncomfortable for me. I offered to help with the dishes, but she insisted she could handle them with no problem. I sat my dishes on the cabinet next to the sink and then headed back out the door and up the stairs to face the lonely memories that waited for me there. I was almost thankful that my body and my muscles were crying out for rest, and I was off to sleep again without much time to wrestle with my thoughts.

For the next several days, I continued to eat my supper on the back porch while Miss La' Shore ate inside at the kitchen table. That was what was comfortable. I assumed it was comfortable for her as well.

Chapter 3

After a couple of weeks had passed, we settled into a routine. Miss La' Shore usually brought me breakfast and left it at my door. Then, she would slip quickly down the stairs, still in her nightgown. I was up and eager to grab it before one of the barnyard cats could get to it. It was always enough to get me started on another busy day. I assumed she was happy to fill me with food if I kept performing. I planned to earn my keep and do my best each day.

I would wash the dishes in my little kitchen sink and then take them down to the house before I headed out on my chores. I kept on top of the garden and orchard, tackling the weeds each day and bringing in whatever was ready for picking. I checked on the cows and made sure they were all doing well. In the evenings, I gave them some feed.

A farmer's work is much like a woman's work—it's never done. I had heard my momma say that a million times about her housework, and I could finally understand what she was talking about. If you have eyes in your head, you can't miss seeing work staring you in the face every day. The secret was to plan your work and schedule it so that everything was done in sort of a cycle, at just the right time.

I was busy working on a special project. It was one I was wishing I had not created for myself. It kept me from my other urgent chores that were in the cycle, and it used up a lot of muscle and energy. I saw some places in the main lawn that sloped and caused the water to drain away before it could soak in the grass. That was probably the cause for the bare patch on the side of the house. Down at the pond, there was a countless supply of rocks. They made it difficult for the cows to get to the water in some places, and they were just in the way. I loaded up a big wagon behind the tractor each day with rocks I gathered at the pond, and then I hauled them up near the house, stacking them at the edge of the sloped area in neat rows. Then, I would place a layer of moist, sticky soil in-between the rows of rocks to secure the rock wall. I also hauled in a little dirt from different places around the farm and filled in the sloped area to where it was now level. With the watering I had been doing in between rainstorms, the edges of the yard were looking much healthier, and the rock wall set off the lawn in a very appealing way. At least, I hoped Astana would think so when she saw it. She kept so busy I wondered if she even knew what all I was doing each day. She must have liked that I kept the fruit and vegetables coming in, and maybe she didn't have time to check on my work with all her canning.

One change that took place was I no longer made my own midday sandwiches. Astana had lunch herself, and she caught me one day my first week there and invited me to join her for lunch. That was a huge asset to my day and to my energy. She usually had sandwiches or a small meal of leftovers. I would quickly eat and then be on my way. I tried to make sure she got her money's worth out of me. I continued to take in her work attire in amazement. However odd or funny looking her clothes were to me, she managed to wear them well. She had a strong posture and a thin build, and her baggy clothes hung nicely on her.

I was busy working on the rock wall and forgot it was time for lunch. I was in the shade of a big oak tree, and I didn't want to leave. Once I got started on a project, it was hard to get me to stop. That was the kind of day I was having, even though I knew I would eventually need to stop and check on my other chores.

I wiped the sweat dripping off my forehead, and when I withdrew my arm, I saw Astana in the distance heading my way. I immediately felt insecure that she would judge me harshly for the rock wall project I had started. Her arms were full, so I jumped up to get to her and help her carry her load. As I got closer, I saw her wardrobe for the day. She was wearing faded blue jeans rolled up to her knees, an oversized man's shirt, and her pearl necklace. On her feet were the infamous black Converse tennis shoes. Her hair was tied up in the back in some kind of twist of hair, with tendrils loosely falling around her face and neck.

Astana was carrying a picnic basket of food and a blanket. When I got to her, she said, "I decided you weren't coming by the house, and I wanted you to have a good lunch."

I took the basket from Astana, and she began to spread out the blanket in the shade of the tree. Once we were seated, she pulled out a plate for each of us from the basket and then a container with potato salad in it. She opened it up and dipped out a huge helping on my plate. Then, she held out a covered basket of fried chicken for me to pick the pieces I wanted for myself. This was better than a sandwich, and it was hand-delivered. The grouchy old woman I feared I was stuck with all summer seemed to have a heart. In fact, I was beginning to think maybe she had a big heart.

I immediately started in on my plate of food. Astana ate quietly, but I could see she was examining my rock wall. "What is this?" she asked, pointing toward the pile of rocks with her chicken leg.

"It's a project I started to help with the erosion of your soil at the edge of your lawn. This rock wall is sort of like a dam, and it will hold the earth above it, and soon, the water will stay in the lawn instead of running down the road, saving you water, and your grass will look thicker and healthier in the future."

"Wow, that's a great idea. How do you know about these things?"

"I don't know. It just makes sense to me. I'm sure you've heard the old saying *necessity is the mother of invention*. I worked in a nursery when I was younger, so maybe I picked up some landscaping ideas from there."

"The wall you're constructing looks really nice. It will help the grass but also add a nice appealing look to the landscape. You are turning out to be a jewel."

"Thanks," I said shyly. I was shocked because she had not seemed to even notice my work before. I had not counted on compliments from her. I was just thankful for her delicious food each day, and I dreamed of the money I would be earning for the whole summer. I had big plans, and I knew right where I wanted to put that money.

I finished eating before Astana, so I laid my plate down in the center of the blanket near the basket. Then, I reclined on my back with my hands behind my head. I was happy I could relax for a minute. Before I knew it, I was asleep in the coolness of that shade tree. When I woke up, Astana and the basket and dirty dishes were gone. I was embarrassed and worried all over again about what she must think. I got my nice compliment from her, and then I blew it by falling asleep on the job.

I hung the blanket over a branch of the tree and began to work again on the rock wall. Right on schedule, I finished that section of the wall before it was time to get ready for supper. I stood back and admired the looks of my special project. I was well pleased.

When I came downstairs for supper, I had the carefully fold-ed blanket in my hands. I got to the door and tapped lightly to let Astana know I was there. When she saw me standing there, she hollered for me to come inside. When I entered, she said, "I think it's time to revisit your forbidden rule about coming inside a White woman's house. You've been inside a few times now, and I haven't given you any trouble. It will be easier for me if you will just join me at the dinner table." She took the blanket from my hands and motioned for me to take a seat.

I was nervous thinking of eating dinner inside the house with Astana, but my hunger outweighed my fear. I cautious-ly pulled out a chair at the table to sit down, creating a slight scraping sound on the wood floor. Once I was seated, I watched her flutter busily around the stove. She had changed out of her blue jeans and into a pretty sundress. Unlike the house dress she wore the first day I saw her at the clothesline, this dress fit her figure, and for the first time, I saw her shape and all her curves nicely arranged. Again she was wearing her grandmother's pearls. Her hair hung softly down on her shoulders. Her feet were bare. This positive change in her looks did not go unnoticed by my roving eyes.

She finally returned to the table and placed a big platter of pork chops down, along with a big bowl of mashed potatoes, and then she added a bowl of green beans and a salad. Her table was already neatly set with nice pottery, silverware, and napkins. Some flowers from her rose garden were in the center of the table in a pretty vase. When Astana sat down, she looked up and smiled at me. "This is nice, having someone to eat with."

I replied eagerly, "It all looks great."

"Brent, do you mind saying the blessing for the meal?" she asked.

Without hesitation, I lowered my head and began, "Dear Lord, how grateful we are to come before You this evening offering thanks for the meal we are about to share. Thank You for our energy and willingness to perform our work today and now for the opportunity to praise Your name. Bless this food and all we do each day. In Jesus' name, amen."

After taking her napkin off the table and placing it in her lap, Astana smiled and said, "That was such a nice prayer, Brent. Thank you."

She handed me a plate of pork chops and then passed me the mashed potatoes. After filling my plate, I followed her lead by placing my napkin in my lap, knowing my momma would be proud. Then, I eagerly ate every bite on my plate and guzzled down the ice tea. We chatted a little during the meal, and I asked more about her farm. She said it was her husband's family farm, but she had worked it alone most of the last few years.

"Do you mind me asking where your husband went?" I asked curiously.

"He went to Vietnam...and never came back. He was killed in action."

"Oh, I'm so sorry I asked you that question," I said, looking embarrassed. "It was inappropriate." Suddenly, I remembered Mr. Turner telling me the lady I was to work for was a widow. It seemed to me every time I opened my mouth around her, I stuck my foot in it.

"No, it's fine. I should have let you know right off. I just told you he was gone, so I understand why you wondered where he went. He was actually killed the first week of combat. He was so proud after finishing boot camp and was ready to do his duty. We had only been married a short time before he was drafted. A few weeks after he went over to Nam, I got news he had been killed."

"That must have been a shock," I said, stating the obvious.

"It was. But later, it occurred to me that I'm glad it happened that way. If it was going to happen anyway, at least Robert didn't have to undergo all the bad experiences of the war, and he didn't have to come home jaded and beaten down emotionally and physically and see people treating the soldiers like they were scum. He would've hated that. I guess it's just a little comfort I tell myself. Anyway, Robert was an only child. Both of his parents had passed away, so I inherited the farm when he died. It was quite an opportunity but also a challenge for a young girl of nineteen."

I nodded my head, knowing it must be hard to lose her husband at such a young age and to have the responsibility of running a farm. Then, she added, almost absentmindedly, "I often wished I had been pregnant so I would have at least had a part of him left with me."

As if redirecting the subject away from her husband, Miss La' Shore asked, "Are you planning to join the military when you graduate?"

"No, I plan to go to college first. If the war is still going on when I finish college, then I may be called to serve."

"I'm glad to hear you're going to college."

"Thank you. I've been planning it for a long time. I've saved my money for years, and my grades are good, so I have a chance at several scholarships in academics and in sports. As long as I keep my grades up in college, I can use my student deferment."

"That's great."

"Thanks. I'm very determined to change the image of most young Black men like myself who can't afford an education. It's so hard to get yourself out of that cycle, so I have to stay focused on my final goal."

"I'm curious." Miss La' Shore asked apprehensively, "Why are you uneasy about going in a White lady's house?"

I looked up before proceeding with caution, wondering the wisdom of revealing too much information. "Well, all my life, I've been told never to do that without there being a witness with you. I've heard of many Black men having their lives turned upside down because some White woman claimed the Black man did something he shouldn't have or stole something, and he didn't have a witness to testify for him. Like what happened in the book To Kill a Mockingbird. You've heard the story of Joseph in the Bible where Potiphar's wife accused him of molesting her, and he slipped out of his cloak to get away from her. Even though he didn't do the crime, he had to serve the time in prison. Who would have believed a slave? It's just a precaution. I hope I didn't offend you by being so blunt."

"No, no. I'm just so sorry about that. It's probably good advice. It's sad you can't trust people anymore. I mean, I know not everyone is like that, but there are some, and it makes it hard on everyone. I will make a deal with you...I will never accuse you of doing something you didn't do. That's just not my way."

"As long as you keep luring me in here with great meals like this one, I will probably take my chances." My remark put a smile on her face.

Changing the subject, I asked, "Is La' Shore your husband's name?"

"No. It's my maiden name. We were married such a short time, and we didn't have children, so it just felt more comfortable going by my maiden name. That's what everyone around here knows me as anyway."

We had both finished eating, and it seemed like the conversation had run its course, so I stood up and scooted my chair back under the table before picking up my plate and silverware and carrying them over to the sink. I put the stopper in the sink and started running water, making suds from the dish soap I had added. Astana brought over the rest of the dishes and then started putting the leftovers in covered dishes. I sank the dirty dishes in the sink and started scrubbing them.

"Brent, you don't need to do that."

"It's okay. My momma made the boys in the family do the dishes just like the girls. She says it's something we will need to know. I reckon she's right."

"I reckon she is too. It's nice to see a young man so at home in the kitchen."

Chapter 4

It had all the makings of a hot summer day when I took off to start my daily chores. At the bottom of the stairs, I saw Astana coming out of the back screen door. She waved me over to where she was standing barefoot, wearing cut-off shorts and a short summer blouse.

"Hey, Brent, I need to wash your sheets today. Do you have anything on your bed you want to get out of the way? I don't want to go in there stripping your bed and disturbing any of your things."

"Oh, yeah. I'll go back up and get my stuff off the bed. I've got some books spread out that I've been studying."

Astana took off toward the stairs ahead of me, leading the way to my garage apartment. She skipped lightly up the steps with me following close behind her. As I observed her from that viewpoint, my eyes roamed from her bare feet, up her legs to the swaying hips in front of my face. She was definitely not the old hag I had pictured in my mind that day I first arrived on the farm. I was glad she couldn't see the expression on my face. Being a young man with raging hormones, it was my natural response to stare. It was like a train wreck that you couldn't turn your eyes away from. She sashayed back and forth with rounded hips swelling in perfect proportion in her faded cut-off jeans that had frayed edges around each leg. Her legs looked soft and shapely down to her bare feet that danced easily up the flight of stairs. I was suddenly surprised at myself for enjoying the show right in front of my eyes. Perhaps my boredom had caused me to delight in any little distraction.

When we got to the door, Astana stood back so I could open the door. She was treating me as though this was my home instead of her own. I appreciated that little gesture of privacy. I quickly began gathering the books and papers up that were strewn around my bed from my late-night reading session the night before. Astana picked up one for me and held it up.

"Hmmm. The Bible," she remarked. "I'm glad to see you reading this."

Feeling immediate irritation, I didn't qualify her comment with a response. Again, my thoughts went straight to negative implications that she was being critical of teenagers or Black people. I wasn't sure which one angered me the most. My natural assumption was that she thought young Black teenagers never saw a Bible or maybe couldn't even read it if they did have one. She probably thought we never stepped foot inside a church. I don't know why I was allowing myself to be upset so easily over a little comment. Astana had been nothing but cordial toward me that morning. But I couldn't get those first remarks from her about teenagers out of my mind. I think I naturally always assumed people were prejudiced against my race because that was what I had experienced all my life. My earlier feelings of attraction to her just a few minutes earlier had suddenly turned into rage. Finally, after taking the Bible out of her hand and placing it with my other books and papers in a stack on the table, I felt the awkward silence deserved some sort of response from me.

"Yes, I try to read a little in the Bible each day. It seems to get my day off to a good start, and it ends my day in peace," I blurted out.

"I could tell from your prayer at supper that you are a spiritual young man," she replied while tugging at the bedspread and ignoring my rude coolness. "I'm glad to see that in you. It will be helpful throughout your life. I often think about my husband in Vietnam, and I wonder if he relied on some kind of trust in the Lord when he was away from home and scared out of his wits." Then, Astana laughed at herself as she started reaching for the sheets on my bed to pull them off. "Don't mind me. Here I go giving motherly advice. You obviously have good parents who have already started your life down the right path. Besides, I'm not that old or experienced to be giving motherly advice, maybe sisterly advice."

I felt ashamed for having had those negative thoughts earlier. I was automatically judging Astana and casting blame on her for things in my past that had nothing to do with her. I had lectured myself many times for that type of behavior and tried my best to remember to judge people for their own actions and not from past experiences. However, it was hard to follow my own advice, especially at the volatile stage of my life as a teenager. My hope was that, with maturity, I would learn to curb my reactions better. I finished grabbing the sheets off the bed for Astana and handed them to her. While she scampered on out the door and down the stairs, I stayed behind and folded the bedspread and placed it neatly on my bed. Then, I took off for the chores of the day.

Chapter 5

That evening when I came down for supper, all squeaky clean from my shower, I grabbed one of the watermelons that had ripened in the garden and brought it with me. I had not seen Astana all day after she got my sheets except briefly at lunch. I did notice the clean sheets drying on the clothesline, and then later, they were gone. When I got back to my room, they were neatly back on my bed with the bedspread all made up for me. When I saw it, I was struck with guilt for getting upset because Astana had asked me about my Bible.

I tapped on the screen as I usually did when approaching the kitchen door. Astana cheerfully invited me inside. Once again, she had a magnificent spread all set on the table. She seemed to enjoy cooking, and she said it made it more worthwhile to have someone enjoying the meal with her. I was more than happy to keep her joy flowing while filling my belly full. She had a big smile on her face when she turned and saw the nice watermelon in my hands. She took it from me and placed it on the kitchen counter.

"That's great that the melons are coming on. I love melons during the summer heat, don't you?"

"Yeah, they're great," I said. "Let me know when you're ready, and I'll cut it for you."

"Oh, I want to put it in the fridge and let it chill for a while, and then we can cut it."

I opened the refrigerator and looked for a good spot for it and then grabbed it off the counter and placed it inside on the shelf.

That night, Astana had a big pot of spaghetti, a nice salad, and some French bread with yummy garlic butter on it. I couldn't stop eating. Astana laughed at me as I tried to get the long pieces of spaghetti in my mouth. I apologized for my lack of manners but told her my hunger couldn't wait for decorum. She laughed again. I was beginning to enjoy her laughter. I also noticed that my lonely nights had started to fade. I was so wrapped up in my chores and my daily schedule that I didn't dwell so much on what I was missing at home. I just kept counting the money I was making in my head, and that put a smile on my face, and soon, I would fall off to sleep each night, a ritual that was much better than counting sheep.

As we ate, we started discussing the upcoming summer chores in our future schedule. Astana started with her plan. "You know, Brent, I've about canned and frozen all I will need for the winter. I think we should start going to the farmer's market each week and try our hand at selling what's left of the crop. What do you think?"

"That sounds like a good plan to me," I replied, appreciating being asked.

"Good. I will get the bushel baskets I have stored in the cellar, and you can start putting the different varieties in the baskets. Then we will haul them in the back of the truck to Echo Falls to the farmer's market. I think we can get a good price. All the beans, squash, okra, cucumbers, and corn are coming in nice this summer. I've made up a batch of pickles and jelly we can try to sell. Everything seems to have a better flavor this year than usual. Maybe it's just my imagination."

"Well, I've never tasted such good vegetables in my life. I'm not much of a green eater, but eating it off the garden like I've done this summer has changed my mind."

"Oh, I'm so glad you like the garden food. What kind of food do you usually eat at home?"

I swallowed my bite of spaghetti and began to describe our usual meal of good home-cooked meats that my dad brought home from his hunting trips and vegetables and sides Momma made, along with great desserts. Just talking about my momma's cooking brought back memories from home. I think Astana could see the homesick look on my face once I finished talking.

"I bet it's been hard on you being away from your family and friends this summer. I'm so sorry. I wish we weren't so far out so you could go home for visits."

"Oh, don't worry about it. My total focus is on my work this summer and making money for college. I will have plenty of time with family and friends this fall."

"I know, but it is still hard when you're actually living through the lonely times. If you want to watch TV sometimes or listen to the radio or stereo just let me know. I don't mind at all."

"That's nice of you. We don't have a TV at home. My dad thinks it has a bunch of rubbish on it that he doesn't want in his house."

"Really? I thought everyone had a TV. Tell me more about your home life."

"Well, I have a big family and two parents who love each other very much and who both work hard for their family."

"That's wonderful. How many brothers and sisters do you have?"

"I've got two of each. There are five children in our family. I'm the oldest boy."

"Do you have a big house for all those kids?"

"No, it's actually quite small. We don't even have an indoor bathroom. We have an outdoor toilet, and we bathe in a number three washtub that we put in the kitchen floor. We heat up the water on the stove."

"Wow, I thought that was only in the country. That's how we bathed before we got indoor plumbing. This is so interesting. Do you miss not having a TV?"

"Yeah, but we often visit people with a TV, and we have a blast watching it with them. Every Saturday morning growing up, our neighbors, Mr. and Miss Powers, would find all of the kids in the neighborhood watching cartoons in their house when they woke up. They seemed happy to share."

"That's so great. It's good to have a community where you can do things together. It's not like living in the country where you have trouble finding friends to play with. It sounds like all you had to do was walk outside your door and you could find a whole bunch of kids in the neighborhood to play with."

"Yeah, you're right about that. We all play together in our neighborhood, and we go to school together, and we go to church together. We're all like one big happy family."

"You know, I'm jealous of you. Growing up out in the country can be rather lonely. You'll discover that before the end of the summer."

"Yeah, I can imagine how it must have been for you growing up in the country," I said. "Do you have lots of brothers and sisters?"

"Well, just my one brother, Jack, and two older sisters."

"What are your sisters' names?" I asked.

"Maypearl and Lillybelle."

"Wow, your folks aren't too country, are they?" I said with a sarcastic laugh. Then, I worried that I may have offended Astana.

But Astana laughed in agreement and said, "You're right. We are downright country. I think they liked sticking to old family names...except for my name."

With a smile on her face, Astana stared at me for a minute. Then she said, "You have such a pretty skin color. It is so smooth and rich looking compared to my rusty farmer's tan." She placed her arm next to mine in comparison. "Do you have some other mixes in your family? I'm just curious. I hope that's not offensive for me to ask."

"No, it's not offensive. My grandmother on my mother's side was White, and most members of our family are lighter-skinned. My grandfather on Daddy's side was a Cherokee Indian, and we have inherited some of his features. A lot of us have smoother straight hair or soft, loose natural curls. My hair is lighter than most of the people in the family for some reason and almost turns blonde by the end of summer."

"Yeah, it's kind of a sandy brown color now. And your eyes are a pretty light tan color that almost matches your hair, and they have a bright sparkle in them that twinkle when you smile. I guess that's why you look so different and why you have a straight nose and high cheekbones. Must be your Indian heritage. And you called me odd? Or was it exotic? Well, you are much the same in your features. I would say you are very unique."

I smiled at her remark.

"That must have been hard on your grandmother and the family with her being White. I mean, not many people are accepting of races mixing, especially back in her day, I imagine. I remember some old lady in town explained why Black and White people shouldn't marry. She said it was the same reason that red birds and blue birds didn't marry. Even as a child, I thought that was a stupid argument. I worried about what kind of bird I was when she made that statement, and I wondered what kind of judgmental church birds got married in."

"I'm sure it was hard on my grandparents," I began. "It was probably illegal for them to marry back then, but they lived in the country and didn't have much interaction with other folks, so they were pretty much left alone. People can be cruel, and in the South, it can be dangerous to live differently. Of course, the mixing of races goes back all the way to the Bible days. God warned His children back then against mixed marriages with the people in the land of milk and honey. But I think His main concern was because of the pagan religions and not because of the races themselves."

"Did you ever hear ugly stories about the troubles your grandparents went through?"

"Oh, yes. There are many stories. But they're too ugly to relive."

"I'm so sorry," she said, sounding sincere.

"What is really sad is that it hasn't changed that much even today. My grandparents loved each other, and they were happy, but they had many trials. My grandmother was disowned by her family when she married my grandpa. Their children suffered tremendously. They sometimes didn't feel comfortable or accepted in either race. But it all worked out. Everyone learns to adapt to whatever circumstances they find themselves in. My momma survived just fine, and she grew up to be a beautiful, happy woman."

Astana seemed to be soaking in all that I had told her, mulling it over in her mind. After a silence, she wiped her mouth and placed her napkin back in her lap before speaking. "What's it like going to a segregated school?"

"Well, I guess I could ask you the same question. How was it for you going to a segregated school? It was all White, right?"

"Yes, I guess it was. I never thought about it from that perspective. We tend to think it's only segregated if all Black people go to school together and not the other way around, don't we?"

"I guess that was rude of me," I replied, apologizing. "It was fine going to a segregated school. Like I said, I've grown up in a segregated neighborhood, school, and church, so that's all I know. We've learned our place, so to speak, so we usually avoid contact with people who hate us. Of course, knowing there are people out there who hate us before they even know us is kind of creepy. It's just hard when you can't avoid being around those people. We never know if White people are friend or foe. It's that *not knowing* that can make you walk on eggshells."

"I'm so sorry you have to feel that way. No one should have to worry about how other people will react to them."

"I totally agree. But I guess if you White folks walked into a group of Black folks, you would probably do a little eggshell walking too."

Astana laughed in agreement while nodding her head. Changing the subject, she started up again, "I bet you're pretty popular in your circle of friends. I bet your teachers love you... and all the girls."

I cocked my head at her and scrunched my eyebrows together, wondering what she meant. "I am pretty popular. I get along well with friends and teachers...and yes, with the girls."

We both laughed. Then, Astana began to pump me with questions. "No, tell me more. Do you have lots of girlfriends?"

"Well, I have lots of friends. Some are girls, and girls tend to like me...mainly because I'm a good guy who treats them with respect. Also, I'm good at sports, and girls love athletes almost as much as they love musicians. But they also know I'm not available, so that makes me even more irresistible to them. I guess because I have my goal of going to college, it has made me shy away from too much fun, especially with girls. Coming from a poor family keeps down the partying. If you don't have money to go places, that keeps you out of a certain amount of trouble. I spend a lot of my free time working to raise money for college and also studying to get a scholarship for college. I guess you would say I'm driven. Girls cost money, and they cost my time. Those are two things I'm very selfish with."

"Wow, I'm so impressed. I would imagine it's hard to be so disciplined at your age...or any age, really. I'm so proud of you.

I want to keep tabs on you, and hopefully, I'll learn one day that you've become rich and famous, and you've broken the racial barrier down to the ground."

"Okay, now I'm impressed, looking at myself through your eyes."

Once again, we got a chuckle out of our conversation. That was the longest and most meaningful conversation we had had since we first met. I was relieved about it after the negative feelings I had experienced earlier in the day.

We slowly got up and started doing the dishes. It had become a regular routine for us ever since my first meal inside the house. I would start washing the dishes, and Astana would put away the leftover food and bring more dishes to me as she emptied the pots and pans. She would then take the dishtowel and dry the dishes while we continued on with our conversations. It wasn't exactly the exciting talks I had with friends back home when we talked about girls, cars, and sports, but they were nice grown-up conversations. The most exciting part of my time with Astana was noticing the transformation of her looks. She was no longer that old hag I had pictured in my mind of a featureless, strangely dressed woman in her work clothes. Now that it was warmer, she had started wearing shorts more, and they revealed legs that were rather provocative to me. All of a sudden, I could see her feminine figure. All her curves were like a winding creek intoxicating me as I navigated them. Where had she been hiding it all before? I loved when she would brush by me when she was squeezing around my back to reach a cabinet to place the dish she was drying. Her soft body felt good passing by me, but it also left a warm sensation on my skin where she had been. Tonight, she had on a flimsy white peasant-type blouse that hung slightly off her shoulder, revealing the pink strap of her bra. Just the thought of a lady's underwear was tempting to a young man my age. Her skin shone like creamy, tan silk in the dim light over the kitchen table, casting golden specks on her body as she moved about.

I usually retired to my room after we finished the dishes unless we decided to watch a TV show. But Astana remembered the watermelon and thought it would be a nice treat for dessert. I got it out of the fridge and, with my newly muscled arms, easily sliced it open with a large knife. I impressed myself and possibly Astana as well. We sat back at the table and started working on the juicy sweet melon slices. There was a lot of slurping going on, followed by a few giggles. Astana sprinkled salt on her melon and suggested I try it. She said the salt brought out the natural sweetness of the melon. Much to my surprise, I agreed with her. I ate so much I started to worry I might be up all night going to the bathroom if I didn't stop.

While we were still sitting at the table, Astana started a conversation, probably stemming from finding my Bible. "Do you miss going to church since you're not at home?"

"Sure. That's always been a big part of my life."

"Would you like to go into town with me on Sunday so you can attend church?"

"Let me think about it. I've never attended a different church other than my home congregation. Thanks for the offer, though."

"Well, keep it in mind."

Astana stood up from the table, so I scooted back my chair and stood up too. She picked up the plate with the watermelon rind sitting in a puddle of juice and headed toward the sink with it. I guess her bouncy step caused the juice to slosh backward over the edge of the plate and soaked her thin white blouse, and then it began to travel down toward her leg. The cold liquid shocked Astana, and she let out a squeal followed by a demand for me to grab the dish towel. "Quick, Brent, take my plate so I can wipe the juice off my leg before it gets on my clean kitchen floor. It's impossible to get up something sticky, and I hate walking on a sticky floor."

I quickly responded by grabbing the towel and twirling back to exchange the towel for her plate of rinds. I could see the juice traveling down her thigh and heading toward her knee. Astana immediately swooped the towel up her leg and thigh to stop the damage and then dabbed at her soaked blouse over and over.

By the time the floor was deemed safely rescued, we were both laughing hysterically. I placed Astana's messy plate of rinds carefully on the counter. When I turned back around, I saw Astana still gently blotting the moisture off of her blouse with the towel. All the while, she continued to laugh and fuss at herself for being such a klutz. I just stood and watched. The soaked blouse began to reveal more of her feminine figure, and I felt uncomfortable staring, but I couldn't stop myself. I started to take my leave, but Astana suddenly tossed me the soaked towel and asked me to get her a washcloth out of the drawer and wet it for her. When I approached her, she took the wet cloth and started washing her leg. She had protected the floor, but she had not relieved the sticky feeling all down her leg. I should have left, but I felt frozen watching Astana slowly wash up and down her leg. Until that moment, I had not completely noticed the beauty of its shape or the soft texture of her skin. My hope at the moment was that my glancing stares appeared to be nonchalant. I prayed my inner thoughts were not written all over my face. Right there, that hot June evening, I probably saw more female flesh than I had in all of my seventeen years of life. Unfortunately, the hurried activity to save the floor prevented me from enjoying it the way I had always pictured it in my mind. Nonetheless, it was a pretty sensational experience.

When Astana finally finished cleaning her leg to her satisfaction, she looked up to see me still standing there. I suddenly felt foolish. She probably wondered why I was still there in the middle of her kitchen staring at her, but she didn't mention it. I went to the sink and quickly tossed all the rinds in the garbage before washing the sticky plates.

When I finished, I turned back around to see Astana continuing to dab at her blouse, "I'm sure you want to get out of those sticky clothes, so I'll head on up to my room. Thanks again for another wonderful supper."

"Thanks, Brent, for helping. Don't say you haven't been fully warned about my klutzy ways and you will want to steer clear of me in the future when I'm handling anything messy." She looked down at herself draped in the wet clingy fabric and laughed, shrugging her shoulders and shaking her head in disbelief.

"Okay," I said clumsily. "I've been fully warned." I looked down at my shuffling feet for a minute and then looked up with a smile and said good night.

When I got to my room, my heart was racing and not from the stairs. Surprisingly, my simple experience that night had stirred something inside me. I tried to analyze my feelings, but it was difficult to evaluate. I had already begun to notice the subtle changes in my attitude over the last few days. What I couldn't understand in my own mind was if the changes were because of my solitude over the short time I had been there. Had my isolation skewed my thinking or changed the way I reacted to things? I couldn't help but wonder if Astana was experiencing any changes in her feelings. She was hard to read, so I could only assume she felt nothing special toward me.

I had also noticed that my Bible reading had developed a much deeper meaning than ever before in my life. Again, I wondered if it was due to having so much quiet time. The words seemed to penetrate my brain and reveal their meaning more clearly. Surely those changes could not be bad, so why should I feel uneasy about my closer, deeper feelings that were developing for Astana?

Chapter 6

When I opened my eyes the next morning, I had a big smile on my face, but it was suddenly wiped off with the thought that I had no one to share my excitement with. It was my birthday, and I was turning eighteen that day. How I wished I could be home celebrating it with my family. They would greet me at breakfast with special wishes for my day, and in the evening, they would shower me with gifts after a delicious special meal and a birthday cake. Far away from home, my special day would be nothing special. Just a full day of work. At least I knew I would get a good meal, and that was always a treat. I tried to settle my mind down like I normally did in the disciplined way I had chosen to live and remind myself that all I needed was work to pay for college and a better life for myself. Nothing else mattered. No need for friends. My family could wait. They would always be there. Just a little more time, and I would have them with me all the time, and I would then be praying for some peaceful quiet time away from them so I could study.

Astana was a little late that morning bringing me my breakfast, and I decided to head on out to start work before it got too hot. When I opened the door, I was startled to see her standing there in her nightgown. She was also startled and let out a little squeal. She handed me my tray and shyly backed away and then quickly ran down the stairs yelling out behind her, "Good morning."

I hollered out good morning to her, too, before she got out of earshot. When I lifted the lid on my tray, there was a mound of pancakes with butter melting and running down the sides. There was a small pitcher of syrup to pour over the cakes, and I dug in without any hesitation. I washed it all down with a tall glass of cold milk. It felt wonderful to have a big meal to get me started. It made my lonely birthday feel a tiny bit special.

I quickly rinsed off the dishes in my sink and then put them back on the tray to carry down to Astana. By the time I got to the screen door, she was dressed and fiddling with her hair that was slipping out of the twisted knot she had at the back of her head. She saw me through the door and quickly opened it for me, taking the tray from my hands.

"Thanks for the great breakfast," I said. "It will fill me with plenty of energy this morning."

"Yeah, at least for a few hours, and then I will need to add more fuel to your fire," she said with a big smile on her face.

Out of the blue, I couldn't help but say what was on my mind ever since I opened my eyes that morning, "Today is my birthday."

"Really. How great. We'll have to celebrate."

"I turn eighteen, so you can't complain anymore about me being a lazy teenager."

We both chuckled. "Hey, I stopped complaining after your first day here. I saw right away that you're no lazy teenager.

You're a full-grown man, and it shows in all the work you've done around here."

That put a big smile on my face. "Thanks. That's the best birthday present I could get."

"You're very welcome. I consider all your hard work a gift to me and my little farm."

I flashed a bigger smile on my face and then excused myself to leave and earn those birthday compliments. My first chore each morning was to check the garden and the orchard to rid them of any new weeds. Then, I picked anything that was ready for picking and placed them in the baskets on the porch so they would be ready when we took them to the farmer's market in Echo Falls at the end of the week. After my morning chores that day, I started mowing the yard. With the new grass I started and with the special watering and attention I was giving it, the grass seemed to grow overnight. Keeping everything trimmed and manicured made the farm look fresh and well kept.

After putting the lawnmower away in the shed, I noticed a rickety old pickup truck pulling up in the long drive to the farmhouse. Astana came running out when she heard the loud motor rumbling as it got closer to the house. An old man on crutches got out of the truck with the help of an attractive older woman. Astana grabbed each one of them and gave them a big hug and then started heading toward the back door with her arm linked through the lady's arm. She saw me out of the corner of her eye heading across the lawn, and she waved me over.

"Brent, these are my parents, Stanley and Anita," Astana said when I arrived. "Mom and Dad, this is my summer helper, Brent Lake." I stuck out my hand and awkwardly shook Mr. La'

Shore's hand off to the side of his crutch and then reached for Mrs. La' Shore's hand responding, "Nice to meet you both."

"Dad, have you noticed how nice the place looks now? Brent has done so much work, and he has made enormous improvements in the short time he's been here."

"Yeah, I could tell as we were driving in," Mr. La' Shore responded in a positive tone. "Even your mom noticed how nice things look."

"Come over here and see Brent's special project he's started for me." As they headed to the side of the house, Astana motioned with a wave of her hand for me to join them, so I tagged along. "See the nice rock wall Brent built to hold the lawn in place and stop all the erosion from running off down the drive. See how nice the grass looks now."

Astana's dad was impressed. He stooped down, leaning on one crutch, and ran his hand over the grassy area. "Wow, this is nice. How did you get it growing like this, Brent?" Mr. La' Shore asked.

"Oh, each week when I mow, I find runners of the Saint Augustine grass, and I pull them by the root. Then, I transplant them in the soil over here in the old beaten-down grass, which probably happened over years of erosion. I have also added some potting soil, fertilizer, and water. It has taken off really well, and I think, over the years, it will completely take over the old grass."

Mr. La' Shore stood there staring at the grass while shaking his head in amazement. Then, Astana walked over to pick up one of the Rose of Sharon starter trees in a bucket that was sunning on the rock wall. "Look at this, Dad. Brent also pulled up all the saplings around my old Rose of Sharon tree and started new ones in each bucket. He said soon he would plant them somewhere around the farm. I have always loved their beautiful blooms, and they make nice shade trees in the summer. If he keeps this up, I can start a nursery out here," she added with a laugh.

Her dad took the bucket and examined it closely, and then looked over at me. I wasn't sure what he might be thinking. I was uncomfortable being scrutinized so closely. After a short pause, he said, "Wow, young man. You have a gift, it looks like. Thanks for helping out our little girl. She is precious to us, and she has had a rough time, so we really appreciate all your help."

"Thanks, Mr. La' Shore. She's been a pleasure to work for."

"Well, I have to be honest, Brent. When I first heard Astana was going to be out here all on her own, I was a little leery of some young man hanging out here, maybe taking advantage of her young age and not putting in a full day's work. God has answered our prayers by sending her a reliable young man."

"Thanks. I try to be."

Astana continued to show her parents how nice the grounds looked. I excused myself, telling her I needed to dig out some rocks that had backed up the creek. I figured the recent rainstorm washed the rocks into the creek and wedged them in tightly. Mr. La' Shore picked up on my news and sounded interested in going with me, so I climbed on the tractor while he got in his truck, and we headed out to the creek. He agreed with my assessment and gave me the go-ahead to pursue the project. He offered to help, but I told him he should stay put. I didn't want him to further injure his knee.

Once the rocks were clear, Mr. La' Shore suggested we go look over the hayfield and see how that was doing. It was obvious Mr. La' Shore was a natural-born farmer, and he had helped Astana out on her own farm as much as he could. He apologized several times for not being there for his daughter now when she really needed him. He said he was very proud of her for doing as well as she had, considering she was doing it mostly on her own.

When we pulled back up to the house, I put the tractor away. I checked it all over before I left, making sure it would be in good working order the next time I needed to use it.

At lunchtime, Astana invited me inside to join her and her parents for lunch. She had a leftover ham meal with potato salad and garden vegetables. They all laughed at my healthy appetite. I just smiled and kept on eating. Astana brought up at the lunch table that today was my birthday.

"Well, happy birthday, Brent," Mrs. La' Shore said joyfully. Mr. La' Shore added, "I wish we would have known it was your birthday. We would have brought you a big cake and some gifts." I thanked them all for their generous thoughts, especially considering they had just met me.

Mr. La' Shore addressed his daughter more seriously as they were leaving after lunch, "You know, Astana, I was worried because of the gossip in town about you being out here with a young man all summer. I'm so glad I got to meet Brent, and I can tell them all where to stick their gossip."

Astana let out an easy laugh. "Oh, Dad, don't worry about it. You know full well how small towns are. If they didn't have gossip to spread around, they would make something up. Brent and I are going to start bringing in some of the leftover fruits and vegetables from the garden and orchard to the farmer's market, so that should cause a few tongues to wag. But I don't pay them any attention. They gossiped about Robert and me for years since we started dating so young. Every other month, they were declaring me as pregnant. What a disappointment I must have been to them with their wild imaginations."

Mr. La' Shore laughed, knowing that it was typical of small towns and a lot of what Astana said had some merit. "Well, once they meet this fine young man, they will stop making up stories."

"Yeah, that's wishful thinking, Daddy," she remarked laughingly, knowing the truth about small-town gossip. "We can always dream."

They all hugged, and Mr. and Mrs. La' Shore got in the old truck and headed on home. I went back inside and started doing up the dishes quickly. I still had a lot of work to do in the afternoon, so I didn't want to waste much time inside. Astana thanked me for the help but released me from kitchen duty so I could get to my work.

As I worked in the afternoon, I thought a lot about the warm reception I received from Mr. and Mrs. La' Shore. I figured they would be suspicious of me, just like the people in town, and they might be wanting to inspect me. Maybe that was what they did, but I seemed to have passed their test if that was their intention.

When my work was finished, I took a little extra time cleaning up and pretended it was a special day just because it was my birthday, fully expecting a normal supper to be waiting for me.

When I arrived, I saw that Astana had taken a little extra care to her appearance. She was wearing a pretty flowing sundress and had washed her long hair and was wearing it down in soft curls. As usual, her outfit was different with her pretty dress and her grandmother's pearls, but there she stood in her bare feet. She looked all-natural in a special sort of glowing way. She had prepared a roast for dinner. I told her that meal was usually set apart as our Sunday meal back home, and it was always special to me. She excitedly said, "Good. I'm glad I found one of your favorites since it's your birthday meal."

I looked over at her with a surprised expression on my face, not expecting that she had prepared something special for my birthday. Then, she added, "I even made you a birthday cake."

"Wow, thanks. You didn't need to do all that."

"Oh, it was nothing. Once you start cooking, it's not all that hard. I want to make some homemade ice cream after we eat, to have it with the birthday cake. You will have to use your muscles and crank that old ice cream freezer."

"No problem. I don't mind working for my birthday surprise," I added with a sarcastic laugh.

Astana laughed a hearty laugh that filled me with excitement, like it really was a special birthday for me, especially after I had figured on such a sad day.

As was the case at every meal, I first said a blessing over the food. Astana was always impressed with my words. I told her they came from my heart and were given to me by God. With my upbringing and my Bible studies all my life, I found it easy to thank God for His blessings in my life. It was never a chore to do so. I thoroughly enjoyed each bite of my birthday supper.

Astana even had some homemade rolls and roast gravy. It was all so good and filled my mouth with savoring flavor.

Over the weeks that I had been working on the farm, we had eased into comfortable conversations as we ate. Astana was always interested in hearing about how it was for me growing up in the segregated South. I enjoyed hearing about her life as a small-town country girl. It had finally reached a point for me where I was no longer worried or concerned about being in her house. Except for the first day when she had looked down her nose at me, she had stopped posing any threatening kind of behavior toward me. I would probably always be somewhat suspicious and cautious because that kind of fear had been bored into my mind since childhood. I know my parents were trying to protect us, but it also put up a roadblock that would be hard to break.

After eating our great meal, I began stacking the dishes and taking them to the sink as usual, and Astana started putting away the leftovers. Later, she came to the drainer and picked up each dish and dried it off. While doing the dishes, we talked about the homemade ice cream we were looking forward to. She said she had already mixed the cream and had it in the cylinder in the ice cream freezer on the porch. All we had to do was add the ice and rock salt and start cranking. We hurried up with the dishes so we could get started on the special treat that was ahead for us.

Astana added the ice and salt as I cranked on the handle. As the ice melted down, she would add more ice and salt and the crank became harder and harder to turn, showing the ice cream was forming into a thicker mass. Later on, the handle became more and more difficult to turn, and the ice cream freezer began to dance around. Astana sat down on it to hold it steady. Her back was up close to my face, and I took in the clean sweet smell of her body and hair. I noticed the slight scent of baby oil and also of coconut oil, which must have been in her shampoo. I closed my eyes and just breathed while enjoying the fragrance. When I opened my eyes, Astana was laughing as she picked up the tail of her dress to keep it from dragging on the dirty floor of the porch. I could instantly see the soft curvy shape of her legs and, for the first time, noticed how pretty her feet were dancing around as I turned the handle in my effort to get the ice cream to harden. I had never liked cranking the ice cream freezer before, but this time, I was hoping it would go on much longer so I could enjoy the view and take in the sweet smell of Astana. When she got really tickled about something, she would lean back even closer to my face and made my birthday even more special with her touch.

Finally, Astana announced that it must be firm enough and I could stop cranking. My right arm was sore, but it was a pain that would remind me later of my joy that evening, not so much the joy of eating the ice cream but of making it.

Astana lifted the cylinder out of the ice and took it to the kitchen sink. She opened up the lid and pulled out the wooden paddle, scooping a bite of the sweet vanilla ice cream to her mouth with her finger, and she smiled broadly. Then, she offered me a bite from her finger to see if it met my approval. I timidly licked it off, causing a stir when my lips wrapped around her finger. Astana went to the laundry room and came back carrying a beautiful cake with white frosting on it and eighteen candles, along with the scrolled words that said "Happy birthday, Brent." She also had some roses decorated around the edges of the cake in a rainbow of colors. I was quite impressed with her artistic abilities in making the beautiful cake. Then, she went to the refrigerator and got out a bowl of fresh strawberries that had been soaking in a sugar mixture. She said I could add them to the cake or the ice cream if I wanted. Even though I didn't have my family to celebrate my birthday with me that summer, it didn't matter. In comparison, with all the work my mother always had to do and with so many children, I had never had so much attention paid to just me before in my life. It was going to be a birthday I would never forget.

After lighting the candles, Astana started singing "Happy Birthday," and I made a wish and blew out my candles. Then, she cut the cake and placed a piece on a plate for me and added some nice creamy ice cream on the side. I added a few strawberries while waiting for Astana to fill her plate, and then we both started in on our treat. We worked hard every single day, so it was a treat for both of us. At first, we ate in silence, enjoying the rich flavor.

We sat at the table for a few minutes with big smiles on our faces. It is amazing how good food can be so satisfying. Finally, we cleaned up the last of the dishes. I was preparing to go back upstairs for bed, but Astana stopped me by taking hold of my wrist when I walked by her. "Wait, I have another surprise for you."

"What?"

"It's your birthday, and you're far away from all your family and friends. You need a birthday gift."

"No, you don't need to do that," I protested.

"Don't worry. It's not that much, really. Come here with me."

Astana started walking through a doorway that led to the hall that led to her bedroom. I had never stepped past the kitchen, so once again, I was hesitant, and my heart was pounding. But she took me by the hand and led me further into the depths of her house. I hoped she didn't feel the pounding of my pulse as she held onto my hand. When we got in her bedroom, there was a stack of men's clothes spread across the bed. "These are some of Robert's clothes. You and he are about the same size, and I thought it would be good to give them to you, especially since I didn't have anything to give you for your birthday."

"Are you sure you're ready to give them away?"

"Yes, I'm sure. They held a strong attachment for a long time, but it's time to let go. I kept some of Robert's special memories, but you can better use these clothes than to have them hanging in the closet getting moth holes in them."

"They are really nice, and I certainly can use them. I'm sure you're tired of seeing me in the same old clothes every day. Thanks so much." I had a strong urge to reach over and hug her, but I refrained. I knew that would be inappropriate.

Astana stroked her fingers over some of the shirts. Then, she looked up at me and said, "I thought you might even want to wear one of these and go to church with me some Sunday. What do you think?"

"I think I would love to go to church with you, but I'm not sure how I would be accepted in this small town of yours."

"What do you mean?"

"Surely you know that Blacks are not welcome in many places around here. Back home, I know which places I'm allowed to go, but I'm not sure here."

"Oh, it will be fine, I'm sure. No one will think anything."

"Okay, we can try it, but I just wanted to put out that warning to you. Thanks for inviting me."

Astana smiled and started picking up the clothes, one at a time, laying them across her arm. Once they were all stacked neatly, she tried to transfer them over to me. In the process, the clothes got tangled up, and so did our arms. As usual, she got tickled at the confusion we were making with the simple task. I was surprised when we both looked at each other, and a flush came over my whole body in a quick second. I could instantly feel my heart racing. We were standing face to face, eyeball to eyeball, with our arms tangled up with each other. The feel of her skin against mine caused a shudder. I don't know if she felt anything. I assumed it was nothing to her, and I tried to untangle our arms and retrieve the clothes without embarrassing myself. Eventually, we managed to escape the grasp of our arms and the twisted clothes, and we stepped back a foot from each other. It took all I had to break my stare from her beautiful crystal aqua eyes and excuse myself to go up to my room. I couldn't believe how heavy my feet were as I tried to turn around and trudge out of her bedroom and walk down the hallway. It felt like the length of a football field. All the while, I kept thanking her for the clothes and for the birthday special meal and cake. The pounding of my blood in my ears kept me from hearing any departing remarks she might have been saying.

Once I got up the stairs and in my room, I tossed the clothes on the bed as well as my body, stretching out on my back across the whole bed. Every thought of that night that came into my head caused that same flush to come over me, wave after wave, and I didn't want it to ever leave. It was a sensation that kept a smile on my face for a long while as I tried to calm myself down. Then, I felt silly allowing my body and my emotions to get so carried away over someone who probably didn't give me a second thought. Eventually, I got up and put the new clothes away in some drawers. I washed my face and got undressed and slipped under the covers.

I found myself going to bed much earlier since I arrived on the farm and had been doing so much manual labor. Usually, I would drift off to sleep in no time, but that night, I started making myself think back on my family and friends back home. For weeks, I had tried not to think about them because it made me too lonely. But that night, I wanted to think about them to get my mind off the beautiful old widow lady who lived down-stairs, the lady I was growing fond of over just a few weeks. All my school years, I had been so disciplined at turning away from the thrill of the girls at school who were always chasing after me. My goal of college kept me on track. But suddenly, my discipline was slipping away from me. I wanted to get it back. I knew I would not be able to do a good job if my mind was con-centrating on things other than my work. It did help settle me down some to reel my mind back to my hometown and my fam-ily. I started thinking about the courses I was going to study when school started and the football practice that would drain my physical energy. Then, I started in on my nightly prayers.

I turned it all over to God and let my mind drift off to sleep with no guilty conscious about the flutters in my heart that had made my eighteenth birthday so special.

Chapter 7

When I woke up the next morning, I decided to get started back to my work as soon as I finished eating breakfast. Work was what would ground me and get my bearings back; I was convinced. Astana had pulled me to her emotionally so tightly I could hardly breathe. Not that she had done it intentionally; it was all one-sided and yet so strong. I had never experienced that kind of power over me by another individual in my life, and in my controlling nature, I had to break away from it. I took my dishes downstairs after breakfast but just left them on the porch table outside and went straight to my work. I knew it would be haying season soon, and I had many projects that needed my attention before that big job hit. I would be preoccupied for days when we started cutting and baling the hay. Mr. La' Shore had told me on his visit that his son would bring over the equipment to do Astana's fields after he finished his own fields, and he had a crew of men who would help. I was very happy to hear that bit of news. I was a hard worker, but I was no farmer, and I didn't have the training or the instincts to know how to handle a big job like haying season.

The rest of the week, I physically wore myself out. All the hard labor helped pull my thoughts off my emotional state.

But at times, the solitude would allow thoughts to slip into my brain, and it was a struggle to keep them at bay. Thoughts of the softness of Astana as she brushed past me at times or the touch of her hand as she led me down the hallway in her house or the smell of her freshness as she sat on the ice cream freezer would enter my mind and soon take over my body. Then, I would imagine her laughter in my ears, and I sometimes had to stop my work and sit for a minute or two and allow my senses to take over for a while, and I would actually enjoy them. I called them my work breaks. But I knew they were not good for me if I wanted to get my control back and keep on track to my goals for my life. I would then shake loose my thoughts and get back to work as if to say, "Break time is over."

At mealtime, Astana and I still talked and laughed at each other's stories. I tried to keep my conversations on the work I had done that day, but it was way too natural for us to slip into talks about life and our feelings, and soon, we would be telling stories that were touching. While we were doing the dishes one night, I could tell Astana was in a pensive mood as I watched her slowly drying a dish over and over. Eventually, she got around to talking about how it was when Robert was there. "You know I miss so much having Robert here making the decisions about this place. All I ever wanted was to be his wife and to be a mother. Now, I'm neither." She sighed and then seemed to realize she had thoroughly dried that one dish, and she put it away on the shelf. Then, while drying another dish, she continued her conversation, "You know we weren't married a year when he died. We never even had our first anniversary."

Looking over at her with sincere sympathy, I said, "I'm so sorry. I know that was not how you planned it."

She looked up at me and smiled a bittersweet smile. "Yeah, you're right. That's not what I planned. It can get really lonely. I mean, living in the country on a farm is lonely anyway, but living on one by yourself and making all the decisions is very lonely." She turned and put another dish on the shelf.

"I'm sorry, Astana. I can imagine how hard it is. I can see all the work that's needed around here. I don't know how you manage to make the decisions and how you live out here all alone. But you have to give yourself some credit. You're doing a great job."

"That's so thoughtful of you to say, Brent," she said with tears in her throat. Then, she laughingly apologized, stating that kindness brought her to tears much faster than harsh words ever could. "No one seems to notice what I do around here or what I sacrifice. And you already know that many big farmers want to take over my place. They would love to wear me down and buy it from me for next to nothing."

"I've heard mention of that," I said with a laugh. "I hope you show them. I hope you don't let them wear you down. Land is very valuable, and as more and more progress moves into the area, this land will be very profitable one day."

"I know, but it won't be if I can't keep up with the taxes and if I can't make a living out here. I guess I will just hang on as long as I can."

I drained the water out of the sink and wiped down the countertop. Astana put the dish drainer under the sink and then hung the dish towel over a rod to dry. For a minute, we just stood there staring at each other, Astana with sad eyes and a dejected stance. I don't know what got into me, but I reached out to her, and she came into my arms for a comforting hug. For the first time, I realized how much taller I was than Astana and how nicely she fit in my arms. I had been so good to keep my distance from her, and there I stood with my arms wrapped around her in a tight embrace. I could feel a little jerk from her as she let out a small whimper, and I could feel some tears leaking from her eyes through my dampened shirt. When we pulled apart, she wiped away her tears and laughed at herself, saying she was being a cry baby.

"No...don't say that," I said with a smile.

We walked over to the couch and sat down before Astana responded in a sweet, soft voice, "Thanks, Brent. You don't know how much I needed that hug. It has been an extra hard day for me. Saturday will be the anniversary of Robert's passing. I have thought about him a lot lately and have needed him so much."

"Oh, I didn't realize. No wonder you're so down."

"I just don't feel like I've been a good wife...or maybe I should say a good widow to him."

"What do you mean by that?" I asked.

"Well, I was just nineteen when he died, and we had been away from each other most of our marriage with his basic training and then his travel over to Vietnam, and I don't think I ever grasped the true sense of his death or got the closure I needed. It's like I am still waiting for him to come home. I mean, I've moved on, obviously, but I'm just in some kind of limbo, not knowing which way to turn. I know I must sound crazy to you."

"Of course not. You don't sound crazy at all. Death is hard for a wife of many years. I imagine it's even more so when you are so young. You haven't really had a chance to live your life. You graduated, got married, and then before you knew it, you became a widow. Someday, I hope you get a chance to live your own life and live it to the fullest. You deserve that." I reached over and patted her hand.

When I looked into her eyes, tears were streaming down her cheeks. I wanted so much to take her in my arms and comfort her, but I was afraid. I just gently placed her hand in mine and continued to pat it softly with my other hand.

After a thick swallow of the lump in her throat, Astana spoke and said, "Brent, that is the kindest and most encouraging thing anyone has said to me since Robert died. People were all wishing me well and telling me how sorry they were, but no one had ever encouraged me to live for myself, and no one had ever said that I deserved to do that. For the first time ever, I feel a nudge in some sort of right direction with your words of encouragement."

With a smile and a soft sigh, I said, "I'm happy if I said anything that will help you feel better. I will say it again. You definitely deserve it." More tears fell from her eyes, and she leaned her head on my shoulder as I draped my arm around her back. We remained there a while, taking it all in. My hope was that something good came out of the closeness we felt there, sharing a moment with each other.

Chapter 8

Friday morning, I got an early start on the work around the farm because I knew later in the afternoon we were taking the fruits and vegetables to the farmer's market in Echo Falls. When I arrived back at the kitchen, I was happy to see the nice lunch Astana had spread out on the table. She had made open-faced roast beef sandwiches over toasted homemade bread, all covered with warm brown gravy. She had some sliced onions, cucumbers, and cantaloupe on the table and, as always, a tall glass of ice tea. Just as we sat down to eat, her phone rang, and it was Mrs. La' Shore calling. Astana instructed me to go ahead and eat while she chatted. When she returned, she informed me that her aunt was in the hospital.

"I think we will stop by and visit her when we finish at the market today. Do you mind?"

"Of course not. Whatever you need to do."

"I wish I had a gift to bring to her. She's my favorite aunt, Dorothy."

"Why don't you bring her one of the Rose of Sharon potted plants we have out at the side of the house waiting to be planted? You could wrap some nice wrapping paper around it or a bow, and then she would have something to plant in her yard when she goes home that would always remind her of you." I continued shoving food in my mouth as she pondered what I said.

"That could be a great idea. I'll check in my storage closet and see if I can find a nice bow for the plant. She would love that. Thanks for thinking of it."

"Oh, no problem. You could name it her *Rose of Dorothy* plant."

Astana laughed and said she loved that idea.

After we cleaned up the kitchen following lunch, I went around to the side of the house and found the nicest looking sapling plant I could find and I cleaned up the pot and then added some water to the plant so it would be nice and fresh. When I brought it to Astana, she was coming from the back of the house with a pretty purple checked piece of wrapping paper that covered nicely around the pot and flared out in triangular edges at the top. Then, she tied a purple ribbon around it, forming a pretty bow to one side. She was thrilled with herself and said, "Wow, Brent! Look how beautiful. It looks like I picked it up at the florist shop in town. But it will mean so much more to my aunt, knowing it came from my farm. Thanks again for thinking of this idea."

We quickly loaded the bushel baskets that were full to the brim with different fruits and vegetables in the back of Astana's pickup truck. She gently placed the decorated plant in the middle of the bench seat of the truck alongside some jars of pickles and assorted jellies. Then, she handed me the keys and asked if I would mind driving to town. I was happy to oblige as long as she gave me the directions. I had never been to Echo Falls before.

Astana said it took about fifteen minutes to get to town. We were a bit excited to be leaving the farm. I had been there a month and had not stepped foot off the premises. As we were driving along, I thought of another idea I wanted to pass by Astana. "I got to thinking last night after our talk about Robert, and I was wondering what you would think if we went by the local nursery in town and bought a tree for you to plant on the farm in Robert's honor. It might be something that would help with your grief. You could watch it grow and talk to him when you water it. It might ease some of your pain."

Astana sat there quietly, but I could tell she was processing the idea in her head, maybe imagining how it would be. Then, she looked over at me and said, "That sounds like a wonderful idea. Thank you so much, Brent. I can't wait to go pick one out when we finish visiting Aunt Dorothy."

When we arrived at the market, several trucks were pulling up, looking for the best stand to set out their wares. We found one that was in the shade of a large oak tree, and we were very happy to get it. I unloaded the bushel baskets and quickly placed them on the stand. Astana started placing them in a decorative arrangement. She had brought a pretty red table cloth that she swirled around the baskets to draw attention to her stand. She had made signs with the prices for the different varieties and stuck them to the baskets. In one section of the stand, she set out all the jars of jelly and pickles. Now, we were all set.

Before long, people from town were strolling by examining the different items the farmers had brought to town. We were pleased that many headed straight to our stand, and we decided it was the bright red table cloth that attracted their attention. I spoke in a friendly way to each person as they approached our stand, and I welcomed them to look around. When Astana saw people she knew, she introduced me to them. Some folks she would grab and hug, and I assumed they were close friends or relatives. She got especially tickled when some of her old classmates came by the stand, and they spent some time catching up. Before long, we had sold all the fruits and vegetables we brought, and many folks asked if we planned to bring more to market the next week. Astana assured them we would bring all we had until the harvest ran dry. I was surprised, but most of the people she introduced me to reacted nicely toward me. I also noticed that there were quite a few Black folks walking around the market and around town. That was good to know. It always felt strange when I was the only one. It made me feel like I stood out from the crowd, and that was never my thing... to stand out.

As we were loading up the empty baskets in the back of the truck, I heard the sound of a loud motor pull up. When I turned around, I saw a beautiful red and white Corvette convertible that was polished and buffed so clean it almost blinded your eyes when you looked at it. A young man got out of the car and headed toward Astana. She began a conversation with him. I could tell he was showing off his car, but I didn't catch if Astana was all that impressed. When I walked over to where she was standing to get a better look at the good-looking car, Astana introduced me to her high school friend, Jackie Jarvis. She explained to him that I had been very helpful with bringing in the harvest this summer. I stuck out my hand, but Jackie ignored it. He just stared at me a minute. I spoke and said, "Good to meet you, Jackie." After a nudge from Astana in his ribs, he responded with, "Hi there."

"That's a beauty of a car you have," I added as I slowly withdrew my hand.

"Yeah, it's pretty hot-looking," he agreed, rather dismissively.

I walked around and looked at it from all angles and tried to imagine having a beauty like that to drive around my hometown. Even though I was disciplined in my actions, it never stopped me from dreaming now and then. I decided to leave Astana alone to visit her friend, so I excused myself and said I would wait in the truck. Astana stopped me and said, "No, I'm ready to leave. We have a lot to do if we're going to the nursery and the hospital." Walking away, she turned and waved goodbye to Jackie dismissively. When we got to the truck, I went to the passenger side and opened the door for Astana before getting the key out of my pocket and going to the driver's side to get in. Looking back, I noticed Jackie pouting dejectedly.

When we got to the hospital, I hopped out of the truck and ran to the other side and opened the door for Astana. She seemed very unaccustomed to having the door opened for her. I told her my parents had trained me well and it was something expected of us. Then, I added, "It's my way of showing the public that I am a well-mannered young man. When you know people are suspicious of you, it makes you want to go the extra mile to prove them wrong." Astana looked at me and then nodded her head, understanding where I was coming from. Then, I added, "Or they might think I'm your chauffeur," which prompted a laugh out of Astana.

When we arrived at the hospital entrance, I opened the door for Astana and then greeted some folks coming out with a hello and a wish for a blessed day. We asked the room number for her aunt and then made our way down the hallway until we found it. Aunt Dorothy was all smiles when she saw Astana coming in with the pretty plant. Astana had a wooden tongue depressor next to the plant sticking up out of the soil with the words *Rose of Dorothy* painted in a pretty lavender color. She was so pleased and felt it was extra special with that personal wording attached to it. Astana turned to me and said, "Aunt Dorothy, this is Brent. He is helping me out at the farm this summer."

"Nice to meet you, Brent. I've already heard good words about you and the wonderful help you are giving our precious Astana out there. Thanks so much."

"Oh, it's nothing. Nice to meet you, Dorothy. I hope you are able to get out of here real soon."

After a few more comments Astana and Aunt Dorothy quickly began to chatter, and her aunt filled her in on the trouble she was having and what all the doctors had planned to do to her while she was in the hospital. After a short while, Astana said we needed to head on home before it got too late.

We stopped at the nursery and enjoyed walking around, looking at all the plants. I helped Astana pick out a good solid tree that I knew would hold up in hot and cold weather and would be there as a reminder of Robert for years to come. I also asked if she would mind if I picked up some potted plants and some potting soil. I had some ideas I wanted to try, and I needed more plants. I got a big pot of orange lilies, a flat of impatiens, and some white daisies with deep violet centers. Then, I spied some white lantana, some beautiful irises, and some daffodils. I promised Astana she would love my surprise when I finished it.

As we were driving through town on our way home, Astana came up with an idea. "Why don't we go get something to eat before we leave, and that way, I won't have to cook supper?"

I was slow to answer. I didn't think she would want to hear what I had to say. Finally, I had to speak up. "Astana, I doubt very seriously if they will let me in any of the café's in town."

"What?"

"Apparently, you have not had many Black friends in your life. We're not usually allowed to eat in regular restaurants. In my hometown, we have one street designated for Blacks, and that street has one café on it, and that is the only place we can eat at in town. We have our own doctors, dentists, barbershops, and everything else right there on that one street. We can't associate with White folks in town."

Astana clutched her chest, looking shocked like the wind had been knocked out of her. "I can't believe it. That's crazy." Then, she motioned for me to pull over to a little drive-in restaurant. When I came to a stop, she told me to wait, and she hopped out of the car. She walked into the restaurant and ordered some hamburgers, fries, and milkshakes. When she came back out with her arms full, she quickly got inside the truck and started laughing hysterically. Soon, I was laughing right along with her like we had just pulled off a big heist, and we quickly made our getaway.

When we got back to the farm, we brought our food inside and started eating away. It was a little later than our usual supper time, so we were starved. The hamburgers were a special treat, and the fries and milkshake topped it off nicely. We still had some birthday cake leftover, so we added dessert later on.

We talked a lot about how well things went at the market. Astana remarked how friendly I was all day to everyone I saw, even the guy mopping the floor at the hospital. That surprised me, and I told her my parents raised us to always speak to people and to be friendly. I talked about the beautiful Corvette, but Astana said she was not that impressed. She then went on to tell me that Jackie was the son of Cleon Jarvis, the man who was so intent on buying her farm. Jackie had liked her since elementary school, but she had always had her eye set on Robert. Since she was a widow now, Jackie had been trying to hang out with her more, and she knew he brought around his fancy new car to the market to try to impress her. She said she wasn't buying any of it, though, and didn't pay it much attention.

"Well, that explains why he was so cold to me when I talked about how nice his car looked. Most guys are eager to talk to anyone who will listen when it comes to their fancy cars. He's probably not too happy knowing I am staying out here on the farm his dad has his eye on...and with the girl he has his eye on."

"Yeah, maybe that's what my dad was talking about when he told me there was some gossip going around town about me being out here all on my own and having a farmworker living here. Now that they've seen how good-looking you are, they will really be talking. There was no problem before when my mom and dad were staying here. But now that I'm on my own, it's a whole different story." Astana sounded disgusted with the thought of people gossiping and making up stories about her.

I decided to change the subject and hopefully change Astana's mood a little, even though I had enjoyed her remarks about my appearance. "Are you friends with some of those migrant workers I saw at the market today?"

"Oh, sure. A lot of them have been coming here for years during the summers, and some were my playmates when we were growing up. In fact, while you were putting the baskets back in the truck, Lorena, one of my friends from the migrant camp, came up to me and asked me about the handsome young man I had working with me. She was looking you up one side and down the other. I think she wanted to throw you in the back of their truck and take you home with her."

"That's funny. Did you tell her I'm not interested in girls, that I am plowing my way to law school, and I have blinders on to keep me from being distracted by girls like her?"

"No, I didn't warn her. I didn't want to shatter her dreams," Astana said with laughter in her voice. I started up again out of curiosity, "It looks like the migrant kids and adults fit in with the other folks around town."

"I guess you could say that. I mean, they don't get too close because they will be leaving again at the end of the season, but they are usually welcomed the next year. People seem glad to see each other. Why do you bring that up?"

"I don't know. I just didn't feel that welcoming vibe toward me, and I wondered if it was the same way with all the Black farm workers that come to work on the farms."

"I'm sorry. I thought my friends seemed happy to meet you. It was your first trip to town, so maybe you need to give it some time. By the way, did you happen to see any of your buddies from the farm truck this afternoon?"

"I don't think so. I saw a few Black guys hauling barrels to the different stands, but I didn't recognize them. However, I didn't get a close look at the guys on the farm truck that brought me here. They were too busy laughing at me, so I turned my back on them."

"Why were they laughing at you?" she asked, and I winced for opening my big mouth. Astana kept prodding me for an answer.

"Well, they were making fun of me for being the unlucky one who got the assignment of your farm."

"Why did they laugh about that?" she asked with a raised voice, perking up with curiosity now.

"The obvious reason was that your farm is smaller than the big ranches some of them were headed to. But also, they knew you were all alone, and they figured it would be very lonely out here with just one woman. Since you were a widow woman, they thought you would be old and grouchy. They like to work on crews at the bigger ranches, and also they like to work for big families, especially families with cute teenage daughters."

"Oh, now I get why they would think you should be disappointed in getting me and my farm. I'm sorry, Brent. I know it's been hard with no one to hang out with. That's important for guys your age."

"No, I'm fine. Of all the guys on that truck, I am the one most suited for this assignment. Because of my laser focus and my self-discipline, I can handle the solitude better than they could have. And by the way...I'm not disappointed."

A slow, satisfying smile crossed Astana's face as she said, "Well, I tell you what, let's make a habit of getting to town more often and letting you have some fun. We don't have to hang out here every waking minute."

"To tell you the truth, I was too tired the first couple of weeks to think about hanging out anywhere but my bed."

We both laughed in agreement, and Astana replied, "Well, things should be slowing down some. Of course, it will be a rough few days when Dad and Jack bring over the hay equipment and we start cutting and baling the hay, but for the most part, you and I have this place under control now, thanks to all your hard work."

I smiled, enjoying her compliment and her company. We finished eating and then put away our trash. We were happy we didn't have dishes to do that night since we were more tired than usual after the long afternoon.

Astana asked me to stay awhile and watch *The Man from U.N.C.L.E.* with her on TV. That was a nice way to wrap up our Friday night.

Chapter 9

I woke up bright and early as usual and got ready for the busy Saturday I had planned. I wanted to get the plants out that I had Astana purchase at the nursery, and I also wanted to plant the tree for her. When she brought me my breakfast, we chatted a minute, even though she seemed embarrassed standing there in her nightgown. I suggested that we plant the tree after we ate our supper in the evening. I wanted to make it special for her. My hope and prayer were that the tree would help her with her grief and she could always look at the tree and visit it when she was having a hard time dealing with her innermost thoughts about Robert.

As soon as I dropped off my dishes in the kitchen, I took off. My plan was to do some landscaping at the entrance of her farm, at the very beginning of the long drive leading to the house. I had already dug up some crepe myrtle trees that had been growing in spots too close to a fence or too close to a more mature tree and had them in pots of topsoil waiting for transplanting in the perfect spot. I figured one on each side of the drive would be perfect.

Once I got two big holes dug and the trees transplanted and packed back down, I started making rows for some of the new plants Astana had gotten. The front row closest to the road was a row of daffodils. They were no longer blooming because they were the earliest flowers to bloom every spring, but they would be ready and waiting next spring. Right behind the yellow daffodils, I planted a couple of rows of purple irises. One row was shorter and had deep purple blooms with black edges, and the next row was taller with purple and lavender blooms. They were usually the next things to bloom after the daffodils. Behind that, I made some mounds of dirt around the new crepe myrtle trees and planted the white lantana. The white would show off the irises and daffodils with their colorful blossoms when they were in bloom and also the dark pink color of the crepe myrtle trees. I did the exact same theme on the other side of the driveway entrance. All the plants were native to the area and were hardy. They bloomed early during the spring rains, so there was no need for a sprinkler system out there. I was finished by noon and headed back to the house to eat the lunch I already knew Astana would have prepared for us.

After lunch, I started on another landscaping project on the side of the house near the rock wall I had built. I got out the impatiens and hauled them to where I wanted them planted. Then, I hauled the topsoil Astana had bought and mounded it up at the edge of the rock wall before planting the impatiens there in clusters that would grow in heaping mounds of brilliant colors and drape a little over the edge of the wall. It was shaded there by the oak tree that had covered me while I worked on my rock wall, and impatiens do well in the shade. I thought Astana might want to plant her tree on the new grassy area there that I had planted. I could picture in my mind how beautiful it would be in future years to come as things began to grow and mature around her farm. I saved the other plants to show Astana how to transplant them into more pots, and in the future, she would have more potted plants to put around the patio and in the yard. The lilies and the daisies were great for that project, and she would be rewarded without a lot of effort when she saw her garden multiply in future years.

After I cleaned up the areas where I had done the planting, I put away my tools and checked the garden and the orchards for any new fruits or vegetables that were ready. We had picked it pretty bare the day before, so there was not much of a haul. After dumping off what I found on the back porch, I headed up for my shower.

When I got out of the shower, I started to put on one of Robert's shirts but then decided that tonight was not the right time since we would be planting his tree later on. I put on one of my few choices of clean clothes that Astana had seen on me many times since my arrival.

When I entered the kitchen, I noticed Astana was wearing shorts. She had a pale, creamy yellow-colored blouse on that was soft and flowing as she fluttered around the kitchen. I marveled at how the pastel yellow went so well with her coloring, both her natural skin color and her hair but also her beautiful aqua eyes.

I sat down and said a blessing over the food, and we started in on our meal. Astana asked what all I did during the day, and I told her about my project. She wanted me to take her on a drive down to the end of the road so she could check it out after we finished the dishes.

I think we were both kind of anxious to get to the tree planting, so we hurried through the dishes instead of standing around talking for any length of time. Before planting the tree, we hopped in the truck and slowly bounced down the bumpy dirt road to the entrance of her farm. I parked the truck, and we both got out to inspect my landscaping work. I was a little worried about what Astana would think about it. She might be upset that I wasted so much time on something that was not needed. Or she might not like the design I picked out. Maybe she would have wanted to design it herself. So many thoughts were going through my mind as she walked around with her hands on her hips, looking at it from one angle and then another. I kept looking down at my feet, wondering how she was going to react to my project. Finally, I had the nerve to look up in her direction, and she had a big smile on her face.

"Oh, Brent, how beautiful. How did you think of it? I've never given much thought about how the entrance should look. You've made it look spectacular." She ran over and gave me a hug. When she pulled away, I started describing how it was going to look next spring when the yellow daffodils would open up first and then the different big purple blooms of the irises. Then, I pointed out how the white of the lantana made the bright pink crepe myrtle blossoms show up more brilliantly. She was beaming, and I could see her picturing it all in her head. Then, she said, "Maybe one day, I will make a big sign to go over the road with a name for this place. I have never given any thought to what I might call it, but now, looking at this beautiful entrance, I will start coming up with some ideas."

We got back in the truck and drove down the long drive to the house. I could tell the mood was changing for both of us. We were excited about planting the tree, but it would cause Astana to draw back on her memories of her life with Robert and on the significance of that day when she lost him. From her remark of not being a good widow, it made me think even more that something like this tree would help her feel more like she had properly mourned her husband. I had already carried the tree to where I thought would be a good spot for it and dug the hole over on the side of the house. When we walked around the house to the side yard, Astana saw the beautiful mounds of impatiens and immediately lit up with a big smile. I asked her if that spot for the tree worked for her, and she nodded her head. I pointed out why I thought it would be good there, and she agreed with me. We both took hold of the tree by the trunk and lifted the root ball into the deep hole. I handed her the shovel and asked if she wanted to put the dirt back in the hole. I held the tree steady while she worked. Once completed, we stomped around the base of the tree to firmly stake it in a nice straight line. I asked Astana if she had any more of that ribbon she put on the potted plant for her aunt, and she said she did. I waited while she went inside to look, and she soon returned with a small piece of the purple ribbon.

"Why don't you tie the ribbon on one of the branches," I instructed, "to commemorate this anniversary of Robert's death? When you come out to visit the tree, you can be reminded of this day. Each year, you can add another ribbon on another branch, and after a long period of time, you will see the ribbons growing higher and higher in the tree and further away from you. You can watch your grief change as the ribbons fade in the rain and sunshine, indicating your healing process. But each brightly colored new ribbon will remind you of your continued love for Robert."

By then, Astana had placed her hands over her mouth, trying to muffle her sobs. I gave her some time to let it all sink in. After a minute, she slowed down her flow of tears and raised her face to look at me before wiping the lingering tears away. "Brent, this is so special. I never imagined you had such a touching ceremony in store for me. This is just what I needed." She reached over to a branch at her eye level and tied the purple ribbon around the branch into a pretty bow. Then, we backed away to look at the new tree with the sun beginning to set behind it. Astana sighed and held her hands across her heart. I opened my Bible and found a scripture to read. I just flipped through psalms for something meaningful and found Psalm 32:1–2 and read, "What happiness for those whose guilt has been forgiven! What joy when sins are covered over! What relief for those who have confessed their sins and God has cleared their record." I had gathered from listening to Astana talk about Robert before that maybe she felt he had not been in the right place with God, and I wanted her to feel that all things were okay. It was settled, and his record was cleared. He was with God.

I closed the Bible and walked closer to Astana and put my arm around her. She rested her head softly on my shoulder.

In a soft, low voice, I said, "I thought if I have time before I leave at the end of the summer, I would like to build you a bench so you can come out here and drink your coffee in the morning or come out any time and visit with Robert."

"Thanks, Brent," Astana said with a sniffle caught in her voice. I nodded my head and then left her alone to spend some time reflecting on her life with Robert.

Chapter 10

I was in a deep sleep when I heard a tapping on my door Sunday morning. I got out of bed and slipped into my jeans before opening the door. Rubbing the sleep from my eyes, I noticed it was Astana there with my breakfast tray. I guess I must have overslept since it was Sunday, and we didn't put in a full day's work on Sundays. "Good morning," I said with a croaked voice. When my head began to clear, I took the tray from her hands. Instead of running down the stairs like she normally did, she stood there looking a little sheepish in her cotton nightgown blowing in the summer morning breeze. I began to feel embarrassed myself standing there with my bare chest. I sat the tray down on the table near the door where I usually ate my breakfast and then returned to find Astana still standing there. "What's up?" I asked as I crossed my arms in front of my chest. "Do you have some chores for me this morning?"

"No, not exactly. I was just wondering...would you be interested in going to church with me this morning?"

I just stood there and stared over her head off in the distance for a minute, plotting what I should say. Then, I hemmed and hawed around, kicking my toe at the knot in the wood floor, trying to come up with some excuse. When I looked into her pleading eyes, I couldn't say no. "Okay. What time do we need to leave?"

"Not until ten o'clock."

"Okay. I'll be ready by then. I hope I won't embarrass you. I don't have a fancy suit to wear."

"Oh, don't worry about that. We go very casual around here. This is farm country, you know."

Astana smiled and then turned to leave. I sat down to eat my breakfast with lots of thoughts going through my mind. My first thought was whether or not Astana was in for a rude awakening. What if they didn't allow me inside their church building? How would she take it? I had tried to warn her, but she seemed determined.

After breakfast, I looked through Robert's clothes Astana had given me. I wondered what shirt and slacks he would pick to wear to church. I tried on a few and then chose some tan cotton slacks and a brown and white checked shirt. I tucked the shirt in but felt uneasy because I needed a belt with it. I got out a towel and buffed up my best pair of shoes, the ones I wore in the evening when I had supper with Astana. They were actually boots, but they were a nicer pair of boots than my work boots. I looked at myself in the mirror and brushed my teeth and then ran my fingers through my clean hair. I noticed it was getting a little fuller since I had not had a haircut since I arrived. I had cut it really short before I left home, so it was not shaggy yet. I kind of liked the new look. Longer hair had become more popular over the last few years, especially after the arrival of the Beatles to America.

Once I felt I was as polished as I could get, I went down the stairs and up to the familiar kitchen screen door with my breakfast dishes. I made a tapping sound and then saw Astana coming from the back of the house like a heavenly vision, all decked out in a nice Sunday dress that showed off her figure. It was that same soft yellow color that was so flattering on her, and it had a scooped neckline that revealed her slender neck, smooth shoulders and showed off her grandmother's pearls nicely. For a change, she was wearing tan sandals instead of bare feet. Apparently, shoes were mandatory at her little country church. Her skin glowed from the summer sun. Astana smiled when she saw me standing in the doorway and asked me to come on in. Looking me over, she seemed pleased with how Robert's clothes looked on me. I guess I made a good choice from her expression. I hoped wearing them didn't cause her to dwell on Robert too much and remind her more of her loss, but she seemed to be beaming, so I guess it didn't trigger any depression. "I'm sorry; I don't have a nice enough belt to wear with these pants. Mine is so worn you can hardly tell what color it was originally."

Astana laughed and said, "I should have thought of that when I gave you those clothes. Let me go find you a belt." When she came back, she had a nice brown leather belt that looked as though it had hardly been worn, like it was brand new from the store. I quickly threaded it through all the loops and then buckled it up and was ready to go. Astana grabbed a wide-brimmed straw hat sitting there on the table by her purse. She handed me the keys again, and we got aboard the pickup truck and headed to Echo Falls, me with fear rising in my heart.

We were both full of energy that morning with our heads on swivels looking back and forth at the different farms and scenery all around. It was a beautiful summer morning, and we were enjoying the drive to town. I kept glancing over at Astana looking so fresh and pretty in her Sunday best. The hat was a nice touch and showed off her exotic features. She also looked over at me several times, and I caught her smiling when we made eye contact. Finally, I asked, "What...do I have something hanging out of my nose?"

She laughed her carefree laugh and said, "No. I was just admiring how handsome you look. You could be a fashion model the way you look in those nice clothes. I hope maybe you can wear them when you go to college soon. I like your hair now that it is fuller. It flatters you." She gently stroked her slender fingers through the strands of hair over my ear, causing me to shudder.

"Thank you," I said, brushing my fingers through my hair. "I haven't paid much attention to my looks this summer. It's kind of nice to have an opportunity to get dressed up for a change." I looked straight ahead, trying to dodge the chug hole in the road. Then, I turned back and added, "You look very nice today."

"Thanks, Brent. I'm happy to have a reason to dress up a little too. I've been so busy I haven't made it to church like I used to. That sometimes happens to me in the summer. I'm so busy, and by Sunday, I just want to rest." Then, as a sad afterthought, she added, "It's also hard to go to church alone. Thanks for agreeing to go with me today."

"Oh, I'm happy to go with you. I go to church every Sunday at home. My only concern is how I will be accepted when we get there. You need to know there may be a problem."

"I find that hard to believe. That doesn't sound very Christian to me."

"Exactly."

Astana directed me to the little church in Echo Falls. It was a community non-denominational church called Friendship Holy Church, where most of the town and those from the surrounding farms attended. I got out quickly so I could get to Astana's door before she opened it herself. It was hard to get my feet to move forward after that. They felt weighted down. I didn't want to crush Astana's naïve, trusting heart. I threw up the imaginary wall I hoped would protect my feelings and said a silent prayer. Then, we walked side by side up the steps and into the foyer of the church, where members were standing around visiting before the service began. Many people greeted Astana eagerly, as it had been a while since she had attended church services. They seemed happy to see her again. She immediately turned toward me and introduced me to her friends. Once again, I did not get a welcoming vibe. In fact, it was more like the parting of the Red Sea the way people were quickly scattering away from me. There were no handshakes or welcoming nods. I spoke first to each person, greeting them with, "Good day. Happy to meet you." But most of the people just stared in my direction, giving me a skeptical look as though I had already stolen a songbook or money from the collection plate. When we started to enter the auditorium to find a seat, one of the older ladies from the congregation, a large busted woman with bushy white hair, took Astana by the arm and pulled her aside. I could hear her conversation because I was standing right there. She didn't bother to hide her remarks from me or anyone else within earshot. "Astana, dear, what are you doing bringing that in here?"

Astana, in her spunky way, came right back at her. "What do you mean that? Are you talking about my hat?"

"No, don't be silly," the old lady said. Then, she pointed her crooked boney finger directly at me as I stood there, taking it all in like I was a manikin in a store with no eyes or ears as she sputtered with droplets flying and repeated the word, "That!" Then, the old lady added, "They have their own church at the edge of town. He should go there."

"Excuse me, but he's my guest. That would be rather inconvenient, don't you think? What about all the sermons I've heard here that said God loves all of us? If Brent's not welcome in this so-called church, then I'm not welcome either." After a moment's hesitation to catch her breath, Astana added, "And by the way, y'all need to take that *friendship* name off your building."

The old lady looked shocked that Astana would speak to her in such a tone, and from the look on her face, she seemed certain Astana was making a colossal mistake if she walked out that door. Several other church members stood around with their mouths open, but none of them offered Astana any support. I noticed Jackie Jarvis standing there off to the side with a man, whom I assumed was his dad, Cleon Jarvis, judging from the identical smirks on both faces. Astana walked over to me and took my arm possessively as we walked out of the building arm-in-arm and straight to the truck, where I opened the door for her. When I got in the driver's seat, Astana abruptly said, "We're going to your church. It's right down there to the right on East Street."

I turned the key to crank the motor, and off we drove with Astana giving me directions. She didn't say a word about what had happened. I could tell she was angry. I had warned her, but she had not been able to wrap her mind around that kind of prejudice until then. I had wanted to spare her the pain, but it was too late. Perhaps it was inevitable. Being a single woman in a small town and being dependent on farm labor to run her farm, she would eventually run into nasty gossip and grudges, especially with greedy farmers coveting her property.

When we turned into the dirt parking lot at the all-Black church on the edge of town, called Whispering Hope Chapel, I looked over at Astana and asked as I shut off the engine, "Are you sure you're ready for this?"

She had the most defiant look in her blazing eyes I had ever seen before when she stared back at me and said, "It couldn't possibly be any worse than what we've already experienced." She opened the door before I could get around to her side. Apparently, she was eager to face the music at the Black church on the other side of the tracks. When I got to her side, she linked her arm in mine and put a forced smile on her face before we took off for the entrance of the building. Several people coming in at the same time greeted us with a warm welcome. Many grabbed hold of us when we introduced ourselves and gave us tight hugs. They were full of questions about where we were from, and they offered to show us to a seat of honor down front. At first, Astana had wide eyes taking it all in, but later she was all smiles, enjoying the warm feeling of welcome we were receiving. Even after we sat down, many people got up from their seats and came to greet us and introduce themselves.

When the singing started, Astana was in for a treat. The voices blended in beautiful harmony, as they didn't have the brash overpowering sound of an organ or piano, just beautiful four-part harmony singing praises to God but with heartfelt soul in their beat and rhythm and big booming voices. They held nothing back. With a big smile on her face, Astana joined in, belting out her beautiful alto voice to the roof top. I joined her with my bass, and we sang to our hearts' content, finding ourselves disappointed when the singing stopped. It was Father's Day, and the church service started out honoring all the fathers. Then, the preacher started talking about the importance of strong fathers as leaders for their families, and his remarks were followed by a round of amens. All the things he said that morning reminded me of my family and my wonderful parents, and I began to get a little homesick, but I relished the words of the fine sermon. Due to my discipline to grow into the kind of man my parents would be proud of, I could easily relate to the advice the minister offered the audience. Then, he came around to the mothers, saying, "As we all know, behind every good man is a good woman." Then, he got started praising the wonderful mothers in the congregation. He ended the sermon reminding everyone with words of wisdom about Momma's saying, "Remember, if momma ain't happy, ain't nobody happy." The audience all got a chuckle out of that.

When the church service ended, several people came up to us once again introducing themselves, and then they invited us to a potluck picnic the church was having. I looked at Astana, and she shrugged her shoulders and said, "Why not? But I'm sorry we didn't bring anything. Can we stop at a store and get something to add to the lunches?"

"Oh no," several folks said, all adding to the conversation at once, "You are our guests. No need to bring anything. We're all meeting over at Lazy Mule Creek just down the road."

We got in the old truck and followed down the road behind the caravan of churchgoers. Lazy Mule Creek was a short drive out of town and down a dirt road that led to a small park area near the creek, a perfect place for a picnic. Everyone got out of their vehicles with arms loaded down with dishes and platters of all sizes. Little children were running back and forth, retrieving more items for their parents. At the park were several picnic tables that the church members quickly covered with table clothes so they could place the different pot luck dishes on top. Astana turned to me, laughing at my big eyes looking eagerly over all the food, and said, "You must be in hog heaven with your big appetite." I laughed in total agreement.

A lady nearby who told us her name was Sarah Faye let out a big laugh and said, "That's what we like to hear. We love young men with big appetites."

After everything was spread out, the congregation gathered around for the prayer by the preacher blessing the food that was about to be shared on this special Father's Day picnic. As soon as the amen was spoken, people started gathering up paper plates and began loading them down. Astana and I were put at the head of the line as special guests that day. We tried a little bit of everything, and before long, our plates were about to overflow. We found a spot on some soft grass to sit and began digging into the great pot luck dishes we had chosen. Several members came and sat near us and had lots of questions to ask us. They were interested in hearing about Astana's farm, and many of them knew her dad and brother from around town. They were anxious to hear how things were going on the farm this season. I mentioned that Astana had lost her husband in the war, and they were all very sympathetic over her loss. They seemed to take immediate pride in knowing she was getting by on her own now. All in all, it was a fun afternoon. We had enjoyed a good sermon along with wonderful songs of praise, raising our voices to the Lord, and we had enjoyed the company of good people at church and at the picnic.

In the late afternoon, we made our way back to Astana's farm. She was quiet on the drive home. As we got closer to the farm, she started opening up. First, with apologies about how things went at her church. "You tried to warn me, Brent, but I didn't believe you. I know God is not prejudiced. I know we are all welcome in His sight." I nodded my head in agreement with everything she had to say.

She went on, "I was so angry when we left my church. My heart was not in a mood for worship. But I pushed forward out of anger. I don't think that is what God wanted, but He still turned it into a good thing the way He always does." I continued to nod, not needing to speak. This was something Astana had discovered for the first time, and she needed to release her anger and describe what she was feeling. "But when we got to your church, the difference was like night and day." Then, she laughed and added, "As different as black and white." I joined her with a soft laugh. "Brent, I couldn't believe how friendly the people were at Whispering Hope. You can't imagine what that meant to me, how welcomed they made me feel. Of course, they made you feel welcome, but they made *me* feel welcome as well.

Maybe it would not have been that way if I had gone there alone. I will never know. But today, I felt like I was one of the family."

"I'm glad you felt so good about it. I felt good too. I've missed that time each week praising God and being with other church-going people. That common love we all have for our Lord bonds us together."

"Well, you would think so, but it wasn't that same bonding feeling at my church. I am so ashamed of those people, and I will never cross that threshold again as long as I live. They think they are so high and mighty, but to me, they are lowly. Their elevation of themselves over other people is despicable."

By then, we had pulled up to the house, and I turned off the motor, but we still sat there quietly in the truck. "Astana, I'm so sorry you had to experience that pain on my account. I understand your hate right now. Believe me. It's hard, I know. But I don't want you to keep it in your heart. That's what I am fighting every single day of my life: to rid my heart of that pain. Now, maybe you can understand why I am so focused on getting my education and getting out of the South and away from this hatred. Not that I can escape it in the city or up north. It will always be there, but I am going to choose to ignore it. As a Christian, I feel my actions have to represent Christ. When I meet people, I think of them as the person they are inside, not what they look like on the outside. I know that sounds cliché, but it's how I truly feel."

"Is that how you felt when you saw me for the first time?" she responded thoughtfully, maybe wondering if I was concerned that she might be prejudiced.

"Hey, that's not fair," I said laughingly. "I told you what stories I had already heard about you before I arrived. When I first saw you all tangled up in the sheets on the line with that frumpy housedress on and your hair braided, I was kind of scared of what I might confront at that moment." Astana laughed, making me feel a little more comfortable. Continuing on, I said, "But you're right in asking that question because if I am truthful, I figured it was going to be a rough summer, and I would have to fight what I assumed would be constant prejudice all summer with no one to console me." Then, thoughtfully, I added in a calm, quiet voice, "But you surprised me. You looked down on me for being a teenager, but I never felt that you looked down on me for being Black."

Astana shook her head back and forth as I finished my statement. "No, I never looked down on you at all. I was just frustrated that day. Cleon had just been to my house, pressuring me to sell to him, and he filled my head with doubts about my ability to survive here. Mr. Turner's remarks didn't help any. When I met you, I took my frustration out on you needlessly and undeservedly. I'm truly sorry about that."

"No problem. I think we have gotten past all our uncertainties by now." Then, changing the subject before I forgot a vital point, I started in again, "I just want to make something clear to you, Astana. What happened today at your church was nothing, probably because I had you with me. It doesn't compare to some of the things I've seen in my life. You don't know what it is like to have to stand and watch your parents be ridiculed in front of their children, and there is nothing they can do to defend themselves. They have to stand there and choke on their feelings and even respond back politely to literal abuse. That is the reason I am getting out, and I won't be looking back. I hope and pray you never have to witness anything like what I've seen." I paused to let it sink in, and then I added, "And I hope I don't cast any of that kind of trouble on you because of your association with me."

Astana looked at me with a sad expression in her eyes and tears streaming down her face. "I understand what you're telling me. I've heard stories, and I've read things, but until today, I've never experienced it. It makes me sick to think about whether I would have even noticed what happened at my church if I had not been with you today, if it had not happened to me. But I will never stand idly by again if I see something like that happening. One thing about me is I am known for my big mouth, and I don't mind one little bit giving people a piece of my mind."

"I believe you. I was so proud of you today when you told that old biddy off and boldly walked out. But I was even more proud of how you handled yourself when you went to the other church. You fit right in, and you treated all the members over there with dignity and respect."

"That's how it should be. We are all God's children." Then, as if shaken by her thoughts, she shuddered and said, "How can they let the kids at my church sing that song about Jesus loving all the little children, red and yellow, black and white?"

Chapter 11

For the next several days, our work schedule got back to normal. I had learned in the few weeks I had been on the farm that there was always something that needed your attention, and it was just going to be that way. I figured that was why God said in the Bible that you have to make yourself stop and take a break one day a week and refresh yourself both physically and mentally. We started going to the little church in town on our day of rest and refreshed ourselves spiritually.

I noticed after our trip to church that Sunday there was a change in my relationship with Astana. For some reason, that day bonded us closer together. Maybe it was because, for the first time in her life, Astana got a glimpse into my life, and it was not a pretty picture. I know she felt the shame and even some fear in the actions of people she thought were her friends. She saw that one wrong move on her part could change how people looked at her from then on. Was she willing to risk being shunned and gossiped about in order to stand up for me? It would be a test for sure. I wasn't positive she was up for that kind of pressure, but I could see she was making an effort. I know that day gave her a lot to think about. I noticed in the evenings when we talked at mealtime and while doing up the dishes, she was suddenly more interested in my life and how I lived than ever before. I willingly shared some aspects of it, but I didn't want to scare her with too much information. I had not personally experienced all the ugliness that was out there. My sleepy hometown didn't have too much energy to put up much of a stink about my part of town. As long as we stayed out of their way and in our place, we all managed just fine. My side didn't want to start a fight they knew they couldn't win, and the other side didn't want to bother with a group of people who were toeing the line, at least so far. I am sure if any of us ever got out of line, they would have mustered up the energy to put us back in our place—at the back of the bus, so to speak—if there had been a bus in our town.

One evening, Astana was especially interested in hearing my stories, and she got me talking about school and what was ahead of me the next year. "Well," I began, "before school starts, I will be busy with football practice. We have two-a-days that almost kill us."

"What are two-a-days?" She asked.

"That's two practices a day. One in the morning while it is still cool, if there is such a thing in late August in the South, and then again in the evening when the sun is going down and it is somewhat cooler. They have us working out and running until we puke. Then, they realize we've had enough, and we can finally go home. When we get home, we eat a big supper if our stomachs are settled enough to handle food by the time we walk the two miles back home."

"I can't believe you have to walk so far to school. Out here in the country, we always had a bus to pick us up."

"There are a few guys who have old beat-up cars, and they sometimes give us a ride home after practice. Sometimes even the coach feels sorry for us, and he will give us a ride. But usually, we just hit the pavement."

"No wonder you are so strong and can do so much work. Do you have a nice football field to play your games on?" She asked curiously.

"Not exactly," I laughed. "We play on an old pasture that someone was nice enough to mow for us, and the parents and kids do their best to dig out the rocks and sticker patches. Then it is marked appropriately."

"Do you ever play on some good official fields when you go to other schools? Do you play any White schools?"

"No. We play other schools like our own, all Black, and we have to travel to get to those schools, and their fields are just as sorry as ours. We have to drive all the way back home after the games no matter how far away or how late it is because we are not allowed to eat at most restaurants or stay in any motels. Our uniforms are hand-me-down ones that some other school is getting rid of, just like our textbooks."

"That doesn't seem right."

"It's okay. That's all we know, so what difference does it make? Of course, when we happen to see the beautiful fields of other schools, then we feel a tinge of envy. We can picture ourselves running freely on their soft turf, and in our eyes, we look like superheroes. We know our athletic abilities are as good as the White teams, if not better, but that will never be challenged, so it's all in our imagination."

"I can see how you would feel. How do you see any other schools if you don't play against them?"

"Well, on our walk to school, we pass right by a White school, and it's beautiful to us, like seeing some mansion. It's funny because during practice at school, we stay late, and I see the bus drop off White kids right across the street from our school. Sometimes we just stand there and stare at each other from across the street, I am sure wondering what it is like to be the other person. Of course, I am also sure they don't want to trade places with us. They are not admiring our pounded down bare field."

"Well, if you get a football scholarship, maybe you can finally play on a nice field with a thick turf, and you can be the super-hero you always imagined."

I laughed at her remarks picturing what it might be like. "Well, first, I have to get a scholarship if I am going to play foot-ball in college. I will be happy even if I can make the team at an all-Black college if it pays for my college. My mom fears that if I get a scholarship to a predominately White college, I will be cheered during the games and then jeered the rest of the week. At least those are the stories we have heard back home from players who made it to White colleges. She feels much more at peace if I go to a Black college. I like sports, but that is not my goal. What I am shooting for in the long run is to go to law school and become an attorney."

With a beaming expression, Astana swooped her hands across the air in front of her face, as if displaying an imaginary sign, and said, "I can picture you now with a bronze nameplate on your office door—Reginald Brent Lake, Attorney at Law. That sounds so distinguished. A perfect name for a lawyer. Brent Lake sounds good too. But I think you can ditch the idea of Butch Lake altogether. It doesn't have that attorney ring to it." I couldn't help but smile at her description, imagining it in my mind.

Astana abruptly changed the subject, as her mind often darted around in different directions. "You know, I think you need to start getting in shape. I've still got Robert's old football in the closet. Maybe we need to get it out and start having you work out in the evenings."

"What? You don't think all the work you have me doing all day is enough of a workout?" I said, laughing. She returned my laughter. We both agreed that it might be good for me to start getting my hands back on a football once in a while.

Another Friday rolled around, and it was time to take the fruits and vegetables to the market. We had some nice melons this time that I added at the back of the truck before shutting the tailgate. Then, we were off to make some money. Astana had offered to buy some more plants for me to decorate around her yard. She had been pleased with what I had done so far. I showed her how to transplant the daisies and the lilies into two other pots from each of the ones she bought a few weeks ago. I told her that the next year, all the pots would be full again and she could transplant more into other empty pots and her garden would grow. She could also plant them in the ground if she found a good spot for them. The week before, I had her buy some short Mexican Petunias to plant as ground cover in some bare spots, but I warned her that they had to have a border or they would take over all the other plants. They were very invasive. The nice thing about them if you can contain them is that they're perennials, and you never have to replant them the next spring. They start coming back in early spring and bloom until almost Christmas. They choke out the weeds, and every morning, you wake up to some beautiful purple blooms.

As usual, we found our good stand in the shade that had become our special spot since we started going to the market, and we both began unloading our garden goodies out of the back of the truck. Astana had a flair for displaying everything, so it drew attention to our spot. After several weeks at the market, we had earned the reputation of having the best stand. I was getting better acquainted with Astana's friends, and they all seemed cordial to me and stopped by to visit quite often. Some of the migrant workers came by as well, and Astana introduced them to me. As she had warned me, Lorena was especially attentive to me whenever she would drop by. Her dad must have gotten wind of the fact that his daughter was interested in me because he usually called her back to their stand once he noticed her hanging out very long with us.

That afternoon one of Astana's friends called her over to where she was selling fruit from her farm because she wanted to share her good news that she was expecting a baby. Astana was thrilled for her friend and wanted to know all that was going on and how she was feeling. While she was gone, I continued to sell what was left on our stand. I was always friendly whenever anyone came to the stand to browse around, and I answered any questions they might have. Usually, there was some friendly banter going on between the customers and me.

When I looked up after selling some peaches to a nice lady who lived in town, I saw Jackie Jarvis pull up to the market with his dad in the passenger seat of his hot car. They had the top down on his red and white Corvette convertible, and it was looking sharp. Jackie saw Astana visiting with her friend, and he headed straight in her direction. I was already feeling sorry for her because I knew she felt he was a pest. Much to my surprise, Cleon Jarvis headed straight toward our stand, strutting along with his shoulders reared back and his chest puffed out, wearing faded jeans and a sleeveless dingy white undershirt that stretched tightly over his pot-belly. There were deep yellow sweat stains under his arms.

"Good day, sir," I said when Mr. Jarvis approached, but like his son, he didn't respond to my greeting. "How's it going?" He just looked at the fruits and vegetables spread out on the stand and fiddled around rummaging through different baskets as if he were checking for a rotten piece at the bottom of the barrel. I noticed his farmer's tan all dark up to his normal short-sleeve shirt line and then milky white on up from there. His rough-looking face was darkened by the sun and all weather-beaten with deep wrinkles etched across his forehead, along with a set of deep crow's feet around his eyes. Speckled liver spots peeked through his thinning gray hair. His arms looked like a dried-up riverbed with wrinkles crisscrossing in all directions. I assumed that was the curse of a farmer's life. Finally, he made his way to the end of the stand where I was standing and spoke a warning to me, "Boy, don't get too cozy there on that farm. You ain't gonna have a job come next summer."

I smiled and said, "Don't worry. I'll be in college by next summer. Where is your son Jackie going to college?"

"He ain't gonna waste his time going to no college, boy. He has a farm to look after. That's where his future is." Then, he chuckled and added, "What kinda future you planning to get at college anyway?"

"I'm planning to be a lawyer," was my quick response. "You might want to remember me. Maybe someday you will need my services."

"Humph!" Mr. Jarvis answered in a huff, and then he asked me how much the melons were selling for. I moved closer and picked up a melon to see if Astana had put any price tags on them or made some sort of a sign to indicate the amount she wanted to ask. Finally, I looked over toward the stand where Astana was visiting not too far from me, and I hollered out, "Hey, Astana, how much are you asking for the melons?"

She looked over at me immediately, and we made eye contact. But before she could give me an answer, Mr. Jarvis grabbed me by my shirt with both fists and lifted me up a few inches off the ground and started shaking me violently, causing me to drop the melon I was holding, and it exploded when it hit the ground. His attack didn't hurt anything other than my pride, but I could see Astana running toward me as if in slow motion the moment she saw him grab me. Once he set me back down where my feet were touching the ground again, he pulled his hand back and, with a strong swing, brought his open palm across the side of my face with brute force, making a loud smack that could be heard all over the market and then he yelled out, "What's wrong with you, boy? You don't ever call a lady by her first name! Don't they teach you no manners where you come from?"

Just as I was able to reel my face back straight again, Astana had arrived to my side. She quickly brought her forearms down across Cleon's arms and hands that still clutched my shirt, and he immediately let go of me, causing my knees to buckle a bit as I tried to regain my balance. Then, she jumped in the middle of his chest with both fists pounding him as hard and as fast as she could. "What are you doing, you idiot? Keep your hands off him. Don't you ever step foot near our stand again or anywhere near my farm again. And by the way...you're paying for that melon," Astana shouted as she pointed to the melon pieces on the ground. Her adrenaline was flowing so furiously she was not even winded by the time she finished her verbal attack.

"Well, it's just not right for a big old Black boy like him to be addressing you by your first name. You're just too dumb and ignorant to know how to handle these kids," Cleon said, thinking he had the upper hand.

"Excuse me, Cleon Jarvis. I ordered him to call me by my first name...as if it's any of your business...which it's not. You have no right whatsoever to interfere in anything here. Do you hear me?" Then, she screamed it even louder so everyone in the market could hear, "*Do you hear me?*"

Mr. Jarvis stood there staring first at Astana and then over to me with a snarl on his ugly face. Then, in a jeering voice, he said, "Just wait until your father hears about this, you little tramp. My boy wants to marry you once he graduates, but I won't let him anywhere near you after this thug has been all over you this summer."

That was the last straw. Astana flew into him again with both fists until he grabbed hold of her wrist. All the while, she continued yelling at him through gritted teeth, saying, "Good. Keep yourself and your son away from me. And don't you worry about my dad. He has the good sense to know a decent man when he sees one, and believe me, you will never be a man that he will respect, especially after tonight."

Mr. Jarvis still had Astana's wrists in his grasp, and I could see her squirming to get loose from his grip. I knew it could be an all-out brawl if I interfered, but my body slowly crept forward in spite of the strong warning sound in my brain, and I drew close to where Mr. Jarvis and Astana were standing. Slowly, in a calm voice, I said, "Let go of her wrists."

Startled, Mr. Jarvis looked at me and then down at her wrists as if just realizing he was still holding onto her. He finally let go of her with a quick gesture like he was tossing off a snake, and she quickly drew her arms close to her chest and began rubbing her wrists. I didn't know if I should expect another blow from him or not, but we both stared each other down. I guess I won because I had Astana on my side staring back at him with those crystal eyes blazing, and slowly, he turned around and then stormed off. All the market witnessed the ordeal that took place. I didn't know the people well enough to know how they would take what had occurred, which side they would be on, or how much influence Mr. Jarvis had over the community. I certainly didn't want Astana to get in the middle of anything on my account, but she had put herself there when she flew into Cleon Jarvis in the middle of the marketplace with both fists flying and her booming voice blasting, demanding that he let me go. It hurt me to think she might have to suffer because of me long after I left at the end of the summer.

Astana immediately started loading up the back of the truck, and I followed her lead. We still had more to sell, but we were in no mood to hang around. In no time, we were ready to leave. Astana sat eerily rigid, staring straight ahead all the way home. I wasn't sure if she was even breathing; she was so quiet and sullen.

When we got back to the farm, she got out of the truck right away and slammed the door shut. I got out calmly and opened up the tailgate and started taking the baskets out of the truck and placing them on the porch. Astana headed on inside. When I had finished unloading the truck and parked it over near the garage, I headed to the backdoor to leave the keys with Astana. When I tapped on the screen door, I saw her moving around the stove in the kitchen. She hollered for me to come on in. She had heated up some leftovers for our supper like nothing out of the ordinary had happened. But we both knew better. In a way, we were both hungry and started right in on our food without saying the prayer. But in another way, we were both so angry that we ended up fiddling with our food, moving it around on our plate with our fork. We didn't talk back and forth or cut up and laugh at ourselves like we usually did at supper time. We just sat quietly and ate slowly, I guess still stewing over in our minds what had just happened and maybe thinking how it was going to affect us from now on. I wondered if it would change our relationship. Would Astana have second thoughts about the friendship that was developing between us?

Finally, we finished playing with our food, and we got up to do the dishes. Still, we were silent through the whole process. It was creeping me out in a way, but it also felt completely normal considering our dark mood.

After I emptied the water out of the sink, I wiped off the countertop, and Astana hung up the dishtowel. We stood there, finally looking at each other for the first time since the whole incident took place. I didn't realize it, but my shirt was all crumpled. Astana noticed it too. She reached over and attempted to straighten out the wrinkles. That's when she noticed the buttons had been ripped off in my scuffle with Jarvis. She started to cry, standing there with her hand resting on my shirt. I guess the shock of all the drama had finally sunk in. "Look what that awful man did to Robert's shirt. Let me go get some buttons and sew them back on for you."

I stood there examining the messy way I looked while I waited for her return. I wondered if she was upset over what had happened to me or if she was just upset over the damage done to Robert's shirt. Finally, she came back with a needle and thread and a handful of buttons. First, she asked me to take off my shirt, but I was hesitant to do so. "Oh, I guess if you don't feel comfortable in a White woman's house, you really don't feel comfortable taking off your shirt in her house," she said with a shaky voice as if she were saying it to herself, only out loud. She first pulled some thread off the spool and then threaded the needle, tying a knot at the end of the thread. Then, she reached over to take hold of my shirt and held a button to the top spot. With nimble fingers, she began to take the threaded needle in and out of the holes in the button. We were both still very emotional. Standing there so close to her, face to face, body to body, with my bare chest in front of her face, made me squirm. The touch of the back of her hand resting softly on my skin as she continued sewing caused a warming sensation where she was touching me, but in a good way. When she finally secured the button tightly, she reached her head close to the back of the button to bite off the end of the thread, and her hair brushed across my chest. Once again, I could smell the freshness of her body and her hair. My heart was pounding so strongly I was afraid it was going to bounce out of my chest and give her a concussion. But she didn't seem to notice. She grabbed another button and placed it in the next spot on the shirt and started running the needle and thread back and forth through all the holes. I was totally aware of my heart pounding, my chest rising and falling, and my labored breathing as she continued on and on, in and out, with the needle and thread. I wondered if she noticed the changes that were taking place in my body as she worked. We didn't speak a word, and the silence accentuated the pounding sounds of my heart and my heavy breathing.

Finally, Astana reached for my shirt at a lower location, close to my waist near my belt buckle, to attach the last button. Her hands touching my body there on my stomach was too much for me. I began to think it would have been less conspicuous and not so titillating if I had just taken my shirt off in the first place than how it was playing out by leaving it on. The closeness of her body, the touch of her skin, the feel of her breath blowing softly on my skin were causing me much discomfort but again, in a good way. I stood silently but ever watchful of her as she moved quickly with her needle and thread. I searched her face for any signal from her. She was so difficult to read as she solely concentrated on her sewing. I couldn't tell if she was feeling any of the same emotions or stirrings I was. Or if the drama of the afternoon had hardened her heart from being capable of feeling anything at that moment. When she finished off that last button, I was screaming inside my innermost thoughts, *Don't stop! Please, don't stop!*

Astana double knotted the last loop of the thread and then reached her head down to that last button to bite off the thread. Again, her silky clean hair was brushing across my skin. She seemed to struggle to bite through the thread, and I thought I was going to explode if she didn't hurry. My breathing by then was so heavy it had become loud enough to notice, like a marathon runner coming to the end of his race.

When Astana looked up at her work, she put on a forced smile, smoothed out my crumpled shirt, and ran her hand down over all the neatly sewn buttons. I know when she stroked my shirt, she had to have felt the heaving of my chest and the pounding of my heart. She looked up in my eyes, and at that moment, I noticed that her breathing was matching mine, and her heart was racing just like mine. With a surprising move, Astana slid her soft hands inside my shirt on both sides of my bare waist, causing me to tremble, and then she stepped an inch closer with our bodies now touching. I had been standing there like a manikin for so long, except for my power breathing and throbbing heart, to the point that I didn't know what to do. I wasn't sure if my arms or hands worked anymore. I just stood there with my limp arms at my sides. As she moved even closer to me, I slowly reached my quivering hands up and touched her bare arms at her elbows. Then, I gently caressed them as my fingers softly and slowly slid up to her shoulders. When I wasn't staring into her amazing eyes, I was staring at her soft arms, her gorgeous body and luscious lips, and the curve of her neck, then back to her eyes. Each view my eyes gazed upon brought me more satisfaction.

Astana brought her hands further around my back and gently stroked her fingers upward toward my shoulders. By then, our foreheads were gently resting against the other, and our noses were side by side. Our lips were inches apart. All the warnings I had ever been taught were suddenly going out the window. The only last warning I held onto was that I couldn't touch her lips no matter how tempting they were. I hated that those fears had to run interference for even a second in the most amazing moment of my life. I wanted to close the door on those warnings and go with my body, with my mind, with my heart. I wanted to taste her lips with every ounce of energy I had left in my trembling body. Where was my discipline? Where was my focus? It all left me that day, that moment. Even the soreness from the slap across my face didn't concern me. It was as if the physical part of the whole incident with Cleon Jarvis never happened. Only the emotions were left. I was convinced I could easily suffer through the pain if I could just have her kisses.

Suddenly, Astana pulled away from me as if she had touched a hot stove. Then, she looked up at me, with a breathless and confused expression on her face, trying to get a grip on her emotions, the same as me. I wanted so much to be able to tell her how I had dreamed of being close to her in that way, but I knew that would be off-limits. Then, I wondered if she might confirm my fears about White women and blame me.

Without ever breaking eye contact, we both stood there with a shocked expression on our faces that slowly changed to odd smiles. We began to gather our senses and straighten out our clothing to calm ourselves down. Astana started fanning her face with her hands flapping like she was putting out a fire. Finally, she spoke up before I could get any words out. "Brent, I'm so sorry. This is all my fault. I don't know what got into me." By then, she was sobbing.

I grabbed her close to me and hugged her tightly, trying my best to soothe her sobs without stirring our passion again. Finally, we moved over to the couch and sat down. Once she slowed her tears and wiped them away from her eyes, we were ready for a more calm discussion about what had happened. "Astana, this was not your fault. It just happened. We were both so worked up with all the emotions of the day, and one thing led to another. Don't you think?"

Astana looked at me bewildered, shrugging her shoulders, not knowing what to think. "I don't know, Brent. I wish I knew. I've never felt anything as powerful as what just happened, and I don't know how to explain it or what to think."

My rational mind was coming back trying to ruin my fun, and I said, "Maybe you are just lonely and missing Robert. The anniversary of his death was not too long ago; I'm wearing his shirt, and you have been alone for so long. Maybe that's what happened."

"Really? That's what you think?" Astana stated, sounding rather ticked off.

"No...well, maybe...I don't know what to think."

"All I know, Brent, is that I am not missing Robert. It's not about the shirt." She looked at me, and her frustrated face turned to a contented smile as she slowly said, "These are all new feelings. I've never had them before. I think it's because

I've learned to trust you this summer, and I've bonded with you. I find myself drawn to you."

"I know. I feel the same way about you," I said as I reached for her hand.

Astana looked as though she was trying to organize her thoughts. I recognized that look because she and I were so much alike and reacted much the same way. "I think what happened today at the market," she said, trying to regain her mature composure, "triggered our emotions in a way that made it where we were unable to control the close feelings that were already there, even though we were trying to keep them buried deep down inside."

I nodded my head, agreeing with her. Then, she added, "I understand you now with your fears because of this experience. I understand why you are afraid of being in my house, and you must be afraid right now about what I'm thinking and how I might react. I might say, 'Hey, let's go to bed,' and then you would have fears about that. Or you may refuse me, and I might get angry like Potiphar's wife did with Joseph in the Bible, and you would have fears about that. I've put you in an awful situation, and that's not fair to you." Astana paused for a minute to gather her thoughts.

When she returned her gaze back toward me, her expression had changed to a contented smile. Then, she softly spoke, "I hope you don't mind, however, if I hold onto the memory of this night so I can think on it whenever I am sad or lonely."

I couldn't help but grin like a silly kid in a candy shop, embarrassing myself, before I turned on my cool teenage persona and responded to Astana's remarks. "As long as you don't mind if I hold onto it just as tightly. It will be a memory I fear may never be surpassed. Thanks for understanding my fears. They are real. Even though I trust you, I am still at risk, and I am very vulnerable. But the fact that you understand makes me love this memory all the more."

We both sat quietly with smiles on our faces enjoying the memory of our special moment. After a bit, I got up from the couch and excused myself to go to my room. I rubbed my chin and winced in pain. Astana jumped up and said, "Let me get you some ice to put on that."

Chapter 12

Astana and I tried to put the emotions we experienced that night behind us. We immediately got back into our schedule the next day as if nothing unusual had happened. I had money to make, and she had work that needed done. We kept our focus on our work and were thankful for the large space we had to work in that put distance between us most of the day. However, there were often times we would catch ourselves looking at each other across the yard, and we would smile a knowing smile, a smile that gave the hint that could no longer be hidden that there was a close feeling between us, that we carried our own little secret. Even in our distance, there was something very familiar in the way we reacted to each other.

As I worked around the farm doing my regular chores, I would allow my thoughts to drift to that night and the excitement I felt. I couldn't help but wonder if her excitement was as fever-pitched as mine. She seemed much more in control of the situation and her body. But was that a woman thing? I wasn't sure. I also couldn't help but wonder if her emotions were maybe associated with the same feelings that she felt for Robert, and they were amplified because of the anniversary of his death and his shirt. But she had assured me the feelings she felt that night were brand new to her. I had to take her at her word. Or was it my fantasy about her that caused me to hold onto that thought? Whatever it was, I knew it was something I would never forget, and I would cherish it as long as my memory allowed me to. For now, the thoughts could instantly cause my body to react much the same way it did that night. If only there was a serum that could recapture the full effect of that emotion and save it for me, I would not have to try so hard to hold it in my memory and retrace each minute of that night.

Astana announced at supper that her dad and brother would be coming over the next day bright and early to start haying. They would have a crew of men to help out. She told me all I needed to do was to listen to her brother, and he would give me plenty to do to keep me busy. I was excited but also nervous since I didn't know what to expect. I figured it would be a nice distraction from all the emotions running rampant inside me.

Just as Astana had said, her dad, brother, and the crew showed up with their equipment at daybreak. I was surprised that her mom came along too. Astana didn't bring me breakfast that morning. Instead, she had a big breakfast for all of the crew working that day. When lunch rolled around, we all headed back to the house for a big lunch, and then she served supper the same way that evening. Astana's mom, Anita, helped her with the cooking and the dishes. They were busy the entire day and just as tired as the men at the end of the day.

I enjoyed the few days of haying, even though it was definitely hard and dirty work. It reminded me of sports. We gathered around, discussing our strategy. Then, we put our plan into action. We worked alongside each other, giving all our energy and strength toward the task. We laughed and cut up with each other, and in the end, we sat back and were proud of what all we had accomplished.

At breaks, Astana would come out to the field to bring me a cold jug of water. She said she didn't want me to get dehydrated. She knew all the other workers brought their own jugs from home. That special attention she gave me felt like a real connection to someone who cared for me. I wasn't expecting that.

My main job on the team was mostly after the hay was baled. I walked along the rows and grabbed hold of each bale of hay and tossed it up on the truck as it was slowly rolling along, and the men on the truck stacked it all in neat rows. Later, we unloaded the bales in the barn so it would be ready for winter and to sell to other farmers. I could feel the muscles, which had already been bulging from my daily work, growing even larger in my arms, back, and chest. I hoped I was building up the right muscles that would work well for me in football that year. I also enjoyed the comradery of the crew and figured that must be how it was for the other farm boys on my work crew that landed jobs on bigger farms or ranches. They got to have friends to work with them and to talk to all summer. But I wasn't complaining. I was happy with my assignment.

It was fun watching Astana with her brother and her parents, laughing and talking around the supper table. I sat back and watched mostly, but now and then, the guys would toss in a joke about me to the ladies about my inexperience, and I got a chance to pop back with a comment or two of my own. I didn't take it negatively because it was just good-natured fun. If they were upset with me, they would not have bothered teasing me.

When supper was over, I started picking up the dishes off the table and carrying them over to the sink. Astana's parents were a little surprised, but Astana assured them that I helped her every night with the dishes, and I was quite handy in the kitchen.

I sat out on the back porch with the other men and visited while the ladies finished the dishes. We talked about how the day went and discussed the plan for the next day. When Anita came outside with her purse over her shoulder, that was a signal that it was time for everyone to leave and get some rest for the next day.

I stood on the porch next to Astana and waved to the family and the crew as they drove off. It felt very comfortable to be standing there. It felt natural. The two of us chatted for a few minutes, but we were both very tired, and we wanted to get our showers and head to bed so we would be ready for the next busy day.

One Saturday after the haying season ended, Astana and I decided to treat ourselves to a second day of rest instead of our regular Sunday. We took off with a picnic lunch and headed to Lazy Mule Creek. We had received a heavy rain a few days earlier, and Astana said that the waterfall there should be really pretty. We parked the truck close to where we had the picnic with the church members that first Sunday we attended church together. From there, we took off hiking along a trail that led to the waterfall. Astana was right. When we got to the clearing where the fall came over the top of the large mountain overhead, I was amazed at its beauty. Astana said Echo Falls got its name from that waterfall, and people said your voice would echo when you yelled loudly in that narrow canyon near the falls. We checked it out over and over, laughing each time at the sound of our own voices. I asked her how Lazy Mule Creek got its name, and she told me legend had it that an old farmer years ago sold his mule to another farmer. He warned him the mule was the laziest mule in all the county. Sure enough, the mule would get out every day and make his way to the creek to drink in the shade of the trees there. Everyone just started calling it Lazy Mule Creek after a while.

We found a nice spot in the grass under the shade of a large tree and spread out a blanket. Then, Astana unloaded the food out of the basket and poured a glass of ice tea from a jug.

We enjoyed our picnic lunch, and we were having a very nice day, talking a lot like we always did, but we were still keeping a little emotional distance from each other after our previous intense experience. Later, after our meal, we stretched out on our sides and rested our heads on our propped-up palms. As we faced each other, I could tell Astana was searching to know more about me and my life. Out of the blue, she asked me, "What is your favorite word?"

I gave it some thought. I had never been asked that question before. But suddenly, a word popped in my head, and I said, "Liberty."

"Liberty?" she questioned with a surprised look on her face.

"Yeah, liberty. That's what I'm going to name my first child, whether it's a boy or a girl. It's the essence of what I'm trying to do with my life. You might say I'm trying to liberate myself. When I get my education, I can go anywhere I want to go, and I can be confident in myself that I belong. You don't know how important that is until you've had people all your life tell you what you can or cannot do and where you can or cannot go. I want to fight for the liberty of others like me."

"That's lovely."

"I have to work really hard, and that's why I am so hard on myself. When you're a minority, you have to prove yourself above and beyond everyone else. You can't just be good. You've got to be better than good to even get noticed. Then, you have to make sure you don't ever slip once you finally prove yourself."

"You don't know how sad it makes me to think you have that kind of pressure. Just the short time I've been around you makes me want to fight for equal rights. I get so angry when I think about how you were treated at church and by Jarvis."

I laughed at her remarks and said, "I can see you now at some college protesting around campus carrying picket signs. You might turn into a real hippy with braided hair and a beaded headband around your head. You seem like a real fighter, so if you were on my side, things would be settled in no time."

Astana laughed at my description of her. Then, sadly, she said, "I doubt that I will ever get to go to college."

"What's stopping you?"

"You see how much I have to do to stay alive as it is," she said, sounding frustrated. "How could I go to college and keep the farm?"

"Maybe you could start out slowly by taking some courses at the junior college. That would get you started, and you could still manage the farm. You don't have as much going on during the winter, do you?"

"No. But I don't know. Maybe I will think about it."

We spent the day talking about our hopes and dreams for life. Astana shared with me how she had wanted so much to be a mother. She feared that dream would escape her. She didn't see any prospects around Echo Falls, and she wasn't looking either. I brought up Jackie Jarvis, and she slapped at me and then giggled at the absurdity of that thought.

"Who knows," I continued, "you might meet some good-looking man at college and get a second chance at love and maybe start that family you long for. Then, you wouldn't have to be so lonely."

Astana didn't respond with words, but a pensive expression veiled her face. Perhaps she was imagining some of the possibilities. After a minute, we both looked at each other as if trying to read what we might be thinking. As for me, I felt a shift in my mood picturing Astana with another man.

By evening, we began to gather up the picnic basket and blanket, and we headed back to the truck. We still had much more we could have talked about, but we would have other times to continue our conversations. It seemed that each day, we started up where we left off the day before, and we felt it would always be that way, at least for the short amount of time I had left there at the farm. However, there was always an underlying urgency that lurked in our minds pressing us to find out as much as we could about each other before I had to leave.

Chapter 13

I was beginning to feel the summer slipping away from me. I thought back to my first days on the farm and how I couldn't wait for the time to fly by. Now, I found myself dreading when it would come to an end. I could picture myself back home getting ready for school to start. I had planned to use some of my work money to buy new school clothes, but with the clothes Astana gave me, I would not need to waste my money on such frivolous things. That meant more money in the college pot.

Astana and I had started working out after supper. We would get out in the yard and start exercises. She had me running sprints as she timed me. We did push-ups and sit-ups, and she had me doing all kinds of drills. Then, we tossed the football around for a while as we cooled down. I was surprised that Astana had a good arm on her and was pretty accurate, too, in her passes back to me. It wasn't the kind of workout I would be doing once football started, but it was a pretty good warm-up to those tougher practices.

One evening, when we were throwing the football around, I noticed some dark clouds coming up in the distance. Suddenly, the wind started blowing, and the tree branches were whipping around in all directions. We could see lightning strikes, and then seconds later, the thunder exploded. We decided we needed to go inside and forget football. I started to head up to my room, but Astana suggested that I wait out the storm with her for a while longer. She was afraid of storms.

We turned on the TV just long enough to check out the weather report, and it was showing storms in the area and suggested that they could become severe. Astana mentioned that she wished they had tornado warning signals out in the country. She had a cellar, but she never knew when it was bad enough to go to it. She told me some stories about her younger days at her parents' farm and how they spent several nights in the cellar waiting out a storm. She figured she would never get over being scared of tornadoes. She told some eerie tales of the kind of damage they could do, how they could tear a house all apart and yet leave something sitting on a table undisturbed. *How strange*, I thought, but I had heard similar stories before.

We turned off the TV because the lightning was getting so fierce, and we unplugged it from the outlet. Astana suggested we open some of the windows around the house a crack because she had heard that the air pressure of a tornado could cause a house to explode if it was closed up tight. The crack in the windows could relieve some of the pressure. At least, that was a common theory.

When I came back to the table, the house felt like it was rocking. Some of the windows were rattling, and the thunder and lightning felt like it was coming right into the kitchen with us. We decided we were scared enough to go to the cellar and wait out the storm there. We both felt it would be safer.

Right off to the side of the back porch was the cellar. I lifted the door that was slanted at an angle, and Astana walked ahead of me down the five or six steps that went underground, and I followed quickly behind her, securing the door shut. The ceiling was just a foot over my head. It was dark down there, but Astana grabbed a lantern and lit it, hanging it on a hook in the middle of the cellar. The glow from the lantern accentuated Astana's spectacular features that I had grown accustomed to admiring. We stood there a minute, not knowing what to do. We felt safer there, but we were at a loss as to how to wait out the storm. Finally, Astana remembered there was a transistor radio in the cellar they had kept there to hear weather reports or to listen to music when waiting out a storm. She turned it on, and we listened again for any updated weather reports, but it was saying much the same as what we heard on television.

Astana was shaking after the last thunderbolt, and I took her in my arms. We both felt comforted by our closeness. Some music started up on the radio, and I asked her to dance. We started swaying to the music of Paul Anka singing "It Had to Be You." We continued dancing to one song after another—Elvis Presley, the Beatles, the Supremes, the Beach Boys. They were all songs we had heard on our radios for years, and we enjoyed listening to them together.

Having Astana in my arms started stirring my passion, and I worried about what might happen to my discipline and my control. Astana looked up in my eyes with the sparkle that I always saw looking back at me. We stopped dancing and just stared at each other, perhaps recalling the memory of the closeness we felt the night she sewed on my buttons.

Suddenly, we were startled by the pounding on the door of the cellar. In a way, we were afraid to open it if a tornado was out there for fear, from stories we had heard, that a tornado could suck you right out of the cellar. But the pounding came again, and there was a jerk on the door. I released the latch and opened the door a crack to see Fred and Jennifer from the next farm down the road, asking if they could join us in the cellar. They had their small child cradled in Jennifer's arms. I pushed the door ajar so they could come on down, and then I secured the latch again once they were safely inside. There were a couple of chairs in the small room where Astana and I sat while offering Fred, Jennifer, and their little daughter the cot. After a bit, Jennifer laid the baby down to sleep, and the four of us started talking, all with different stories about scary storms of the past. We heard a lot of racket going on outside, and I could tell that some of the potted plants may have blown off the porch, along with some of the metal lawn chairs. Even though it was a scary time, we had fun visiting with each other and not being all alone during the storm. We all enjoyed hearing the music on the radio to pass the time, and soon, our fears slipped away.

I loved listening to Astana that night talking with her neighbors. They would get tickled about some of the stories they were telling, and Astana's infectious laugh triggered uncontrollable laughter from all of us. I loved that about her.

It felt good being with Astana in a group setting, almost like we were a normal couple enjoying an evening together with friends. Astana couldn't keep her eyes off the baby sleeping soundly on the cot. Watching her probably brought about memories of her desire to have her own baby. Her memories soon turned to words. "Remember how sad I was when Robert left for the military?" she whispered.

Fred and Jennifer nodded, and Astana continued, "I missed him so much and often wished I had gotten pregnant so I could have a part of him with me. That would have been hard, though, since he didn't come home. I don't know if I would make a good mother. I'm so overprotective and controlling. Robert was the complete opposite. Remember how wild and crazy he could be, always getting hurt or breaking something?"

They all laughed at the memory in their minds. "I was watching Robert's baseball game one night, and I noticed Sophia Tucker's little girl sitting on the ground playing dolls in the parking lot with all those crazy teenagers being reckless in their cars, probably not aware of little children playing. I couldn't concentrate on the game for worrying about that kid. I remember thinking it must be so freeing to not be overwrought with worry all the time and to just let your kids run wild."

Jennifer spoke up and said, "That worry over someone else's child shows what a good mother you would be." I smiled, watching Astana enjoy her compliment.

Finally, about midnight, things seemed to calm down, and we all ventured out to assess the damage. It was not too bad. There appeared to be some broken tree branches and some damage to the porch area, but that was all we could see in the darkness of the late hour since the power was out. Fred and Jennifer got in their truck with the baby still asleep and headed back home. I got Astana inside the house, and then I headed on up to my room over the garage with a flashlight in hand.

The next day we worked around the farm, picking up broken limbs around the property and putting the chairs back up on the porch and salvaging the potted plants that had taken a beating. Later in the day, we loaded up the truck with what we planned to take to the market. This time we had a bunch of potatoes. Earlier in the week, I had dug up the rows of potatoes, and Astana and I both gathered them up, dusted off the dirt, and hauled them to the cellar, spreading them out on some lower shelves so they would last a long time.

As usual, we had a good time visiting with people at the market. We didn't have any more problems after that last experience with Cleon Jarvis. I wasn't sure if he had given up or if he didn't think I was worth the effort of harassing. We had become friends with all the other vendors over the summer, and the customers were usually friendly and had become regulars to the market.

We had made it a habit after we left the market to go by the nursery and get more plants for the farm. I knew Astana was not making much money off what she sold at the market when she was buying new plants each week. But I also felt they were good investments for her farm. That day they had a bunch of Rose of Sharon trees on sale that had a beautiful mauve-colored bloom to them with a dark pink center. I suggested that Astana buy several and let me plant them all down the drive leading to her farm. With the pretty landscaping at the entrance and then the trees lining the lane, it would make an attractive, appealing look to her farm that would make it stand out from other farms. She laughed and said, "I don't know why I am spending so much money and hard work to fix up this farm for old man Jarvis." We both laughed, knowing she would never sell to him.

The next day, we both worked at planting the trees along the lane. First, we planned out the location and spacing we wanted for the trees by measuring it off to have them line up perfectly. Then, I dug the holes, and Astana drove the truck down the dirt road, and then we unloaded each tree near the hole. Once we had them all ready, we lifted them into the holes and then covered them with dirt and patted them down firmly.

We were quite pleased with ourselves when we finished our work. They looked beautiful, and I could picture in my mind how nice they would look in the future as they matured and provided shade all down her lane. I reminded Astana that she could get saplings from these trees every spring and pot them and even sell them at the market in years to come. That put a sparkle in her already beautiful eyes. She was beginning to see the investment that was developing in her little farm.

When we got the truck back up to the house, we unloaded the shovels and stored them away. I hated for Astana to have to cook supper. I spoke up and said, "You don't know how much I wish we could hop in the truck and drive to town, and I could take you out to eat tonight. You deserve that."

Astana smiled, grateful for my thoughtfulness. Then, she said, "Let's go. We can at least go to the hamburger joint and get some hamburgers to go."

"That sounds good to me. I'm paying, though. I don't want you to have to cook, and I don't want you to have to pay tonight. It's my treat."

We enjoyed a fun Saturday night out like two young kids on a summer date. It was special to get something different to eat and to not have to do a lot of cooking or cleaning up. Astana turned up the radio loud in the truck, and we laughed and sang along with the songs all the way home and then enjoyed eating our burgers once we got back to the house. After supper, we turned on the TV and watched *The Lawrence Welk Show* and enjoyed all the music and dancing.

Sunday morning, we planned to go to church as normal. One of the ladies named Opal was having a birthday, and Astana wanted to bring her a gift. She picked out a Rose of Sharon pot and cleaned it up and wrapped it in pretty floral paper like the one she gave her aunt and tied a ribbon around it. Then, she painted a sign that said "Rose of Opal" on it. She decided to also take her one of the white daisy pots with the dark purple centers she had transplanted, and she decorated it nicely with a pretty bow. We both walked in the church that morning with our arms full and handed them over to Opal. She was tickled when she saw they were for her and was soon busy showing them to all the members. They were amazed at the thoughtful gift, especially knowing it came from the farm and could be planted in the ground later on, and Opal could have that memory for many years. They were quite impressed with Astana's green thumb, but she gave me the credit.

We enjoyed the church service after we settled in our pew. Over the weeks we had been attending church there, we had gotten to know the minister and many of the members. They were still all very friendly. Astana loved playing with the babies, and all the little toddlers loved running up to her and clinging to her legs for her to pick them up. I could see what a beautiful mother Astana would make. She had a special way with the children. From the first day we stepped inside that church, we both felt at home. No one ever mentioned anything about race or that we were different. It was nice to be accepted and welcomed no matter what.

A lot of Sundays, Stanley and Anita would come over for Sunday lunch after church. Many times, Stan and his wife and kids came along too. And on special occasions, the two sisters visited with their families. They lived out of town, so it was not often that we saw Maypearl and Lillybelle. They were sweet ladies, just like Astana, and it was fun watching them visit together. They all had fun personalities and that same contagious laughter. Everyone would bring their favorite dishes, and they were added to the table, and the eating began. I didn't expect to be invited to join them, but Astana would insist that I sit down and eat with them like I was part of the family. We would end up talking and laughing, and they had lots of family stories to share with me. Just like church, it felt good to be able to feel comfortable. I had never been around White people with me being the only Black in the group, and it had always been a little tense to think about it. I began to see that I would be fine someday going to an integrated college. That was the first time I had ever allowed myself to imagine it before.

After lunch, we would sometimes go out in the yard and toss the football around and have a little family football game. Stanley and Anita would watch from the porch. Stanley was still recovering from his knee surgery. We all had fun running around in the yard keeping the parents entertained.

One hot summer morning, while I was working out in the garden, I saw a truck coming down the drive up to the house. I wondered who it could be since, by now, I was quite familiar with most of the people who came out to visit with Astana.

When I finished picking the last of the green beans, I headed to the kitchen to drop them off. I was surprised when I turned the corner around that section of the house and saw Opal, from church, sitting on the porch with Astana.

"Look, Brent," Astana said when she saw me, "Opal dropped by to visit and to see about getting one of our Rose of Sharon plants."

"Great. Nice to see you, Opal. How are things going over at your place?"

"Oh, Son, they are just fine and dandy. It's been a good summer for us. Can't complain...who would listen anyway," she said with a big laugh. Continuing on, she said, "I loved that plant y'all brought to me for my birthday, and I have a good friend, Ella Ruth, who is sick right now, and I thought I would come out here and see if you have any left. I would like to buy one from you. I know she would treasure a gift like that."

Astana spoke up quickly, "Oh, no, you don't need to buy it. We would be happy to let you pick one out."

"Oh, but you need to be selling those beauties. Would you mind showing me the mother plant so I can see what mine is going to look like when it matures?"

"Sure," Astana said as she got up, and then we both led Opal around the house to where the original Rose of Sharon tree was standing. It was a strong tree, creating lots of shade. It was covered with white blossoms that had deep cherry-colored centers. It looked really nice with the white daisies I had planted beneath the tree. When Opal saw it, she let out a little gasp of air in excitement at how pretty it was.

"That is so beautiful. I can't wait to get mine planted and to watch it grow. How fast do they grow?" she asked.

I spoke up and told her that they grew fairly quickly. "It should be a foot or two by next summer, maybe more, and that is a lot considering how small the sapling was that we gave you. Then, each year, it will get bigger and end up being a tall tree unless you prefer to keep it as a bush. Be sure when you first plant it to put something around it because it is deciduous and will look like a dead twig in the winter."

"What does that mean?" Opal asked.

"That means it will lose its leaves in the winter. But they come back early in the spring, and you have a beautiful tree most of the year. The blossoms start in late spring, around May. But if you don't protect it when it is small, people sometimes mow over them, thinking it's dead. Once spring comes, you will see tiny green buds that will turn into nice green leaves in no time, and then pretty flowers will pop out."

"Thanks for sharing that with me. It's such a pretty color."

"That's another thing," I said. "It might not be that color when it blossoms. My mom had a mauve Rose of Sharon tree, and we transplanted the saplings, and they turned out white like this one. Then, we transplanted the saplings from the white blossomed tree, and those grew into mauve-colored trees."

"Wow, that's amazing," Opal said. "No matter though, whatever color, it will be beautiful, I am sure."

"Yes, you can count on that," I said in agreement. "You can see what the mauve ones will look like. That's what is on the side of the road up to the house."

"Okay," Opal said, "I'll check those out when I leave. You may remember that the Rose of Sharon is mentioned by Solomon in the Bible. It symbolizes beauty."

Astana asked Opal to stay for lunch after she picked out the plant she wanted. She was thrilled to get it and already had some pretty paper picked out to wrap around it for when she took it to her friend, Ella Ruth. Astana asked me if I was ready for lunch, even though it was a tad earlier than we usually ate. I told her I was always ready to eat, which made her laugh. I got in the kitchen and started helping her get the leftovers out to heat up for our lunch. I set the table while she stirred the food on the stove.

While we were waiting for the lunch to warm up, Opal started rummaging around in her purse, recovering a memory. "I almost forgot," she said, "I brought some pictures of y'all that I took at one of our church picnics. I took pictures of all the folks on my little Brownie camera, and they turned out so nice. I am really fond of these I took of you two. You are such a cute couple. Your looks complement each other, and it really shows in photos. I think the camera loves y'all. Here, look for yourself."

Astana took the photos and flipped through them slowly, one at a time, handing the top one over to me after viewing it. Astana was giving each one close examination. I was amazed when I got a chance to look them over. Opal had taken pictures of us sitting quietly eating our meal with smiles on our faces. She had some of us walking along the creek and splashing in the water. They were all black and white candid shots catching us unaware, and I could see that the camera did capture something special, like it could secretly see the bond we had with each other and, just like our own faces, that bond could not be hidden in those pictures. I realized when I looked at them that people around town must be able to read something into what they saw in our faces when we were walking around town together and working at the farmer's market. That must be why the gossip got started so quickly about Astana. Sure, they would have gossiped anyway, but seeing how we reacted to each other in those photos made me see how that look of closeness could be interpreted as something worthy of gossip. I wondered what Astana thought when she looked at them.

When Astana finished flipping through all the pictures, she looked up at Opal with a smile and asked, "Can I get a copy of some of these?"

"Oh, dear, those are your copies. I took photos of all the folks at the picnic, and I have been out delivering them around."

"That's so sweet of you. Thanks so much."

We enjoyed our lunch together and visiting with Opal. She had lots of stories to share, as she had lived in the area all of her life.

"That is sad," Astana said. "We've both lived here all our lives, but I never met you until I walked into Whispering Hope Chapel that Sunday morning."

"Yes, dear, it is sad. It just goes to show how things could change if we just learned to cross over the lines that divide us."

Astana smiled and said, "That's so beautifully put."

"Seeing you two together gives me hope for the future that someday people can see each other's hearts instead of what's on the outside. Having you come to church with us is a good start. That divide I'm talking about is like how a deformed person or a mentally slow person is treated in society. Sometimes people are afraid of them. They don't ever make eye contact with them, much less talk to them. But once they give them a chance and sit down and talk to them, they stop seeing the differences and see the real person. The same is true with old folks. They are so lonely because people are scared of them. Maybe they remind us of what is coming for ourselves, so we try to avoid them, but it is sad to let them be all lonely. If you stop to talk to them, you find that they are so full of interesting stories, and they can tell you some history that will make you want to sit and listen to them all day."

Nodding, I said, agreeing with Opal, "Yeah, sometimes they sit off to the side so quietly that we often ignore them. But when you take time to approach them and let them talk, they are so interesting, and you can see a light come on in their eyes. I love the proverb that says, 'The glory of young men is their strength; gray hair is the splendor of the old.'"

Opal and Astana sat there with big endearing smiles on their faces like I had just quoted Shakespeare or something. "What?" I asked.

"That was just so touching and showed us what a wonderful character you have," Opal stated, still smiling and nodding while patting my arm over and over like I was a precious baby. I was just waiting for her to reach over and pinch my cheek like my aunts always loved to do when they saw me.

Opal left with her new plant under her arm. She had gotten Astana to paint a sign for her plant that said *Rose of Ella Ruth* before she took off for home.

I had plenty of work to do that would keep me busy all afternoon, so I took off after Opal drove away, and Astana went back to work in the house. My newest project was making the bench I had promised Astana I would make for her to go over by Robert's tree. I also wanted to make her a porch swing to hang at the end of her porch. As always, I hoped she didn't think I was wasting time by coming up with these extra projects. I guess I was not a farmer at heart, and I liked the different projects to keep my mind off the boredom of farm work. I had just about finished the bench, and I planned to paint it white. I thought it would give kind of an angelic look to it and make for a peaceful setting there on the side of the house with the nice grass growing there now and the pretty impatiens blooming galore and the tree spreading its branches with the purple anniversary ribbon blowing in the wind. At least I hoped Astana was going to like it.

Later that evening, after we finished the dishes, Astana reached for the photos that Opal had dropped by. She kept flipping through them one by one. When she finished, she looked over at me and asked, "How do you like these?"

"They're great," I replied.

"Really?"

"Yes, really. Why? Don't you like them?"

"I love them. I usually hate pictures of myself, but these draw me in. I actually like the way I look in these candid shots when I am not posing for them. I guess I'm saying I'm not as bad as I thought I was."

"What? How could you even think you look bad? You're absolutely beautiful. Stunning even."

Astana got a big smile on her face. "I've never been called beautiful or stunning before. I kind of like it. You know, I could become vain if I got compliments like that all the time."

"Well, I don't want you to become vain, but you are exquisite, and don't ever forget it. Now, you have these pictures to always remind you of how lovely you are."

"I'm so glad to have them. I don't have a camera, so I never think about taking pictures. It would be a shame for you to leave without me having a picture of you as a reminder of this wonderful summer."

Now, I was smiling.

"Would you like to take some so you will also have a reminder, that is, if you want a reminder of me?" Astana remarked. "Reminders of here may turn into nightmares, though, when you recall all the hard labor you did over the summer."

I moved over closer to where Astana was standing and picked up the pictures. Twisting my head in her direction, I said, "There is nothing about you or this farm that I will ever consider a nightmare." Then, I began flipping through the pictures.

"Not even your shakedown from Cleon?" she asked.

"Hush your mouth," I said laughingly. "I'm working on blotting that memory out of my mind." We both started laughing at what was once a disturbing memory. Finally, I came across a picture of Astana and me together and pointed that one out as one I would like to have. She slapped at my arm and said, "No, that's the one I want." Then, she started laughing and said she was just kidding. I could have whatever one I wanted. Then, I reached for one more. It was one of Astana by herself standing by the creek looking out across the water. "Can I have this one?"

"Sure."

Then, I flipped to the perfect one. It was a close-up shot of Astana's face. Opal must have been standing behind me because a small piece of my shoulder was in the bottom of the picture on one side. Astana was wearing her straw hat, looking at me with a big smile on her face like I had just said something hilarious. The photo captured all of her exotic features that I admired so much, even in black and white. If I could only have one photo, that would be the one. "Can I have this one?"

"Sure?" she said, laughing.

"You are being awful generous."

Astana started laughing again and said, "No, I'm not all that generous." Then, she lifted up the film envelope and showed me that there were duplicates of all the pictures in the flap of the envelope. "You picked out the same photos I wanted, so there would have been a fight over them if I hadn't noticed the duplicates."

I picked up the photo of the two of us together and examined it closer. I had a fascination for it for some reason, and it wasn't just the fact that I was so pleased to have a picture of the two of us together. It was something else. As I continued to look at it and hold it with tender care, Astana asked me what I was thinking.

"Look at this picture," I said, holding it up to her. "See how well we match, but also contrast, in a beautiful harmony that blends together and compliments the two of us, just like Opal said. And it's not just our colors; it's also our different features."

Astana took the picture from my hand to examine it closer. She softly traced her fingers over the surface of the photo as if caressing it. "You're right. We blend so well together like a painting on a canvas, and yet we contrast in an eye-catching way. I'm so happy Opal brought them to us, and I will always have a visual memory of you instead of trying to conjure you up in my mind."

"Me too. Now, I can have these pictures to remind me of the summer, and they will help me in the hard days ahead of me in football practice and in the years to come in college."

"Even without the pictures," Astana said softly, "I will always have reminders of you everywhere I look when I see all the improvements you've made to the farm, and I will automatically think of you. Every spring, when the new plants you put in start to bloom, I will think of you. You have left your touch in all directions around here, sort of like Johnny Appleseed."

That night before I went to bed, I looked at the three pictures I took with me and savored the memories they brought to my mind. Then, I placed them in my Bible to keep safe until I got home and could find a better place to keep them.

Chapter 14

Over the next few weeks, I made preparations around the farm for my departure. I wanted to tie down any loose ends and not leave unfinished work for Astana to worry about. It kept me busy but didn't wear me out like the work had done when I first arrived. Perhaps, I had built up a stamina for farm work, and that was why I didn't feel beat at the end of the day. Memories of my few weeks there kept rolling around in my mind as I worked. Mundane work gives the mind ample time to think and dwell on things. I thought back to how miserable I was my first few days there when I was missing my family and my home so much. The hard work was all that saved me in those early days. I was too pooped to linger in my homesickness for long.

One of my fears back then was that my time there would drag out like a prison sentence, and I would feel as though I was in solitary confinement living there with someone I felt was so foreign to me at the time. It's amazing how things can change in such a short period of time. Here I had not done any fun social things all summer, but it was turning out to be the best summer of my life. It all felt so strange to me to be having these feelings. They continued each day those last few weeks. I found myself worrying about how lonely I was going to be when I got back home. Nothing made sense to me anymore. Nonetheless, I kept plugging along with my chores and wrestled with my thoughts.

When we went to the last farmer's market day in Echo Falls, we saw many friends who stopped by to say goodbye and to wish me luck when I left. I appreciated having had the opportunity to meet them and to see how we all got along together. Those experiences with Astana's White friends had been new to me, just like so many of the experiences I had shared with her over the summer.

On my last Sunday at the little church in Echo Falls, they had a watermelon feast planned after church. It was actually a regular picnic but with watermelon for the main dessert. The church service was touching, and my heart swelled with joy being there with so many friends I had made in just a few weeks. The sermon rocked, and so did the singing. There was much fellowship following the worship service as we sat around the picnic area, slurping on our watermelons. I warned everyone how messy Astana could be when she was eating watermelon. She started giggling that contagious laugh that triggered our memories from a wonderful summer night that now seemed like ancient history. How much closer we had grown since that night.

It was especially difficult that afternoon hugging all my friends from church goodbye, knowing I would never see them again. They all had good wishes for me, and some of them had farewell gifts to remember them by.

Chapter 15

My heart was heavy when I crawled out of bed my last full day on the farm. Then, I laughed at myself, thinking about how often I had dreamed of this day when I first arrived. If I had had a calendar on my wall, I would have been marking off the days, and I would have been jumping for joy when this day finally arrived. But that wasn't how it turned out. It's funny how life doesn't always turn out the way you plan, even when you have worked so hard to plan your life carefully as I had done. I think it was that day when I first said to myself, *Buddy, you just can't always know what is ahead for you.* It wouldn't be the last time I would make that statement.

As usual, Astana brought up breakfast and said good morning. I ate it quickly and then cleaned up my dishes and took them down to her. She asked me what I had planned for the day. I told her just some odds and ends. She asked me not to work too hard since it was my last day. She said she wanted to have a nice quiet evening together. The thought of being together one last time brought excitement to my heart and kept me whistling as I worked throughout the day.

That evening, I got cleaned up and put on my favorite set of clothes that Astana had given me, hoping that by now, the clothes didn't remind her of Robert when I wore them. When I went downstairs and got to the kitchen door, Astana was not there. I walked on in because I saw that the table was set and food was on the stove, so I knew she must be around somewhere. Thoughts of my first time in her kitchen and my forbidden rule to not go in a White woman's house crossed my mind. Now, it felt perfectly normal to be there. I walked around nervously, wondering how the night would turn out. I picked up the photo of the two of us that Astana had framed on a shelf, admiring it, before setting it back down. I had so many things on my mind I would have loved to tell her, but I was certain I would not have the nerve to get it out. The longer I waited for her, the more anxious I became, and the more my emotions rose to the surface. Finally, I heard the soft sound of Astana's bare feet coming down the hall to the kitchen. She was a little startled, not expecting to see me there. I was startled, too, seeing her standing there in that pretty pastel yellow dress she had worn to church and, of course, her grandmother's pearls. It made my heart sing to know she went to extra trouble that last night to wear a church dress for me. Her loveliness was on full display that night. Her face had a healthy glow, and her cheeks were a soft pink. Those eyes. What could I possibly add about those eyes? They always took my breath away. She had the figure of a young girl who had just blossomed into a beautiful woman with all her curves showing gracefully in her creamy yellow dress. Her brown hair was shiny and hung down her back with soft curls, some falling forward over her shoulder to rest on the neckline of her dress.

I know I must have been gawking when she saw me, but she just laughed her normal laugh and started getting the food off the stove and adding the finishing touches to the meal. When we sat down to eat that night, I reached for her hand before saying the blessing. She smiled, and I began, "Thank You, Lord, for all Your blessings You have showered on us today. Thank You for the friendship that has grown between the two of us while I've had the opportunity to work here. Please, Lord, watch over both of us as we depart and go our separate ways. Lord, I offer a special thanks for bringing us together so we could experience the bond we've shared this summer. May the Lord bless us and keep us. In Jesus' name, amen."

Astana looked up, and I saw that tears had welled up in her eyes. I had a lump in my throat, and I was beginning to wonder how we were going to be able to make it through this last meal together. Astana squeezed my hand before releasing it, and we gathered ourselves together so we could start to eat another good meal she had prepared for us. Soon we started talking about different things that had happened during our day. There was not as much laughter that night, but it was jovial enough to feel normal. I guess we both had lots of memories to dwell on.

After we did the dishes, I told Astana I had a surprise for her. I took her by the hand and led her out on the porch. There, she saw the porch swing I had just hung that afternoon. I had painted it white with the leftover paint from the bench. It gave the porch a nice warm country feel. She started jumping up and down enthusiastically. "Oh, Brent, I have always wanted a porch swing."

I led her to the end of the porch, and we sat down to enjoy swinging slowly back and forth. For a few minutes, we were quiet, deep in our own thoughts. I had my arm around Astana's back but still resting on the back of the swing. Astana reached her hand over and rested it on my knee. I felt an immediate rush. I looked over at her face just as she looked up at me. Our eyes were locked in a magnetic stare that seemed to be expressing our thoughts without speech. I took my arm from behind her back and reached for her hand there on my knee. We then sat there holding hands like a nice romantic couple who might be courting each other. It felt so natural, and yet, the thought of how natural it felt created so much excitement in my young heart. I knew this night was going to end in some kind of emotional conversation. There was no way around it. I was so immature, though, and didn't know how to respond to my emotions. After planning my whole life so carefully, I was suddenly at a loss as to what to do this last night with this wonderful woman. Finally, my emotions were too high, and I had to cut the tension. I stood up abruptly and startled Astana for a minute. "I just remembered I have another surprise for you. I have the bench finished and placed over by Robert's tree. I want to show it to you."

"Wait," she said. "I want to get something for the tree. I'll meet you over there."

We parted, and I went straight to the tree. As I paced back and forth, I stopped now and then to admire my work on the bench, and then I investigated the lawn I had started there and checked out the impatiens I planted. It had turned into a very pretty tranquil setting and a nice memorial to Robert. Finally,

I saw Astana heading my way, the breeze gently blowing her hair around her face and causing her dress to swirl around her pretty shapely legs.

"I wanted to bring a ribbon from this dress that you like so much," she said as she approached, lifting it up for me to see. "I want to tie it on a branch on the tree to remind me of the day you left." I could see there were some tears in her eyes as she reached up and tied the pretty, creamy yellow ribbon on a branch of the tree. Then, we both stepped back and gazed at the tree with the purple and yellow ribbons fluttering softly in the breeze. I had Astana turn around and examine the new bench I had placed there. She smiled, and we both took a seat and sat quietly for a few minutes, looking at the tree with runaway thoughts racing through our minds.

After a while, the mosquitos made their nightly appearance, and we decided to go back inside. I opened the screen door for Astana to walk in ahead of me. She entered the room and walked toward the couch. I assumed she was preparing for our departing conversation and was probably just as nervous as I was. We both sat down and remained in silence.

Being plagued with insensitive male genes, I was positive I would not be able to say the right words. My heart was confused as I sat there drowning in my emotions, not knowing how to reveal them in a proper way. Feeling uncomfortable, I decided I needed to face the music and see where my sad song took me.

"I'm glad you wore that pretty dress tonight," I began. "I can have this picture of you in my mind to take back home with me."

Astana laughed that laugh that I loved so much. "Well, you should have seen my second option I was pondering."

"Oh. What was that?" I asked.

"I had planned to wear that baggy old dress and my Converse sneakers that you saw me in when you first arrived."

We both laughed remembering that memory from what seemed like ages ago, and I loved to see her sense of humor to think of wearing that outfit. "Well, that will be another memory I will never forget. What I loved so much about those first impressions of you was how struck I was with how you carried yourself. You didn't need fancy clothes. You showed me right off that you were a strong woman, and you wore your old clothes with pride, and they began to sparkle on you."

"Oh sure," she laughed. "I wore them out of necessity for the work I had on my plate." Then, looking down at her hands for a minute as if thinking back to those days, she said as she raised her head back and looked in my eyes, "But after I saw all that you were capable of doing, I could take off my old work clothes, and for a short while, I didn't have to be the strong woman."

"I'm glad I was able to give you a break and let you be yourself for a little while." She smiled and nodded at my words. Then, I added a question for her, "What did you think when you first met me?"

"Well, I've already told you about the altercation I had just experienced with Cleon Jarvis about the farm, so I was in a sour and defeated mood. I'm sorry I wasn't more welcoming when you first arrived. All I could think of was the stress it would be on me if I didn't have someone who could step up and do the job. I was worried because you had zero farm experience. But

I was impressed when you stood up for yourself when I rudely asked if you had flunked. I was also impressed by your good manners. After I got to know you better, I began to notice your striking good looks and strong muscular body. The more comfortable you became with me, the more your sweet, caring personality came out, and then your humor began to show. You came through for me in a big way." A bright smile crossed her face but with sadness in her eyes. "I'll never forget you and all you've done for me."

Knowing I should have immediately responded back to her and let her know that I would never forget her either, I was, instead, drawn in another direction. I felt the need to warn her about something that I feared in my heart. "Well, you will be getting another worker next summer."

Astana abruptly looked at me with raised eyebrows and a tilt of her head, maybe not believing what I just said. "You think I will feel the same way about the next farmworker that is dropped off here? Really?"

"No...at least I hope not. I think I have been worrying about it, though, for a while now. I didn't get to know those guys long on the truck. Just the few hours on the drive to the different farms. But I was around them enough to know I don't want them around you next year...or the next...or the next."

By then, Astana had moved closer to me and patted me on the knee. "Brent, you don't have to worry about any other guys coming out here working for me. I love that you feel protective of me. But I will have my dad next summer barring any other accidents, and I think I am pretty savvy about how to handle

155

myself with men and especially young boys. And by the way, you were no boy."

"I know. I don't mean any disrespect. I just know how young men think. I can see now why Daddy is so cautious with my sisters when it comes to men. We are onto that male instinct in other guys, but we are afraid you women are not aware of how they are."

"Believe me," Astana said, "I am very aware of how men can be, young and old alike. I think that is why I've bonded so well with you because you never gave off those vibes that would cause me to ever think of you as a threat. I could relax around you and get to know the real person you were inside."

"I'm glad you felt that way. I worried that you would forever think of me as a snotty teenager." We both chuckled, remembering her remarks from the past, and then I started again, "You know, if I had not stayed back a year in school because of sports, you might have looked at me differently. You might have instantly thought of me as more of a man or your equal if I had already graduated. But with me going back to high school, you will probably always think of me as an immature teenager."

Astana sat there listening to me talk. She was recalling her own memories of our time together. "You know, I think I did start thinking of you in a more adult way after you told me you had stayed back a year and you were turning eighteen. But then you proved your manhood to me over and over again during the rest of the summer. And you are right. If you were not in school, there probably wouldn't be the imagined gap between us. It's funny how that is. But once you are out of high school, age doesn't seem to matter much."

It felt good to go over our memories and to get words at-tached to them, explaining our feelings that would have other-wise been left to interpretation. I knew I had grown very fond of Astana over the summer, but I was not sure of her feelings for me. I still wondered if her feelings were just a close-friend kind of fondness for me. However, remembering the night when she sewed my buttons back on my shirt, what we expe-rienced didn't feel like a friendship kind of emotion. We made an effort that night not to get carried away, and we passed it off as the emotional state we were in that night due to our rage over Jarvis. I was still painfully aware of my place as her em-ployee and also as a Black young man in a White lady's house. Yes, we had grown closer over the months that followed, and we made a real connection with each other, but I was too inex-perienced to know what those feelings I had for her were, and I definitely couldn't figure out what her feelings were for me. I had seen so many guys over the years with that strong male ego who automatically assumed that all women were crazy about them. I was wishing, just for tonight, that I could grab hold of some of that self-assurance for myself. All I knew was that I hated to leave her, and I knew she would stay in my mind for a long time to come. Finally, I returned back to the conversation and said, "I know we come from two different worlds, and you might even say, two different time zones if you let our two-year age difference bother you, but I feel if we had met at another time under different circumstances, there might be a place for us. Does any of that make sense to you?"

"Yes, it does," Astana responded quickly. "It already feels that way for me. Like our bond is special. Like our meeting each other was meant to be, and our differences are a positive instead of a negative."

My practical thinking started creeping into my brain, and I said, "But it is probably just because we are out here away from everyone. Away from our own environments. Things might be a lot different if we were trying to live in the real world, yours or mine. You have seen how unaccepting people can be toward me, but can you imagine how they would be if we tried to navigate in the real world as a couple? Folks are even more intolerant of people who dare to try that."

Astana looked at me with disappointment in her eyes. I searched them, trying to read what was on her mind. But I didn't have to wait long before she shared her thoughts with me. "So you think I am too naïve...that we're too far apart?"

"No, but I think it would be extremely difficult. And it would be hard to see someone suffer because of me. I still worry about the problems my time with you this summer may cause you, even after I'm gone. It burdens my heart to think of any pain coming to you because of me."

"Brent, any pain I may suffer because of you, I would consider a badge of honor. I've had people talk about me before, and I got over it. These eyes of mine that you call exotic, well, growing up, kids used to make fun of me and call me ghost eyes. The freckles on my nose that you think are so cute caused me many tears when I was called *freckled face* as a kid."

Astana stopped suddenly and started rapidly shaking her head back and forth as if she had made a huge mistake. "Don't get me wrong. I know those things are nothing in comparison to what you've had to suffer. I have no authority whatsoever to make such a comparison. That's very presumptuous of me to even hint at such a thing. I'm just trying to let you know I'm tough enough to take what comes."

I looked down dejectedly and uttered, "But I don't know if I'm tough enough to watch you take it. I could never forgive myself if any harm came to you. We have been accepted pretty well here this summer, but your friends and family accept me because they trust your judgment. Our friends at church accept you because you're with me, and they trust my judgment. We've not tested our relationship out as a couple yet. We're accepted because people think we're just casual friends."

I could see Astana was exasperated, thinking of all the negative. Finally, she looked up at me with a flicker of hope in her eyes. "What if we just stay in touch with each other and see what happens later on after you graduate? Maybe race issues will get better. I could go to some of your games this year and watch you play sports. I could dress like a man and carry a clipboard and pretend to be a coaching scout."

"There's no way you could pass as a man," I said, laughing. Then, I began again, hating to bust her bubble, but I couldn't see a future in us staying in touch. "Astana, I would never want you in some of the neighborhoods where I play my games. It would not be safe for you. And I don't take much stock in long-distance relationships. For me, it will be a very long time before I am settled enough to have a relationship. I have high school, college, law school, and then setting up my practice. That's not fair to you. What if I end up getting drafted? I would never want you worrying about another man off at war. I know we haven't really discussed us as a couple before, but I feel we are touching on it right now, and those are my thoughts on the subject."

The silence between us lingered like a thick fog. I couldn't read what Astana was thinking, but I didn't think they were good thoughts. When she looked up at me, tears were beginning to pool up in her eyes, and the lump in her throat made her words sound strained. "I guess you don't have enough faith in me...or in us. And I can understand how you are thinking because you have disciplined yourself your entire life so you will be able to reach your goal. I would never want to stand in the way of you reaching that goal." She sat still, nodding her head as if agreeing with herself.

"Astana, I know I sound selfish, but it is hard to let go. I have worked so hard, and I can't envision letting go of my plan right now. If I did let it go, you would be the one person who would definitely be worth it. But please believe me when I say this. You have made such an impression on me, and I will never forget you. I will never forget how you have made me feel...how you have made me feel like a man this summer."

I could see Astana's body shaking in coordination with the tiny sobs that were now slipping out. Tears were starting to run down her cheeks. Then, she began to apologize for her tears. I guess, after being the strong woman all summer, she didn't want to appear weak. "I'm sorry, Brent. I didn't mean to do this. I'm just thinking ahead of myself. I can see me tomorrow night sitting here all alone at the table over there eating a meal that is meant for two people. I will have no one to talk to. No one to laugh with. No one to get excited about. I don't know how I'm going to make it. I feel like I will be grieving all over again. I know I was just grasping at straws thinking we could stay in touch with each other being so far away. You don't even know where you will end up going to college. I want you to reach all your goals; I really do. I want you to have a happy life. I just wish I could know about it and see how it all turns out."

I scooted over closer to Astana as she sat there, still whimpering a little. I took both of her hands in mine, and we sat there eyeball to eyeball. "I am going to miss you so much, and I will definitely miss not being here each night to join you for supper. I hope you will find someone who will make you happy because your happiness will make me happy, and yes, I know how cliché that sounds. But it is true. I have to admit I will be jealous thinking of you being happy with someone else and imagining it in my mind. I pray that you find the perfect person to fulfill all your dreams. All I have been doing is thinking about my own dreams, but you have dreams too, and you deserve to have them come true."

My words triggered more tears and sobs from Astana. Chokingly, she said, "Brent, I have never taken time to have a dream of my own. I don't even know what I want, so it is hard to dream about it. My only dream until I met you was to marry Robert and be a wife and mother. That dream was ripped away from me. Maybe I am scared to try to have any other dreams. My time with you this summer was like a dream come true for me, and now it's over."

"I believe in you, and I know you will find it. It may take some time, but you will eventually find what it is you really want." I reached up and wiped away her tears with my thumb. The touch of Astana's skin sent a spark all through my body. I know she could feel it too. I quickly stood up from the shock I felt, and Astana stood up along with me. I reached over and placed my arms around her. Then, I gently pulled her closer to me and reached for a hug, thinking of it as just a goodbye embrace on our last night together. When I pulled away, I suddenly wanted another hug, and I held on tighter this time. From the passion I was feeling, I suddenly began to fear we would get carried away and not be able to stop. I wasn't sure I wanted to stop. We stood there staring intently at each other. I wanted to kiss her more than anything I had ever wanted in my life.

Suddenly, we were startled by car lights shining into the house through the windows, and we automatically jerked apart and began straightening our crumpled clothes. Astana walked quickly over to the door to look out and then turned to me and said, "It's Mom and Dad."

Slowly, we saw them get out of the truck and head toward the house. Astana looked back at me with sorrow in her eyes and then opened the screen door and went out to greet them. I followed behind her.

"Hi, Mom. Hi, Daddy. What are y'all doing out here this time of night?"

"Oh, honey, we were over visiting with Aunt Dorothy to see how she's doing. She's much better, by the way. We got to talking and ended up staying too long. Look, we brought a going-away gift for Brent. We knew it was his last day, but we had planned on getting here a little earlier than this. Sorry, it's so late."

We all walked into the kitchen, and Mrs. La' Shore placed a small cake and the gift on the table. I thanked them and then sat down at the table to open the package. Once I got the paper off and opened up the box, I saw that they had gotten me a nice leather wallet, and it had my initials engraved on it—RBL. It was beautiful and something like I had never had before. Mr. La' Shore laughed and said, "That's to keep all the money you are going to make one of these days when you're a big lawyer."

Astana came over close behind me, placing her hands on my shoulders to look over at the wallet. I ran my fingers over the engraving. Looking up, I graciously thanked both Mr. and Mrs. La' Shore. "I will keep this always, and I hope to do just that, fill it with lots of money."

We all sat down and enjoyed the cake and then visited for a while. I thought for sure Mr. and Mrs. La' Shore would be leaving, but then Mr. La' Shore asked if he could turn on the TV. He said he didn't want to miss the news, and he couldn't make it home in time to catch it at his house. I was disappointed, but it was getting late, and I figured that was all the time Astana and I were going to get. I am sure her parents had no clue what all was transpiring between the two of us when they arrived. But the mood had been broken, and I felt we had said all there was to say. Anything we had left to say would probably get us in trouble. I had spent my life avoiding trouble, and there was no need to start now. I had become a master of avoidance.

Chapter 16

I don't think I slept a wink all night. A part of me had wanted to bolt down the stairs as soon as Astana's parents left and start up where we had left off. I wondered if Astana was expecting me to do just that and if she had eventually fallen asleep waiting for me. I was being a coward just trying to protect my heart.

I got up early, knowing Mr. Turner would be picking me up that morning. I got dressed in some of Robert's clothes and then started packing. Astana had given me an extra bag since I was going home with more than I came with. What a metaphor for that summer. Yes, I was going home with much more than I had come there with. I had become a man over the summer in more ways than one. I was flooded with so many memories, and with all the transitions those memories created in me. It was overwhelming, and I felt a lump come up in my throat that was way too hard to swallow. I feared tears might creep up and start to trickle down my cheeks if I didn't stop my thoughts, and that would be hard to explain to the guys on the truck.

I was startled by the tapping on my door, and I quickly wiped my eyes. I wasn't expecting Astana to bring my breakfast, as I didn't have time to eat, and I felt we had said our goodbyes the night before, with nothing left to say. The door opened before

I could get to it, and Astana walked on in instead of standing outside like she normally did. She closed the door behind her, and I could see she was nervous from the shaking of the tray in her hands. I understood because the sight of her caused me to quiver myself. She placed the tray on the table and took a step closer toward me. My quivering changed to all-out trembling. I opened my mouth to say something even though I didn't know what words would come out. Then, at that moment, we heard the sound of a horn honking outside. We both looked at each other wide-eyed, not knowing what to say or what to do. Then, instinct kicked in, and I reached on the bed for my two bags and picked them up.

"I'm sorry to rush off," was my feeble response, showing my lack of maturity in dealing with my emotions. "Thanks for all you did for me this summer. I'm going to miss you." Then, I headed toward the door. Astana was as dumbfounded as I was. I could tell she wanted to say something, and I knew she would be kicking herself later on for not having the gumption to speak up. But I couldn't pry the words out of her, and I didn't have time to press her for them. She just stood and stared with a bewildered expression. I reached for the doorknob and opened the door, looking back over my shoulder at the beautiful, exotic woman I had grown to love.

I ran down the stairs and hopped on the back of the old truck, and Mr. Turner took off slowly down the bumpy dirt road, while I left behind a heart full of emotions that was growing more twisted with each turn of the tires. Immediately, the other guys started poking fun at me with questions and jokes. "Look at the muscles you grew over the summer," Ralph said.

"How was your old lady friend? Did she knit you some socks to take home with you?" The other guys hooped it up with laughter, but I just stared ahead as if I didn't hear them because I didn't really hear them. They were just words bouncing off the sound barrier covering my ears like balls in a pinball machine. What they had to say meant nothing to me. They had no way of understanding all that had taken place with me over the summer. They had no depth or measurement to calculate my feelings.

I tried to direct my thoughts on going home; on seeing Momma and Daddy; on seeing my brothers, sisters, and friends; on sleeping in my own bed; starting school in the fall; and on eating my momma's home cooking. I thought that would help me recover from the whirling emotions that were spinning around inside me like the spin cycle of a washing machine. But none of my attempts seemed to help. My mind kept going right back over the memories of my summer, memories of Astana, from the first day I arrived until the last moment I saw her standing in my room. Every place I looked driving down the road away from the farm was a sign of my work there. All the new trees lining the dirt road that she and I planted and the special plants I had put in over the summer. The garden and the orchard had become intimate friends to me with all my devotion to them day in and day out. Again, my thoughts went back to Astana standing there in her pretty silk nightgown I am sure she wore for my benefit. Usually, she wore a cotton gown that was impossible to see through even with x-ray vision, but that morning she wore a soft, flimsy pink nightgown, and it screamed out to be touched. I could feel the pain Astana must have felt as

I quickly left her, walking by her with no regard to the courage it must have taken for her to allow me to see her in that beautiful lace gown. She must have felt tossed aside, as if her feelings didn't matter to me at all. With my talk all summer about my focus and self-discipline, she could easily imagine that I didn't even notice her. But I did notice. Suddenly, I could no longer stand my thoughts. I was overcome with an urgency that could not be stopped. I jumped up and made my way to the bed of the truck and banged on the side. Mr. Turner leaned his head out the window and yelled, "What?"

"Stop the truck," I yelled back. "I forgot something important."

Mr. Turner stopped the truck and yelled, "Make it snappy, kid."

"I'll be quick. Be right back." Then, I hopped out of the end of the truck and took off, running down that dirt road with all the speed I had ever known. My feet were flying, kicking up dust as I ran swiftly down the road as if I were running a race in the Olympics.

When I reached the end of the drive, I was surprised that I didn't even feel out of breath yet. I was too pumped. I raced to the back door and opened up the screen, yelling for Astana. She didn't answer. I looked all around the house and then ran back out on the porch. Suddenly, I ran back up the stairs to my room and yanked the door open. There she was, standing with her face buried in my sheets she had pulled off my bed. When she looked in my direction, tears were streaming down her cheeks. Suddenly, words started coming out of me briskly, tumbling over each other, "I couldn't leave. Not like that. I had to come back. I know you think I will forget you, that I have no need for you. I have spent all summer convincing you that I don't need women in my life. But I was wrong. I can't leave here without you knowing that. But not just any woman. Just you. I know I can't do anything about it, and I have to go forward with my life and my plans, but I couldn't leave here without you knowing how I feel."

Astana dropped the sheets back on the bed and then started in my direction. When she got close to me, I took hold of her hand and spun her gently around, pressing her back up against the closed door as I drew close to her. She wrapped her arms tightly around my waist. When our lips touched, they were scorching with passion. The longing was painful. The thought of not knowing when or if we would ever see each other again made us cling for dear life. When I finally needed air, I placed both of my hands on the door, one on each side of her head, and lifted my head back away so I could run my eyes slowly over her sweet face, her beautiful eyes, her silky hair, her smooth skin, and the beautiful nightgown she had worn for me on my last day. I smiled with raised eyebrows, and she knew I was pleased. I softly whispered, "You don't know how long I've wanted to kiss you." Then, I closed my eyes and breathed slowly like a person doing yoga, but making a sizzling, sucking sound through my teeth.

Astana finally asked, breathlessly confused, "What are you doing?"

"I am recording every sensation I am feeling in my body; I'm recording every emotion I have ever felt for you, and my eyes have already stored your image in my memory forever. I never want to forget this feeling I am experiencing right now."

Astana took hold of my face and planted one last, long kiss on my lips. When we separated, she said, "I will never forget how this feels either. Please, promise me you will do all that you've planned to do. Be the man you are meant to be. Know I will be secretly cheering for your every achievement all of your life."

We were both next to tears at that moment. I choked out the words, "Astana, I promise you I will succeed. I will be hearing you cheering me on in my mind. If it is at all possible, I promise I will see you again someday. You may be married and have little ones running around here, but I will come back and prove to you that I made it, and you will know you played a big part in me making it."

Suddenly, we were rudely interrupted by the sound of the truck's horn honking again. I didn't want to be left behind, so I peeled my body ever so slowly off of Astana and stepped away. She moved away from the door and reached for the doorknob, opening it apprehensively. I sauntered by her, slowly taking in one last look at the whole woman I had learned to love that summer. I stepped out the door halfway and then suddenly turned around once more and grabbed a biscuit off my breakfast tray and grabbed one more kiss before taking off down the stairs.

Mr. Turner had backed the truck most of the way down the drive and was waiting impatiently for me. As I was running to hop on the truck, I heard Astana yell at me from the balcony of the garage apartment, "Hey, Brent, you might want to go out for track. You're pretty fast, you know." I laughed and waved after hopping on the back of the truck. All the guys gawked in disbelief at the beauty they saw standing that morning on the balcony waving to me—just me. Then, Ralph laughed and said, "You ran all that way back to fetch a biscuit." Then, he gave me a wink, understanding the real reason for my urgent detour that morning.

Chapter 17

I sat quietly in the back of the truck on my three-hour drive to the city of Hampton, where I was to catch the bus on to my hometown of Horseshoe Junction. The entire ride was torture for me. All the other guys were cutting up and telling lies about all the things they had done over the summer. Most, if not all, of their lies were X-rated. That's a definite sign you can tell it's a lie when it is directly from some smut magazine. I paid them no attention as I was drowning in my own memories. Some of those memories put a smile on my face, but the thought of leaving them all behind for good pained my heart, and it felt like a dark cloud hovered over me. I had heard people before say something about certain things dampening their spirits, and that was exactly how I felt, like I was drenched in a storm cloud of sorrow.

I gazed out at all the farmland as we drove lazily by on the country roads. When we went through towns, we were given stares. Looks of fear showed in the eyes of people walking the streets or passing by in cars watching a truckload of young Black men all piled together like maybe we were being hauled off to prison. How I wished I could be looked at as just a person instead of a Black man who might be a fugitive. That thought reminded me of how accepted I was around Astana and her family and friends. When we walked around town together, people greeted us in a friendly way. Maybe it was Astana's bold personality and the way she carried herself with such confidence. And then, with my training from my parents, who taught me to be friendly and to greet everyone, we were soon just Brent and Astana walking down the street. Like Opal said that day, maybe we were a glimpse into the future of what life could be. I tried to hold onto that dream.

Many times on the long drive, I tried to reel my thoughts toward my home where I was headed instead of back where I had just left. But no matter how hard I tried, I could not keep my concentration on home. My life had become too tangled with Astana, and it was like pulling up a deep-rooted weed to try to separate my thoughts from the memory of her. Everywhere I looked, I was flooded with memories, in the breeze, the trees, the passing creeks, and the neatly plowed fields all around us as we drove down the road. Even the smell in the summer air reminded me of her.

Off and on, some of the guys tried to draw me into a conversation. I just answered their questions in short answers so I could quickly get back to my own thoughts. I decided against fighting my memories, so I leaned back against my bags and put my cap over my eyes. I allowed myself to doze off in hopes of dreaming and having my memories feel more real once I let go of my inhibitions. My hope was to have more freedom in my dreams where my senses would be stronger, and for a moment, I could still be in Astana's arms.

I was shaken awake when the truck came to an abrupt stop at the bus station in Hampton. We each gathered up our bags and hopped off the truck. Mr. Turner was standing at the front of the truck with our final paychecks and our bus tickets home. I took mine and then wandered over to the group of busses all lined up, ready to go somewhere. I found the bus that had the number matching the number on my ticket, and I climbed aboard.

It was not long after I got settled in my seat that the bus driver climbed up in his seat and offered some announcements before taking off. His words sounded kind of garbled over the little speaker he held in his hand, but that didn't matter to me. I wasn't listening anyway. I noticed the smell of the diesel fuel, the sounds the bus made when it opened and closed the door, the sounds made when it shifted gears, the sound of the tires turning, and then the rolling sounds the tires made as we finally hit the pavement heading in a straight line back home.

Thankfully, it was not a long bus ride for me, and soon, I heard the driver announce my stop at Horseshoe Junction coming up. It wasn't until that moment that I finally started looking around at what had once been so familiar to me. I started remembering the history of my small town where, in its beginning, people came from all over to get their horses shoed by the most talented men in the business. Eventually, schools were established to teach the trade. Men from the school traveled around the tri-state area to shoe horses on the different farms. That day my town seemed new again. As I started to recognize different sights around town, a tinge of excitement started creeping into my soul. It surprised me that it took so long to spur my emotions. I knew Momma or Daddy would be at the bus station to pick me up. Exciting things like bus trips were not regular occurrences in my family, so it would be a big deal to pick up the eldest son of the Lake family.

The bus driver started a big turn of the giant steering wheel, twisting it around and around, before heading under the garage overhang that served as the bus station back home. I looked out the window in each direction and finally spotted Momma standing there, so beautiful, with an excited look on her face. She was beaming when I walked down the steps, and she could hardly wait to get her hands on me. I had always been close to Momma, and I had to say she was a welcome sight to me, even in my depressed state. She went on and on about how much I had grown and matured while I was gone and how much she had missed me. She loved the new clothes I had on, and she wanted to get me home so she could hear all about my summer. She linked her arm in mine, and off we went walking down the street.

Our little town was small, so Momma had not driven the car to pick me up. She was never much for driving anyway. It was a nice day and gave us a chance to talk before we were surrounded by the rest of the family waiting at home. Momma said she had prepared a big meal, and my sisters were finishing it up for her, and it would be ready when we walked through the door. Now, the thought of seeing my family and eating Momma's home-cooked meal became exciting. The closer to home, the more comfortable I became. It didn't mean by any means that I was already forgetting about my summer and about where

I had just spent the last months of my life. It just meant that what was so familiar to me was coming back slowly but surely.

When we walked through the door, Momma was squealing with excitement announcing our arrival. Everyone gathered about me like I was Santa Claus coming to town. I felt sort of like a celebrity, and I planned to enjoy it as long as I could, knowing I would soon be put back in my place as just another member of the Lake family. I guess being the first one in the family to go away from home and being gone for so long did kind of make me a celebrity in their eyes. Momma took my bags and placed them on my bed, and then came back in and gathered her family around our dinner table. By then, the frown I had worn so proudly all day was starting to reverse its course. Then, a bigger smile came over my face when we started passing dishes around the table and filling our plates while all talking at once, just like I remembered home to be.

After dinner, my sisters remained in the kitchen to do up the dishes, and my younger brothers took off to go visit friends. Momma and Daddy sat down with me and asked me how my summer was. I told them about the farm and explained about many of the projects I had worked on and the different things I had learned. Momma got my checkbook out of a drawer and handed it to me. "I wanted you to see how much money you have in the bank now with all that you earned over the summer added to what you had already saved. It is quite an amount. I went straight to the bank each time you mailed me a paycheck, and I deposited it in your account."

I opened up the checkbook register and saw the amount that was recorded there. It had grown quite a bit with my summer pay and with the amount that was added by the government, and I still had the paycheck I just received to add to it. I was happy to see my savings growing, even though I knew I would need a lot more than that for my goal of college. I also had to rely on my brain in my studies all the next school year to try to win a scholarship. I saw a huge challenge before me. Most of the time, I had no doubts about my ability to meet the challenge, but right then, at that moment, it felt a little overwhelming.

The next morning, the Lake family got all dressed in their Sunday best and headed out the door to church. There was excitement in the air for me to be going back to church and to gather around all my old friends from school and the neighborhood. I was also a little nervous, the kind of nervous you feel on the first day of school each year. I was greeted and hugged as soon as I walked through the door like a war hero returning home. When the service started, the crowd was rocking to the music. Then I got a picture in my mind of Astana standing next to me at the little church in Echo Falls with a big smile on her face, just swaying and clapping to the beat of the music. She would sometimes get so excited she would tap her foot on the floor and dance around and swing her hips like she was dancing with Elvis to "Jailhouse Rock." I loved her uninhibited way in which she could be herself and not worry about what people were thinking. I had teased her about everyone in church scrutinizing her White dance moves, but she sarcastically shot back that they were just jealous of her, being the only one with rhythm. Her actions would put a smile on everyone's face around her. And now, her memory put a smile on my face right there in my hometown church. People may have thought my smile was due to my happiness about being back home. No one could have imagined my thoughts were so far removed from where I stood that morning.

As soon as church was over, all my classmates gathered around me as we exchanged stories about our summer adventures. Some of the girls were huddled together over to the side of the group. I could see them whispering and giggling and pointing in my direction. I picked up on one of the girls talking, who was all a tither saying, "He's back," while eyeing me and pointing in my direction. Most people around those parts never got more than fifty miles from home and returned after a day or two. If they were ever gone for long, you never heard from them again. Word would come back that they had vanished from the South and moved up north to Chicago or New York. I was one of the few who took a lengthy journey and returned back home. It made me wonder how they would act when I left for college and would be gone for a year or more. When we started to depart, the guys reminded me of football practice early the next morning, and there were loud groans from all of us. As I was heading to the car, Sherry Kaye, one of my neighbor friends, came up to me and said, "Hey, Brent, I'll see you tomorrow at football practice."

"Oh, really?" I responded.

"Yes, remember I made cheerleader, and we'll be practicing too."

"That's great, Sherry Kaye. See ya tomorrow."

I got in the car Daddy had parked there idling. I knew he would be impatient after waiting around so long for me to talk to my friends, but with me having been away from home so long, he cut me some slack that day. Since my two sisters had boyfriends now, they got rides home with them, and that made more room in our car with just me and my two younger brothers. With our big family, there had been many times when we had tight squeezes, but we always managed. It was a good thing cars were so roomy on the inside so we could pack ourselves in like sardines if necessary. Now though, without the girls, we all had plenty of room to stretch out.

Momma got me up early the next morning for football practice and fed me a good breakfast. It reminded me of the big breakfast that Astana used to bring me. Those first few days back home brought back many memories of Astana. I assumed they would fade in time. It was just that it had been such a short spell since I was last with her. I could imagine how she must be feeling all alone now on her farm.

When I arrived at the school, I could hear laughter from the other guys on the team joking around with each other. I knew that laughter would soon turn to moans. I was very happy a cool breeze was in the air that morning, but I knew it would soon fade, and the hot humidity would soak us in sweat in no time. After a few remarks from the coaches, they started us doing drills. I was surprised that my wind and stamina were strong, especially considering it was the first day of practice. Usually, I would be dying in the first hour, but after each drill, I felt fine, just a tad winded, but not huffing and puffing like the other guys. Maybe the hard farm work I had done all summer had prepared me for practice. The coaches were pretty easy on us that first day. I think they wanted our muscles to be broken in gradually and then rebuild them slowly instead of wearing them all out that first day to where they were too painful to function the next few days. I thought that was a wise move on their part.

Sherry Kaye came over to me and her brother, Earl Dean, on one of our water breaks. She remarked in a shy voice about my big muscles and then ran off to kick up her heels with the other cheerleaders.

We went home for lunch and had an afternoon break to re-group and rest up. Then, we were back in the evening for more practice. This would be the routine for the next two weeks, and then, school would be starting up, and real football games would begin. It was my senior year, so this would be my final year to impress whatever scouts might be looking me over. I put forth my full effort so I would be prepared when the time came for me to perform in a real game. Just like my studies, I never wanted to be unprepared. Then, I chuckled to myself, thinking of Astana suggesting she dress up like a scout to watch my games.

At practice and at home, I began to hear rumors about some upcoming events around town. The state had ruled that the next school year, after I graduated, the schools would all be integrated. I guess we were one of the last states to integrate. Change was hard, and rumors were flaring up about what might happen when the people in our town were forced to change. People were already talking about protest marches. Both sides of town had their own fears about the future. Momma was worried about my two younger brothers and what might hap-pen to them. They were closing down the school in our part of town and sending those students to one of the White schools in town. We wondered how they would be accepted and what trouble they might face. Some tried to imagine what the nice White school would be like and how well supplied it would be there. I felt sure all the talk would calm down eventually because my hometown was not known for too much mischief or action on either side of town. We liked to keep the peace, as they say. Yes, people would be on their guard for sure. Hatred can create a bunch of unnecessary energy, but if nothing out of the ordinary happened in those beginning weeks, then I felt sure things would settle down. After all, this was inevitable. We couldn't go on forever living in a segregated world. Things had already started changing in the rest of the country, and they were changing in the South as well, just a little slower. The sooner we got started, the better it would be in the long run, kind of like ripping off the Band-Aid or diving in the swimming pool all at once instead of wading in slowly trying to adjust to the cold water. That was my prayer anyway.

One night after practice, I came home, and Momma had a plate of food waiting for me. She was such a jewel, and I appreciated her always watching out for me. My sisters were out on dates with their boyfriends, and Daddy and my brothers were off somewhere hunting. Momma sat down next to me while I ate. I was not very talkative that night, so Momma took up the slack. "It's so good to have you back home, Son. We all really missed you this summer."

"Thanks, Momma. I missed y'all too," was my reply.

"I've seen some of the girls up at church checking you out since you got home. You interested in any of them?" Momma asked.

"Momma, those same girls have been checking me out for years."

"Yeah, but they're at the age when they'll be doing more than checking you out. Soon, they'll be having their claws out for you."

I had to laugh at Momma thinking she understood the young girls of today. "Well, they can just show their claws all they want. Just like all the years before, I am too busy for them."

"Are you telling me you don't plan to date this year again? Are you just going to keep your head in your books all the time? I don't think that's healthy."

"Momma, you make me laugh. Most parents would be telling their sons to stop looking at the girls and get to studying. Now you're telling me it is not healthy for me to want to study all the time."

"Well, Son, you need a break. You need balance in your life. All you do is study and play sports. You need to work on a social life too. Whenever you become some big shot lawyer, you're not gonna know what to do when you're out socially."

Again, I was laughing at momma. "I guess I will take a crash course on social skills once I become a lawyer." Then, I patted Mom on the back and said, "Don't worry, Momma. I will balance my life out just fine. Besides, I'm looking for a woman just like you. Until I find that kind of woman, I'm not interested."

Momma couldn't help but smile with pride at my compliment, but I meant every word of it. I had been telling her that ever since I was a small boy, and it was still true.

I got a bath in the warm tub of water Momma fixed for me in the kitchen floor. It felt so good to soak my sore muscles, even all scrunched up in that small tub, and to get all the dirt, grime, and sweat off my body. But as I sat in the soothing water, I felt my mood sinking. I always found my mind wandering in all directions whenever I would take a bath. It was the only time I had quiet all around me, and I could relax inside my own head. Before long, my head was back on memories of Astana. In my busy day, I didn't have time to think about her so much. But whenever I had peace and quiet, I would quickly slip back to memories of her, and they could consume me.

That night, I was remembering so vividly my last night there. I could picture us on the bench looking at the tree. I saw us spilling out our hearts to each other on the couch. I saw myself running up the stairs to my garage apartment the next morning and finding Astana standing there holding my sheets. Then, a vivid picture of us up against the door, kissing with all the passion we both possessed. It was a feeling I had never felt before, and I didn't think it was possible that it could ever be surpassed. Those mental pictures caused my heart to ache for her, and I felt a flush come over me and then a tremble. At that moment, I needed Astana so badly. I wanted to feel her arms around me and taste her lips. I wanted to look in her eyes, and I wanted to hear her laughter.

With my long-range goals and the great distance between us, we would probably never meet again. I remembered telling her so passionately that I would come back and I would prove to her that I achieved my goals, and then I began to doubt my own promise. I meant it that morning. I really did. But the thought of it actually happening seemed too far removed from reality. How arrogant of me to even think that she would be waiting for me if I did go back. She was young and vibrant. She wanted children. She needed to find a good man who could give her babies, and she should have all her dreams come true. That was so selfish of me to even consider holding her back from her own accomplishments. I was the one who had encouraged her to pursue her dreams, and then I left her with the hope that I would return. I was suddenly ashamed of myself and my actions.

Everything in my mind whirling around like in a wind tunnel felt so confusing. It was more than I could handle on the weekend before starting my senior year of high school. If I kept thinking of Astana all the time, I would be a dismal failure in my last year of school, and I might ruin my chances to get into college. I had to get a grip on my life. There I was again, surrounding myself with my own selfish desires. Once again, everything went right back to being all about me.

I got out of the tub, dried off, and got my jeans on before I dumped the bathwater out the back door onto the lawn. Then, I sprayed the tub out with the water hose and hung it on the hook on the side of the house so it would be ready for the next person who needed a bath. When I came back inside, Momma was putting away my dishes and remembered something she had forgotten to tell me. "Honey, did you know we are finally going to put in a bathroom this year? Daddy has saved enough for it, and we got a contractor who is going to do it for us. He's going to let Daddy and you boys help him, so that will help to cut the costs. Won't that be wonderful?"

"Yeah, Momma. That'll be great. Finally, just as I'm leaving." Then, I laughed so she would think it was a joke. But having a bathroom at my garage apartment had spoiled me a little over the summer, and it was frustrating that such luxuries, as an indoor bathroom, had eluded me all these years. There I was again, being selfish. It had eluded my parents much longer than me. I went over and hugged Momma and said, "Really, Momma, that's great. I guess me being out of the house all summer and not eating all your food helped you save up for the new bathroom."

Momma chuckled and gave me a squeeze, adding that she did notice a measurable dent in her grocery budget while I was gone.

When I got to my room, I sat on the side of the bed in my jeans with a fan blowing on me, waiting for the dampness from the humidity to dry off of my chest before I put on my shirt. My mood was sinking even lower than it had earlier. I was thinking about it being Friday night, and most kids my age were out on dates. Then, I remembered the night when Astana and I went to the drive-up restaurant and got some hamburgers and brought them home. It had seemed like a date, like a real teenage experience that other kids enjoyed every weekend. I knew my lack of normal teenage fun and games was of my own choosing, but it didn't hurt any less knowing that fact.

I reached up on my table next to my bed and took my wallet that I got from Astana's parents. I stroked my initials on the outside. Then, I slowly opened it up, not looking for any money but searching for the plastic covers that held the three pictures I had of Astana. I had trimmed them down, cutting out some of the background scenery, so they would fit in the plastic picture covers. I flipped to each picture, one at a time, stopping on the last one, which was the shot of Astana looking at me with a big smile on her beautiful face. Finally, my heart cracked. I closed the wallet, and tears that had worked their way to my eyes began to flow. I put my face in the palms of my hands and cried, an act that did not come naturally to me.

The door to my bedroom was open, and Momma saw me hunched over crying when she walked by. Immediately, she came on in and sat on my bed, putting her hand on my back. I straightened up and quickly wiped away my falling tears.

"Honey, what's wrong?" Momma asked with concern in her voice.

Maybe it was because no one else was home, or maybe it was because I was always so close to Momma, but suddenly I heard my voice say, "Momma, I found that woman. I found that woman just like you." Then, I bent over and sobbed louder and with more tears.

Momma reached her arms around my broad shoulders and attempted to pull me toward her in a hug like she did when I was a small boy, but my larger man-size body made it awkward. Again, I got control of myself, and Momma looked me in the eye. "Do you want to tell me about her, Son?" she asked, expecting an answer.

"Momma, she's wonderful. Here, let me show you a picture." I reached for my wallet again and opened it up to the pictures I had of Astana, wondering what she would say about her being White. I knew she would be more understanding than most since her own mother was White. Momma gently took it from me and examined the pictures as if I had given her a valuable document. I appreciated that she was taking my broken heart seriously like that. When she turned to the photo of Astana and me together, she let out a soft sigh and traced her fingers softly over the plastic cover. She looked over at me and smiled.

"Are you shocked that she's White? I asked.

Thoughtfully, she replied, "Perhaps."

"Are you disappointed?"

Looking at the photo again, Momma said, "Seeing you two together in this photo gives me some insight in how my momma and daddy fell for each other. So no...I'm not disappointed." Then, she added, "She's lovely, Brent. You look perfect together. Do you want to tell me about her?"

"Oh, Momma, there is not enough time in one day to tell you all about her. She is just a special woman. I feel so blessed to have gotten to know her this summer. She is the woman who owns the farm where I worked. She lost her husband in Vietnam." Then, pausing, I put up my hands in defense and said, "I know...I know what you're thinking. She must be too old for me. But she is only two years older than me. Momma, she's a good cook. She is so caring. She's a hard worker. And as you can see, she's beautiful."

I stopped for breath before continuing on, "And Momma, when she walks into a room, the whole room lights up. Her laughter is so contagious she can have everyone laughing along with her over the simplest thing you can ever imagine."

I stopped and sighed before moving on. Then, a little more solemnly, I looked up at Momma again and said, "See, I told you I didn't have time to tell you everything. She is all I can think about. And I am trying so hard to not think about her right now. You know how hard I've worked all these years to concentrate on my studies and to make it to college. I guess being away from home this summer and not having studying on my brain allowed me to slip a little and let my guard down. Now, I'm doomed, and I finally know why I've had such a huge wall around myself all these years. See how I'm falling apart. Momma, I don't know what to do." I stopped and hung my head again, feeling embarrassed that I had shared so much of my feelings with my Momma.

She sat there nodding to herself as if she were mulling things over in her mind. Then, she patted my back softly in her own comforting way. "Brent, I understand how you feel. On one hand, you have experienced extreme joy, but on the other hand, you are now experiencing extreme sorrow for your loss. All loss feels like that. But joy and loss so close together must be extremely hard."

"Thanks, Momma, for understanding. I feel so foolish."

"Why would you feel foolish? Do you think you are immune to feelings?"

"No, of course not, Momma, but I have spent my life trying to avoid them. I just feel foolish for allowing my feelings to take over and then for letting them spill out on you just now. I think men are supposed to keep their feelings inside."

"Well, Son, I don't mean to burst your bubble, but the reason you kept them inside this long is because there was nothing so important on the inside that had to come out. You've never experienced love before."

"This is what love feels like?" I asked, sounding exasperated.

"Sometimes. It definitely has its highs and lows. But love can cause you to lose control of your feelings altogether like you are doing now. If you didn't feel what you're feeling now, you would never be able to relate to others in the future. If you kept that wall around your heart, you would be like some kind of frozen man. I don't want that for you."

"So you would rather have a son who is falling all apart like this?"

"No, Son. I want a son who is capable of feeling. I am happy to meet your nice lady friend, even if it's just a photo. I'm glad you had those wonderful experiences with her. Are you going to keep in touch with her now that you're back home?"

"No, Momma. I didn't give her my address. She wanted to come to my games this year and keep tabs on me, but I didn't encourage that. She lives too far away, and I wouldn't want her to be in some of the neighborhoods by herself where we play our games. And it wouldn't be fair to have her hanging around waiting for me for years while I finish up my education and start my career."

"Oh, so you made up her mind for her? You didn't allow her to decide what she wanted to do in this situation?"

"I guess so, Momma. Maybe I couldn't handle the thought of her growing tired of waiting on this kid to grow up, and someday, she would stop coming to see me and stop writing and move on with her life. Or she might put pressure on me and divert me from my goals."

"Well, even if it did happen that way, it would have been a more natural course for the relationship to take. Now, you are suffering greatly, and you'll always be wondering...what if? Sadly, you only have yourself to blame."

"I know, and it's driving me crazy. Here school is about to start, and football games are coming up, and I'm all torn up inside. I have to get myself together, or all I've worked for will go up in flames here at the very end."

"Honey, thank you for sharing this with me. By the way, what is your young lady's name?"

"Astana," I said, smiling at the sound of her name on my ears.

"That's a very pretty name," she said, looking again at her picture. "Now, I suggest you try to relax and not try to figure everything all out tonight. Just keep praying and wake up each day and see where that day takes you. God led you to her this summer. He has watched over you all these years. I think He will keep on watching over you and preparing you for whatever He has in store for you. Trust in Him. At least for now, you have these sweet pictures and your memories, and nothing or nobody can take those away from you."

"Thanks, Momma, for understanding," I said as I reached for a hug and felt the comfort only a mother can give. Then, she got up and left the room, and I lay down on my bed, trying to gently release my emotions. It felt good to get them out to Momma. I knew they were safe with her. She always seemed to be able to see into my heart, and I didn't have to strain to try to get my feelings across to her. She took in as much as I was willing to give, but she could also read between the lines and understand more than I even knew myself. She was good at that.

Chapter 18

Once school started, it really got busy. My oldest sister went off to Mississippi State College for Women, so that gave us a little more room around our house, which was nice, but it was still crowded trying to get ready in the morning.

I was exuberant the first day of school, arriving that fall with my friends as the big shots on campus, being seniors at last. We often got nostalgic, thinking we would be the last graduating class at our old high school. Everything we did that year would be the last time for any student, and the other classes looked up to us with a kind of superhero worship, knowing we were making history. We heard rumors that the school was going to be demolished, but then there were other rumors that they were going to turn it into a museum to celebrate the history of Black education. People didn't want to wipe out that history of what happened in the segregated South completely, even though it represented something negative. Nonetheless, it was our history, and we were proud to be a part of it and to have survived it. The old school would be sort of a memorial to what once was, even though many people wanted to forget how it was. But to us, since that was all we had ever known, we were happy with the rumors of keeping the school as a museum.

My plan that year was to pour myself into my studies immediately. I knew I would be consumed with football until the end of the season, leaving me little time for homework. I did most of my homework in our study hall period at school, and then I had a schedule for study time after I got home from practice at night. My only problem, even with as much structure as I had planned, was I still found myself slipping back into my memories of Astana. When I went there, I found it difficult to concentrate on my school work. Even my teachers noticed in the beginning as I sat staring out the windows. I had to work to get my mind back on track. Sports left little time for thinking, and that was my refuge. I had to put everything I had into my goal of graduating at the top of my class, and that was all there was to it.

Momma often worried about me since she was privy to my broken heart story, and she kept an eye on me, checking in with me from time to time and offering to let me vent. It was a good escape when I needed it, but I tried not to allow myself that luxury very often.

Our football team was on a roll, winning most of all our games that season. In the end, we brought home the championship trophy. That gave our superhero status an even higher ranking. My stats as a receiver were high, and my hope was that the right college coaches were watching me.

Every now and then, I would attempt to go on a date, but I found it was best to date girls who were friends. I wasn't emotionally ready to let my heart be burdened with any more turmoil than was already visiting me on a regular basis with memories of Astana. Dating, however, only reminded me of the fact that I wasn't with the one I wanted to be with. I never dated anyone in a steady pattern, and eventually, that was a drag on the girls who were interested in me. They didn't want an *on-again, off-again* relationship. I totally understood.

I made the varsity basketball team, and we had a good season. I actually enjoyed basketball because it was indoors, and we didn't have to withstand the extreme cold like we did in football. Once again, our team won the championship, and we took home another trophy for our high school display case, although it would be the last year for trophies for that school. Maybe that was what drove us so hard, knowing it was the last of everything.

When baseball rolled around, I was ready and in the best shape I had been in my high school athletic career. I played first base and sometimes pitched. A funny thing happened before baseball started. I was approached by the track coach, and he suggested I might like to try out for track. I told him I was playing baseball, but that didn't deter him any. As I was walking home from school that afternoon and began thinking about the track coach's proposition, I suddenly remembered the words of Astana shouting at me, saying, "Hey, Brent, you might want to try out for track. You're pretty fast, you know." I couldn't get those words out of my head, and they put a smile on my face remembering how fast I ran down that dirt road to find her that day. When I returned to school the next day, I went in to see the coach and told him I would be glad to try out for track as long as it didn't interfere with baseball.

As it turned out, I ended up with a good baseball season and track season. I was highly ranked in all the different races I competed in, and when I ran, I often thought of that run down Astana's long drive and who I was running to see.

Our spirits were high in the spring of that school year. Plans were being made for our last prom. I had not attended the prom before, but Momma was pressuring me to ask someone to the dance. She thought it would be good for me, and she even suggested again that it would help my social skills that would come in handy as a big shot lawyer someday. I looked around the school but couldn't think of anyone I would like to spend my hard-earned money on or who I would want to spend an entire evening with. Nothing seemed to jive for me, and I didn't want it to feel forced.

One evening, when I was in the kitchen eating my supper after baseball practice, Momma sat down with me. That was a habit we had developed over the years. We discussed the normal topics of the day. Momma asked me how my plans were going in my search for colleges. I reminded her that I was waiting first to see if a college team offered me a scholarship. Several colleges had contacted me to talk about football and baseball. One college had even contacted me about a track scholarship. Both my parents were happy about the interest the different colleges were showing in their eldest son.

Finally, Momma got around to the subject that had caused her to want to sit and chat that evening. "You know, Brent, I was talking to Mrs. Henderson over at the church the other day. She is worried that Alma Faye may not be asked to the prom this year. She wasn't invited last year, but that was her junior year, so it wasn't as important. She's afraid Alma may be the only senior who doesn't have a date to the prom, and it's breaking her heart."

"Really?" was my brilliant answer.

Momma slapped at my shoulder softly and laughed. "That's not what you're supposed to say."

"What, Momma? What do you want me to say?" I asked.

"Well, I was just thinking it would be really sweet of you to ask Alma Faye to go with you to the prom. She's a cute girl and very sweet. You've known her all your life, so what would be the problem?"

I sighed a heavy sigh and rolled my eyes in my head. "Really, Momma? You expect me to ask a girl I am not interested in to the prom? You want me to spend the money I have saved for college on a corsage and all the other expenses of a prom just so someone doesn't feel left out?"

"That would be the honorable thing to do." Then, she added, "Your Honor."

I couldn't help but smile at Momma for that little courtroom jab at me. "I'll think about it, Momma. Alma is sweet, and I don't mind her company. My main problem is that I didn't want to take my own self to the prom, much less someone else. But if it will make you, Mrs. Henderson, and Alma Faye happy, then I guess I will consider it."

Momma laughed her beautiful laugh and gave me a big squeeze. "You're such a sweet boy. You make me so proud."

Alma was thrilled when I asked her to the prom, even though she realized it was not an act of romance but more of an arranged date. She got busy planning her dress for that special night, and I was happy when Momma offered to cover the cost of Alma's corsage. I guess she felt guilty for twisting my arm a bit. When the night rolled around, I got dressed in my church suit, and Dad let me borrow the family car. We got our pictures taken at both houses, and there were lots of laughs. It was easy to be with Alma since we had played together since we were young, and we had gone to school and church together all our lives. It gave me some practice dancing, which I had missed out on since I was always too busy with school and sports. I faked my way on the dance floor, and we all had a fun night cutting up with our friends. All the girls looked extra special, and the guys looked quite handsome as well. When I dropped Alma off at her house that night, I managed to give her a gentle, friendly kiss, and then I told her good night.

As I drove home that night, I pondered that kiss. It was not a kiss that begged for more. It was just a formality. I remembered some kisses in my recent past that did scream out for more, and those were the ones I cherished that night as I was all dressed up in my suit. I then thought how childish a prom probably would be to Astana, a woman who had already passed her high school years. Then, I pushed my memories of her kisses to the back of my mind feeling embarrassed, and I began to rip my tie off from around my neck. When I was with Astana that summer, I felt like a man. Driving home from the prom that night in my suit, pretending to be a man, made me feel like a kid.

Toward the end of my spring semester, I got word that I had been chosen valedictorian of our class. I was honored and immediately thought that it would look good on my college resume. Then, I felt shame that all I could ever think of was how things would look on my record or how my awards would elevate me in the future. I guess that was the personality of a goal-driven person. It didn't look very admirable in my eyes.

After checking over the different college offers for athletic scholarships, I had narrowed it down to an offer from a Black college not too far from home. First of all, I knew that it would tickle Momma for me to be close to home and going to a Black college. However, in my mind, I felt I needed to get into an integrated college soon. That would be my future. I figured my integration experience would come when I got in law school. The sport I settled on was a track scholarship. My reasoning was that I felt track would not take up so much of my time and not beat up my body as much compared to football. I wanted the financial opportunity a sport could offer me but one that allowed me the most time to study. I thought track was a good balance. It made me smile to think that Astana had been the one to suggest it to me.

The last few weeks of high school flew by. We had finals to study for and a baseball season to win, and our hope was that we would take home the championship trophy to add to our senior year trophies there on display in the trophy case at the entrance of the school building. I was also thinking over what I wanted to put in my speech to the graduates. It seemed to me that every minute of my life was crammed with activity that spring. Even though I had controlled most of my actions and my emotions, a sense of joy started oozing out of all of us, me included, that spring. We could see the end, and we had dreams of the future. In the final weeks, I aced my finals, and we did indeed bring home the baseball championship trophy.

You couldn't tell us nothing. We were the big shots on campus. It was a feeling that would be hard to replace after we walked out those doors for the very last time.

We had our graduation in the auditorium of our church building. I was a wreck that night getting my cap and gown on straight and thinking about speaking in front of all the kids at school and all our parents. I knew the auditorium would be packed and all eyes would be on me at the moment of my speech. Then, I calmed myself down and tried to put things in perspective. It was not all about me. Graduation was about all the kids that had stood together over the many years. Immediately, I calmed down.

I was so proud when I walked down the aisle of the large auditorium and up on the stage, all decked out in my cap and gown. In our school colors, we looked united, and it felt wonderful and even kind of powerful.

I sat in my seat on stage, bouncing my knee nervously up and down. I wasn't sure if my nerves would let me hear my name when I was called forward to give my speech. Perhaps, they had already announced my name, and I didn't hear it. Was everyone waiting for me now? No...just calm down...breathe.

I had thought long and hard about what I wanted to say in my speech. I had listened to many graduation addresses over the last few weeks, trying to get a handle on what to say, but I didn't like any of the speeches I heard. They were all so formal. They talked about gestures of grandeur and accomplishments. They talked about outer space and great accomplishments. I wanted to look to the future, but I also wanted to look at the past and point out how important the past was to our future, despite the difficulties we had faced.

Finally, I heard the announcement, "And now, for our valedictorian address tonight, let's welcome Brent Lake." Then, I heard a round of applause as I headed down the stairs to the podium. I had chosen not to have a written speech. What was I thinking? I quickly let out a silent plead to my Lord to give me strength and wisdom when I opened my mouth and to please not let me embarrass myself or my parents. When I arrived at the podium, I grabbed each side and held on tight. Then, I slowly looked out over the audience, seeing so many familiar faces, and my nervous tension began to fade. Those faces were what my speech was about. I was suddenly overwhelmed just thinking of all our parents and all they went through to get us where we were that very night. They must be bursting with pride.

I cleared my throat and started, "Good evening, faculty, parents, friends, and relatives from near and far. Thank you all for coming to share this important night in our lives. What you see standing behind me on the stage tonight is an army. We are united as one. Our caps and gowns are our uniforms. We have fought in the trenches together all these years, and now we have arrived." Lots of clapping rose from the crowd, and then I began again.

"But what I see when I stand here tonight is that morning years ago when my momma dropped me off at the elementary school we all attended so I could start first grade. I was scared, and I think Momma was too." There were a few chuckles around the crowd from people who knew exactly what I was talking about.

"Momma introduced me to my teacher, Miss Coats, and that woman scared me. Suddenly, I wanted my momma." Laughter broke out in the audience.

A lump rose in my throat as I started again with a strained voice, "I hung on tight to Momma's hand that day, and she had to absolutely pry my fingers off of her strong hand. I thought to myself, *How could she abandon me like that?* What was she doing? I had tears in my eyes, and when I looked at Momma, I think I saw tears in her eyes too as she hurried out of the room. I shyly sat at my desk when she left, not knowing what to expect or how that day would change everything I had known about the world before that morning when I walked innocently into that classroom. When the rest of the students arrived, Miss Coats started the class. She taught us a cute song that morning, *welcoming us to her class.*" I softly started singing the first lines of the song, and in a minute, the rest of the class behind me started singing along impromptu with me. When we finished, we all clapped for ourselves, and the auditorium was filled with laughter seeing big high school students singing our first grade *welcome to school* song from so many years ago.

Then, I started up again, "Think about it, folks, from that song on, we have marched the halls of this school together and have ended up right here tonight. There were so many more songs we learned together along the way and so many lessons about life. We've had some of the best teachers here who have fought for us the entire way. Sometimes, they had to kick us in the pants to get us motivated, but they loved us that much.

They never let us be less than what they knew we could be. I want to give all our teachers, not only at the high school but in elementary and middle school, a round of applause." The room broke out clapping, showing their appreciation for all the teachers and their many efforts for their students.

"Our coaches have been more than coaches to us," I continued. "They have been mentors and taught us about life. They protected us when they saw possible harm on the horizon, and they gave us rides home if they sensed danger. That was so special to boys trying to be men but who were really scared inside. The same was true for the lady coaches and the young women they developed over the years. Please, give a round of applause to our coaches. Please, stand up, all of you coaches." Again, the auditorium broke out with loud clapping.

When I began next, I wasn't sure what I was going to say. But I started by opening my mouth, and words started pouring out. "I could stand here and talk about the future and all we plan to accomplish. I could tell you that we plan to set our sails towards the office of the president of the United States. Or maybe we will go on to be an astronaut. Those goals, all are lofty, yet they are still within our reach. But tonight, I want to concentrate on what got us here. I want to talk about our foundation. That foundation is because of all of you in this audience. You are the ones who have sheltered us and encouraged us and even nagged us at times. But you believed in us. You taught us our values and what is really important in life. Without all your patience and love, we could never have made it this far. And if we go on to become president or an astronaut or a teacher, then it is because of you. Yes, all of us here on this stage worked hard, and we are quite proud tonight to be standing here. But we know in our hearts that we would not be here if not for all of you out there. Not only have you pushed us to get through school, but you got us to church. You taught us manners and workmanship and work ethic. Now, don't get me wrong. We hated it every inch of the way, but now we look back, and we thank you. We thank you for loving us enough to push us.

"Tonight is our final night together in a school setting. I can see my momma now in my mind coming to pick me up that first day of school all those years ago, all nervous to see how I did that day. Her face lit up when she saw me laughing with some new friends and hanging back, not wanting to stop my play and come to her right away. It may have hurt her feelings a little bit that day to have to let go, but she was also proud that I took that first step with making new friends, just like she was proud when I took my very first baby steps. But then I said goodbye to Freddy, my new friend I had met that day, who is still my best friend today, and I took off running into her arms. I couldn't wait to tell her all the adventures I had experienced that first independent day I spent away from her watchful eye. I think tonight, those early tears that were in all of our eyes that first day of school may have returned as you parents see us cross over from high school students into working adults of the future. I think we all look back to those early days and wonder how it could have possibly gone by so fast in a blink of an eye. But here we are. We made it. Thanks to all of you. We owe you, our parents, the biggest applause of the night." Then, all the students behind me immediately stood up, and we applauded our parents, who indeed did have tears in their eyes by then.

When everyone sat down, I began once more, "And now to our future. We all know slaves received their freedom many years ago. In the beginning, some didn't know what to do with themselves. They had been told what to do and when to do it for so long that they didn't know where to turn. They had been denied an education, so they needed to fight for knowledge so they could succeed in their new freedom. Even today, we have also been denied certain rights. The right to go to an integrated school, the right to walk freely in certain parts of town, to sit in any restaurant around town, or even drink from a public water fountain. But times are changing, and we are embarking on a new era. In the beginning, we may function like the first freed slaves, and we may stumble at first, trying to find our footing in this new world. The one sure thing we have that those early slaves didn't have is a good education, and we need to take full advantage of that."

The crowd broke out in an unexpected applause that startled me for a minute. When it ceased, I gathered my thoughts and began again, "I think back on a saying I've heard many times about the best revenge when you've been dumped is to be happy. When we have heartbreak in our lives or have been treated unfairly, we need to be so happy and successful, and then we can stuff our happiness in the face of the one who broke our heart. That is the best revenge for us as we receive our marching orders tonight and leave the halls of our high school behind. We need to seek to overcome and be all we can be. That is the best way to show all the people who may have tried to keep us down in the past. Someone recently asked me what my favorite word was, and I told her 'liberty.' Liberty is freedom. It is escaping the things that bind us, whether real or imaginary, because sometimes we hold *ourselves* back. Let us live our lives as though we really believe we are free. We need to *take* it. It *belongs* to us. We have seen a lot growing up here in this town and going to this high school. We have seen a lot of changes in the world in our short lives with the Vietnam War and the civil rights movement. We're not sure what we're going to face when we leave here, but when we get scared in our future uncertainties, I want us to remember back to this night, to this army standing here together in our cap and gown uniforms. Together we are strong. I want us to remember our friendships and our love for each other, and I want us to fight to keep the hate that is out there all around us from stopping us in our tracks. We don't want to get bogged down in the hatred. We need to rise above it. We have things to accomplish. My advice to the graduates is to move forward with hope in our hearts, knowing we are standing on a strong foundation that our parents and teachers have prepared us for. We have been liberated. Congratulations, graduates. Now, go with God."

When I finished my last words, the audience began clapping as well as the students behind me, and then they all stood up and gave me a standing ovation. I didn't know if it was because I had given such a short speech, but my heart was swelling, and I feared I would find tears of my own running down my face. I had not been reciting memorized lines. I had been speaking from my heart. Then, I had a crazy thought. I wished Astana would have been there to hear my speech, but then I immediately became embarrassed to think she would be interested in a high school graduation.

After my speech and before we walked across the stage, the principal got up and announced the different plans for the graduates. Many of the guys were heading off to different branches of the military to serve their country. Some students had plans for college, and their choices were announced. Then, the principal announced the different scholarships. I was in the group of athletic scholarships, and we each proudly stood up when our names were announced. Then, the principal announced the different academic scholarships. My heart soared when I heard my name mentioned as receiving my academic scholarship as well as my track scholarship.

Soon, we walked across the stage and received our diplomas and switched our tassel to the other side of our cap. Then, when it was all over and we were officially announced as graduates, we all tossed our caps high in the air, and I don't think I had ever seen so many smiles on faces in one room in my life. It was a hallelujah moment for us all.

We began to congregate with our families and friends, and we received tons of congratulations and hugs. I was happy that I had made my parents proud. It was a good feeling and one that I would keep in my heart for years to come. I had definitely hit a major milestone, but I still had many more ahead of me.

That night, I went out with my friends to celebrate our graduation. We laughed and cut up with each other. We talked about old times and about new plans for our future. I got the feeling that night that, although many of my friends had teased me for years about my disciplined life, they were a tad jealous that they had not followed my lead and put some of my practices in their own lives. After four years of their fun-free high school life, what did they have to show for themselves? I felt a little vindicated about all the partying I had missed out on as I held my certificates in my hand, representing my two scholarships.

I had already passed my SAT test with high marks and planned to get a head start by attending summer school. My college, Winston State, was about a hundred miles away from my hometown. That was far enough away to feel like I was on my own but close enough to go home when I got lonely. I wanted to get ahead over the summer by tackling some of my required courses. I also wanted to get on the training program for my track scholarship. It was an easy adjustment starting in the summer session as there were fewer students at the college then. It allowed me some time to get familiar with the campus and to get acquainted with a few folks before the larger crowd hit campus in the fall. Momma and Daddy were not too happy about me leaving so soon, but they were happy by comparison when they remembered that I could have been going off to war.

As it turned out, college was a lot of fun. I met interesting people from different parts of the state and different parts of the country. It was nice to learn other points of view about life. There were a lot of brilliant people who came by their intelligence naturally. And there were lots of smart people who had come by it like me, through hard work and discipline. Then, there were those who were there to play. They were interesting to observe and to converse with, but socially, I stayed as far away from them as possible. My early training in life sent up red flags that warned me they would be a total distraction and a hurdle in my future plans. I was thankful for the godly training I had received from my parents and from church, which helped me keep my focus on God and away from all the temptations around me.

I was happy during the summer to get a few of the required courses out of the way. I was anxious to get into classes that were going to head me in the direction of obtaining a spot in law school. Once I got into those courses that were of benefit to me, I began to love to study and to learn. Spending time at the library or in my dorm room reading books, doing papers, and researching information became kind of an obsession for me. I was very happy I had worked hard to earn scholarships, and I had saved my money, so I didn't have to work on top of going to school. I wanted to go to school full-time all year round and finish as quickly as possible. Having worked so long for my goal and thinking it would never be accomplished made this time in college seem like there was a light at the end of the tunnel.

My track coach had me training all year long, providing me a proper diet and plenty of workouts. I had never thought of myself as a fast runner before, but in my daily workouts, I saw that I had above-average speed. With the training I was receiving, I kept pushing for faster records. One thing I noticed about track was all the time I got to spend inside my head. It was a sport that was all on you. In most of the races, you didn't have to rely on other members of your team, just yourself. I saw that I had made the right choice by going for the track scholarship. It allowed me time to think and reflect; it helped my body build, and it also gave me time to continue on with my studies. When spring rolled around, I got a little frustrated when we started going to track meets. Not that I minded the events at all. I loved them, and I seemed to excel in them. It was the wasted time in between, sitting around waiting for my events, that bothered me most. It reminded me of what I had heard actors complain about when they sat around all day in their wardrobe waiting for their scene. It was the *hurry up and wait* syndrome. I brought a bag full of books with me to the meets and spent my time studying while I waited.

There were many beautiful girls at the college. They wowed me from the first glance. Not that the girls back home were not beautiful too, but these were newer models of the female persuasion, and they caught the attention of most of the men on campus. I was thankful for my disciplined training, and I didn't go wild over the girls like so many of the guys on campus did. They couldn't study or even go to their classes because all they thought about was how to meet those beauties. That was a real danger sign for me to see how crippling that strong attraction could be on a person. I allowed myself to eye the ladies and even become friends with many of the girls at college, but like always, I didn't want to spend my time or money on anything that would hold me back from my dream. Maybe I was too driven, but that was all I knew. What I didn't think about at the time was that I was in the one place with the most available single members of the opposite sex all together and I would never be in a position like that again. I came to the realization that college life is the worst place on the face of the planet to get an education. Where else are you more distracted from your studies than in college, where you are all bunched up together, and you are all overflowing with hormones? For so many, studying was the last thing on their mind at college. Already many of the students were pairing off, and some were getting engaged, and

the pickings were already narrowing down. By the time I finished college and law school, I guess I would finally get a chance
to check out the leftovers.

I went back home during holidays and whenever I got lonely. It was always good to be around my family and to remember
my roots. My older sister, Bonnie, got married but continued
her education. We all figured my younger sister, Becky, would
be getting married before long. She was always with her boy-
friend. She had plans to go to college too. Momma and Daddy
were surprised but very happy that their children were pursuing college and, for the most part, had not needed financial as-
sistance. Being as they had not had much of a formal education
themselves, they never dreamed their children would be so successful. Daddy always said he would be happy with us no matter what our careers, as long as we were honorable citizens and
worked hard and did right by others. He was a strong believer
in picking friends who had a strong faith in the Lord. That was
always the first thing he would ask when I talked about new
friends. He would say, "Son, do they go to church?"

With the South busting out of segregation, there were lots
of discussions about the subject everywhere in the country, and
they were discussions that could bring about a lot of anger and,
many times, violence. Sometimes change was so slow that you
didn't feel the change at all. Back home, we still remained on
our side of town. We didn't try to cross the line even though we
had the freedom to do so, according to the law. I was kind of
protected by going to an all-Black college because we were basi-
cally self-segregated and not bothering anyone. Life was like it
had always been for me back home. It was only when we went

outside the protection of our campus that we noticed some of the ruckus that was going on around the rest of the country. I guess I thought we could just wave a magic wand, and everything would automatically change overnight just because the civil rights bill was passed. Seeing all the injustices during those first stages of moving away from segregation was helping me, without me knowing it, to decide what direction I might want to take my law studies once I got to that point. I wanted to learn everything I could to try to help bring about social justice for those who needed it.

I noticed more prejudice when it came to my track meets because we were meeting with other colleges, and for the first time, I was competing against White athletes at integrated schools. Back in high school, when we walked by the White schools, I remembered imagining that we would outrun all those students if we only had a chance to compete against them. Well, my chance finally came to prove myself. Every time I got in my stance to take off on a race, I thought to myself about walking by Will Rogers High School, and I pretended I was racing against those students back home, and I wanted so badly to show them my stuff. Much to my surprise, I usually did beat my imagined enemies, and my heart was thrilled. My hope was that eventually, I would not have that determination or need to prove myself. I didn't want to lose my competitive edge, but I wanted to move past the class distinction that was deep-seated in me. I felt in my mind that if I was always competing to be the best because I was Black and because they didn't allow me to compete with them in the past, then I wasn't moving beyond prejudice. I was being a part of the prejudice. On the other hand, I was willing to use any motivation that would help me win. I also had the other motivator, and that was the memory of running down the dirt road after Astana, which was a more exhilarating motivation.

At those meets, we were usually at fine schools with nice facilities. At times we were treated like we didn't belong there, like we needed to be put in our place. When we arrived at some schools and would walk off the bus, there were often racial slurs thrown in our direction. I was shocked a little in the beginning because I had lived my whole life in the little cocoon of my segregated neighborhood and school where we were all accepted as equals. My college coaches had prepared us for the possibility of abuse when we were at track meets, and their words of encouragement gave us strength to withstand the insults. They reminded us of Martin Luther King's peaceful approach to racial issues, and we tried to follow his example. We didn't want any unforced errors on our part. Before I knew it, I was no longer shocked at remarks, and I let them bounce off of me. I also remembered my graduation speech when I said that the best revenge was to be happy. In this case, the best revenge was to beat the socks off my opponents like Jesse Owens in the Olympics. But in my secret moments, I still longed to be accepted for myself, as Reginald Brent Lake, all American citizen of the United States of America and an exceptionally fast runner.

I managed to maintain my grades all through college, so that kept me out of the draft, and I kept both of my scholarships intact, so I had most of my college paid for. By the end of my four years there, I started looking at law schools, and I hoped they were looking at me as well. I had applications out to several schools.

On one of my trips back home, I was surprised to find Momma sitting at the kitchen table in the middle of the day. She usually worked long hours cleaning houses for different rich White families around town. She was sitting at the kitchen table drinking a cup of coffee when I walked in on her. When she looked up, I could see she had been crying. I immediately went to her side and sat in the chair next to her and asked, "Momma, what's wrong?"

Surprised to see me home and grasping for a response, Momma said, "Oh, Son, nothing you need to worry yourself about." Typical of my parents to keep their problems hidden from their children. Momma wiped her eyes before patting my cheek with a sudden, forced smile on her tear-streaked face and said, "So good to have you home for a spell."

"Thanks, Momma, but I want you to tell me what's wrong." My first thought was that maybe my college education was a strain on the family. Then, I questioned her and asked, "Why are you home in the middle of the day like this?"

Slowly, Momma's fake smile withdrew from its arch, and her lower lip began to quiver. As she looked down, she realized she could no longer hold back her tears, and she placed her hands over her whole face and started sobbing.

I put my arm around her and asked again, with more urgency in my voice, "Momma, what's wrong? You have to tell me."

"I'm sorry, Brent, to bother you like this."

"No, Momma. Tell me," was my firm reply.

"Well, Son," she began, "this morning, I worked at the Ward's house cleaning all morning. I was nervous because I told Mrs. Ward that my wages had gone up on cleaning houses these days, and I told her what I was getting from other folks. With the cost of living going up all the time, I had to raise my prices. She didn't say a word. She let me completely clean her house, thinking I would be getting my new salary. I probably even whistled a little while I worked. Then, she got out her purse and pulled out the same amount she has been paying me for the past twenty years. I cleared my throat and stared at it without moving. I couldn't summon the right words to say to her. But she had a few choice words for me. She reminded me that I had agreed to that salary when she first hired me and she had no intention of changing it now. I was speechless, but I finally asked in a very calm and collected voice, 'Has your husband received a raise in the past twenty years?'

"She said, 'Yes, of course?' raising her voice at the end, as if questioning my question. Considering she was a woman with at least half a brain, I figured she got my point. I picked up my money and my purse and walked out of her house. I will never step foot back there again. She can scrub her own toilets from now on. I heard her holler after me as I was walking away, saying, 'Portia, you and your people are just fine as long as you stay in your place. You just need to remember your place, you hear?' Son, it was all I could do to keep from turning around and walking back in there and hitting her up aside of her head with my purse, you know, with all the heavy weight it had now with her stinking money in it."

I reared back and launched into a huge belly laugh and then rolled forward in a ball with uncontrollable laughter. "Momma. I love that. Hooray for you. How did you manage to carry that heavy old purse all the way home? It's a wonder the strap didn't break."

By then, we were both rolling around in our chairs, laughing. Once we calmed down, we sat silent for a few minutes letting out some laugh sighs, and then we were finally all calm again. Momma reached over and stroked my cheek and said, "I'm so glad you came home. You are just what I needed today."

I smiled and reached up to pat her hand that was resting on my cheek. "It's good to be back home. But I have some news for you."

Momma jumped in immediately, "What? What's the news?"

"I was going to tell it to all the family tonight, but that was because I didn't expect you to be home in the middle of the day like this. I got accepted to Stanford Law School."

"Oh, that's great, Son." Then, her smiling face quickly turned to a furrowed brow look of concern when she asked, "But isn't that all the way out in California?"

With a laughing voice, I said, "Yes, Momma, it's in California. But it's a really good school, and I am thankful for their offer."

"Wow, I can't bear the thought of you going so far away from home. I'm going to have to take a minute to adjust to that fact. It kind of reminds me of when you went off for the summer to the farm job and I had never had you so far away from home before and for so long. I didn't like that feeling, and I don't think

I will like you being all the way out in California. When will we ever see you?"

"It won't be easy, Momma; I'm not gonna lie to you about that. But it will be a short detour, and then I will be on my way, and I will be able to go anywhere I want to go, and no one will be able to stop me after that. I will be able to make some money and not have to pinch pennies all the time. I can help you and Daddy out, and you won't have to put up with people like Mrs. Ward again."

That evening was a time of mixed emotions. Everyone was thrilled for me, and family pride was all around our table because they all knew how hard I had worked for my goals. But they were also sad to think about me leaving, and they were afraid of what I might face out in California. I assured them that steps were being made with racial equality, howbeit they were the baby steps of an awkward child. I was learning of more and more government programs that were pushing for the employment of minority workers, and that would be beneficial in turning things around in the South and all over the country if people took advantage of their opportunities. Some labeled them as *token Black* opportunities, but I was not ashamed of being a token anything as long as I got my chance. I knew I would earn respect as a valued employee if I were given the chance.

After supper that night, Daddy took me walking around town. It was fun watching him stick out his chest when he told his friends his son had been accepted to law school. He was beaming, but in a humble way, because that was the kind of man he was. Daddy had always been strict on me but always fair. He never flew off the handle, even in his anger. I admired how firm but calm he could be when he dished out punishment and advice. I had always planned to pattern my demeanor as an attorney after him. Daddy had a mountain of intelligence inside him, and I could imagine how far he could have gone if he had been born in a different time and if he had been allowed to have more than a sixth-grade education. But he was successful beyond measure despite the hardships that fell on him. That night, I came home more proud of my dad than he was of me.

So much was running through my mind when I tried to fall asleep that night. Plans were racing around, needing priorities set to them. Thoughts of finishing up college and graduating were front and center. I ranked high in my graduating class but was not chosen to give the final speech. That was fine with me. One less thing to have to worry about. I had already been accepted to law school, so I didn't need any more padding of my resume other than to have it look good to prospective employers someday.

Just as I was about to drift off to sleep, I remembered the comment Momma made comparing law school in California to when I went off to the farm. It had been such a long time since I had allowed myself time to dwell on those memories. That night, I dreamed of them and felt a deep sense of comfort. I longed to let Astana know how much I had accomplished and that I was going to law school ahead of schedule. Then, I wondered if she still cared to know. Maybe I was a forgotten memory to her.

Chapter 19

After graduation, I was busy finishing up paperwork in preparation to enroll in law school and also packing up my dorm room and heading back home for a few weeks before leaving for California. I tried to spend as much time with family as I could, knowing we would soon be so far apart. I also got in touch with old friends and enjoyed hearing about all their adventures. Often, their stories were far more exciting than mine. Many friends were getting married, and some already had children. That was so far beyond my comprehension, but they seemed happy and fulfilled, and I was happy for my friends, maybe even a little jealous, if I was honest with myself. It was difficult to hear about classmates who had lost their lives in Vietnam or see friends return home from war, all broken in body and spirit.

Momma and Daddy were taking a rare break in their lives. They decided they would drive me to California when it was time to go to college. They had worked most of their lives without ever taking a vacation. We had some relatives who lived in San Francisco, and we planned to stay with them for a few days until I could get settled on campus. Momma was thrilled to death to know there would be some family nearby if I needed anything. It was a bit of a relief to me, as I started getting an overwhelming feeling the closer we got to California.

It was a long drive, and we had to make stops along the way, but we planned ahead to know what part of each town offered lodging for people of color like us. Momma packed a basket of food, so we didn't have to stop at cafés along the way. That was the fear of leaving the safety of our own home, the fear of the unknown. We were careful all along the way. We wanted this to be a fun trip and not one spoiled by troubles. We were thankful that our vehicle performed well the whole way. Time in the car with my parents gave me time with them that I had been missing in the years away at college. I loved watching them react with each other. They had been married a long time, but they still showed such caring feelings toward each other. We chatted a lot about all the different sights we were seeing as we crossed the United States. Almost everywhere we looked in all directions was something of God's beauty.

I was suddenly flooded with strong memories of Astana when driving through farm country. Memories that were so vivid. Everything about her and that summer moved to the front of my brain, reminding me why I had functioned better over the past few years, filling my brain with my studies and avoiding free time for thinking because it always led straight back to her and made for a painful distraction.

Our spirits soared when we started getting closer to San Francisco. The Pacific Ocean was more beautiful than I could ever imagine. All the tall buildings of the city were amazing, rising so high in the sky we had to strain our necks. I loved the architecture of the bridges. We saw Alcatraz Island with small boats heading out in the choppy water in that direction. We toured the Golden Gate Bridge, Fisherman's Wharf, Golden Gate Park, Chinatown, Lombard Street, with its hairpin curves, and the Presidio. We had our heads on a swivel, swinging back and forth, checking out all the amazing sights of San Francisco.

We were thrilled to visit our relatives and to get reacquainted with them. We shared our first impressions of the beauty of their fine city. My uncle got us all laughing when he commented on his early memories of California when he moved there as a young boy from the Deep South. He saw so many different races of people walking around out there in California, and he was shocked in the beginning. He said the first time he saw a Black person hug a White person at church, his immediate reaction was, Oh no, there's gonna be a lynching tonight. He was happy to report that people were a little more easy-going regarding race issues around there than what we may have experienced in the South.

After visiting with our relatives for a few days and looking around the city, I think Momma and Daddy were feeling a little better about leaving me there to stay. But on the day they were leaving, I saw tears slipping from Momma's eyes all morning and a good amount of sniffling. I would have been doing the same thing if I had not been so excited about getting to campus and starting this final chapter of my education that would lead me to my ultimate goal. Momma clung tightly to me when she gave me that last hug before getting in the car to head back home. I felt a little pain in my heart as well, seeing their car get smaller and smaller on the horizon and not knowing when I could see them again. I knew I would worry about them until they were safely back home. I had spent a lot of my money from my savings and would have to scrimp by during law school. I wouldn't have money for trips back home any time soon. Daddy said he would be putting some aside in their budget, so maybe by Christmas, he would have enough for a bus ticket. That little tidbit was the bait needed to help me and Momma ease our departure tension a little.

The Stanford campus was beautiful, and I learned my way around fairly easily. When I saw the courses in my lineup, I was scared but also excited. I dug into my books and did my usual thing, keeping my nose to the grindstone. I realized that on my epitaph, it would say, "Here lies a very boring man." I knew in law school my fellow classmates were just as determined as I was, and this was going to be the most difficult leg of my journey. My competition was going to be fierce, and I couldn't relax yet. I doubted, though, that there were many students who had the same amount of drive and self-determination that I had. My goal at this point, beyond passing my classes and passing the bar in the end, was to be chosen by a prestigious law firm. I was not sure how in demand young Black men were to the firms looking for new talent, no matter how impressive their grade point average or ranking. But with the civil rights movement pressuring the government, my chances were improving each year. I was not proud. I would be happy even if I was the token Black candidate. I had enough confidence in myself to know I would prove myself, and they would not be sorry. All I needed was to get my foot in the door.

If everything went well, I planned to get my law degree in three years. I met many interesting and fun people over the years there at Stanford. It was my first experience in an integrated school environment. I was pleased that I was quickly accepted, and campus life went smoothly for me. Over the years, I became friends with people of many different races. As usual, I classified my classmates as to how they might benefit me in the future. At this point in my college career, I was already networking. I figured all the best minds in the country would cross paths from time to time, and I wanted to make some good connections so I might call in favors if necessary in my future career. There were many of my connections who turned out to be good friends, despite my lack of social activity. I did just enough socializing to get acquainted with people but not enough to distract me from studying. Whenever I got lonely or needed a break, I would get in the beat-up old car I had purchased, and I would take off driving around California. There were so many sights to see in every direction. My closeness with nature was a relationship that soothed me and didn't put a hold on me emotionally the way a dating relationship would have. It would just revive me, and then I could get back to campus and move on with my studies.

As my years at law school were winding down and coming to a close, I thought to myself boldly, almost bragging, that *I love when a plan comes together*. That is how I felt about my life up to that point. It had mostly been a good plan, and it all turned out just as I had hoped. In many ways much better than I had dreamed because each year, more strides were being made with civil rights that gave me more opportunities as places needed to meet their quotas of minorities. But there were also many atrocities against humanity going on at the same time, and that would lead me to opportunities to practice law in a meaningful way to help overcome those atrocities.

Chapter 20

My last spring at Stanford, the campus was flooded with law firms, both large and small, from all over the country looking for talented young lawyers. I graduated with the top of my class and knew my resume would have to be considered. I tried to apply with most all the firms that arrived on campus that year. Soon, I was called back for interviews with many of the firms. After the preliminary interviews on campus, the firms narrowed down their lists, and I was among those invited to interview at several firms around the country. I was shocked to discover they provided us with all-expense-paid arrangements to each interview. For the first time in my life, I was flying around the country. Some interviews were as far away as New York City. I was nervous navigating around in the big cities but also exhilarated. How could a small-town Black boy like me have ever possibly dreamed that one day I would be catching a cab in New York City and going on interviews at prestigious law firms? I don't know if I ever pictured my dream that far. All I had planned out in my mind was the work getting through school. I wasn't sure what to do once I arrived at the end of that journey or how to step out and grab hold of my future.

In the end, I was asked to join a large corporate law firm in Dallas called Brighton & Wakefield. Dallas was a large city, but I felt more comfortable there than in a city like New York or Chicago. I felt closer to my roots being in the south central part of the country. I would be closer to home, and Momma and Daddy would be happy about that. Dallas was also very metropolitan and had contacts and influence around the country and the world. They were interested in using my talents in the civil rights sections of their practice. I was just happy to have landed on my feet, and I planned to prove myself, just like I had done all my life. I knew they were taking a chance with me and they were expecting a lot from me. I had experienced enough of life to know I had to prove I was not chosen strictly because of minority opportunities but on my own merit. I was interested in that part of the law, so I knew I would pursue my work with a passion that was even more fulfilling and intense than competing against my classmates all those years in school.

After accepting my position with the firm, I went back home for a long visit before reporting to work. I had spent so many years away from home while at college and law school and had not often returned home. I had to admit it was great to be home again. My younger brothers were now in college. My sister Becky had gotten married but was still pursuing college. Bonnie, my older sister, had finished college and was working as an accountant for a large company, and she and her husband had moved to Chicago. Momma and Daddy were pretty much living in their empty nest and probably making some adjustments of their own after so many years cramped in a small house with five children. The house was all modern now with a nice indoor bathroom and even a television. They had enlarged the kitchen, and Momma now had plenty of room to cook right at the time when she didn't have that many to cook for.

While I was in town, Daddy took me around visiting with his old friends, and Momma took me shopping for new clothes for when I went back to Dallas to begin my career as an attorney. I had taken good care of the one suit I got for my college graduation and had worn it on all my interviews. But Momma said I needed to dress in style for my new job with more fine-looking suits, ties, and dress shirts. Also, fine new shoes. She said it was high time I took that crash course on social manners and rules I had missed out on for so many years when I had my nose stuck in my books. She checked out a book on etiquette from the library and was brushing up on all the rules with me. I enjoyed those moments with both of my parents. It was the most time we had shared together in many years, and I cherished every moment.

My last weekend, Momma and Daddy had all their children come back home for a visit. We spent the entire weekend laughing and enjoying time together and sharing great meals again like old times. I also visited with my friends around town and caught up with them. I was surprised how many of them had started families and were still living right there in town.

Sunday morning, we all went to church together. Once again, it was fun seeing old friends, and we enjoyed visiting before church began. Then, my family all sat together on one pew according to Momma's wishes. We took up a whole row since we had all grown up and had added two new members to the family with my sisters' husbands. In my mind, I could picture us all sitting together like that when we were children and twitching around getting into trouble during the church service.

Daddy was one of the deacons of the church, and at the end of the service, he went forward to give some announcements and to offer a blessing for the week. Before he sat down, he did something out of the ordinary. He just started talking, "I am a very fortunate man today. I have my whole family with me, and it is pure joy. I would like for all five of my children to come up here with me. I don't know when we will all be together like this again. Momma, you come up here too." We all looked at each other, wondering what was going on, but then we stood up and followed behind each other up to the front of the church and stood there by Daddy, wondering what he was up to.

"Most all of you have known my kids since they were born," he began. "They grew up in this small town and have worshipped at this church all their lives. Now, they are all grown. My oldest boy, Brent, has just accepted a position at a law firm in Dallas. My oldest daughter, Bonnie, is married and has started her career as an accountant in Chicago. Then, there is Becky, who is married and still working on her college degree. And both my younger boys here, Bobby and Daniel, are in college and are doing well. They have big plans for their future." Daddy stopped and just looked over at all of us for a minute. Then, he started again, "My precious Portia and I are humble people. We have not accomplished so much in life as the world considers success. But when I look at what we created and the family we raised to be fine citizens on this planet, I consider the two of us to be quite a success." Daddy barely choked those last few words out. I looked at him when he turned toward us, spreading his arm out in our direction as if showing off some fine display, and there were tears in his eyes. I could feel the lump in his throat from the sound of his last words as he croaked them out shakily. I had never seen my daddy cry in all my life. I probably had my mouth wide open as I stared at him in disbelief. I couldn't understand what made him cry like that right out in front of the whole church. Momma went over to him and hugged him, and they both cried together. I looked out over the audience, and most everyone in the audience was crying. My brothers and sisters and I were all looking back and forth at each other, taking it all in and trying not to ruin the moment by shrugging our shoulders or asking questions.

As I stood there that morning, I experienced something I would never forget for the rest of my life. I had seen my daddy get hurt physically with injuries or with severe illnesses over the years, but he had always remained strong. I had seen him humiliated with violent words from prejudiced people over the years, but he politely stood strong and never raised a complaint, even when he got back home out from under the pressure of the abusers. He had never been bitter or shed a tear. But that day, Daddy was standing there crying like a newborn baby, being comforted by Momma's arms around his neck. I realized that the pride he had in his family was the straw that broke the camel's back that Sunday morning in front of the whole church body in our small-town Baptist church. As proud as I had always been of Daddy and his strength, I think I was never more proud of him than I was that day.

The next morning, we all left Momma and Daddy to return to our own residences, and it was really hard to say goodbye to each other. As for me, I was finally back in the South after so many years on the West Coast, so I could visit home more often in the future. However, I had grown angry over many years, remembering my life back in my hometown when it was segregated. I had grown accustomed to my integrated college life, and the anger I felt was like a repellent that would keep me from coming home very often. But then, I would remember my momma's words before I left when she told me, "Son, please don't blame your daddy and me for the anger you have in your heart when you say you don't ever want to come back home. Remember we are here, and that is all that should matter to you. Look how far you have come. You are no longer shackled by the restraints that once held you back when you were young. Heck, you never let them stop you anyway. You broke the barriers down, and you should be proud of yourself. You have inspired other youngsters around here to do the same. So please, Son, come back and see your momma from time to time." How could I deny my sweet momma?

Chapter 21

Thrills and nerves were the words that best described my first day at my new law firm. First, I visited the Human Resources Department and got squared away with them, signing all my papers and getting my insurance packet. Then, I was shown around the office and introduced to many of the associates there before I was finally led to my office. It was small but perfect for me. I could instantly feel myself being surrounded by such knowledge and discoveries that would happen in my near future time spent there working on cases.

My supervising attorney, Mr. Jenkins, had me take a seat in his office for a while to go over what I could expect as I got started. He was looking at my resume, glancing over my accomplishments. "Well, Brent, it looks like things have been easy for you throughout your college career from looking at your records."

I didn't know how to take what he said to me. I knew I was just arriving on my job, but I felt I had to speak up about his remarks. "I beg your pardon, sir. Things have never come easy for me. I have never received any breaks. What you are looking at are years of hard work devoted to my studies to the point of denying myself a normal life. Those accomplishments came with my own blood, sweat, and tears."

Mr. Jenkins looked up from my folder and stared at me over the top of his bifocals that were resting on the end of his nose. I didn't know if I had already gotten myself in trouble for speaking so boldly. Finally, he closed my folder and neatly added it to a stack of others on his desk before answering. "That's even better, Brent. That tells me a lot about your character. First of all, you just revealed all your hard work. You obviously take pride in hard work, so that shows me the kind of work ethic you will bring to this firm. And you spoke up for yourself despite what I might assume could be rather scary. You didn't just let my remarks stand. I think we may have picked a gem when we picked you." I sighed with relief that I had not already blown my career on my first day of work.

As with every chapter in life, it took a while to get acquainted and to learn the ropes of my new position. Most of my first year, I was doing research on other people's cases. I was accustomed to working hard and studying longer than was really normal for most people, so I felt I was in my element right away. It was sometimes boring to do research for other lawyers, but I watched the cases they were handling and followed through to see the results that took place. I realized, even in the boring part of research, that I was learning my trade. I also knew myself well enough to know that I was on my way. I could see that I was making an impression. I had learned long ago that hard work and focus paved many roads for me, and I expected it would continue as I became better known around my firm.

Because of my work ethic, I couldn't exactly say that I had a lot of free time on my hands. But I was feeling a little more relaxed after my first couple of years with the firm. I was being accepted and appreciated, finally, and with that came more confidence. That was something I had not allowed for myself through the years. I had always been confident I could out-study most people, but I never felt completely confident that it would pay off in the end. I was starting to feel the tide was finally turning.

I was invited to some office parties and social events, and I was happy to have those nice suits that Momma had insisted I buy. As Momma said, "You are a fine-looking young man, and you will look sharp in these suits." I was often teased by some of the guys around the office for looking like a fashion model. Many of the secretaries often complimented me on being a sharp dresser. There were not many female lawyers at the firm in the late seventies, but times were changing, and I figured the color and gender of the firm would be changing too, eventually. I was careful about my reputation and made sure to stick to my work at the office and not socialize there. I knew office romances could lead to trouble if anything went awry.

When I first moved to Dallas, I got established in a church and started meeting people there. That was where I did most of my socializing. What I discovered, though, was just what I told myself back in college when I was overlooking all the pretty college girls so I could study. I had said that by the time I got out of college and law school and got settled in my career, the single playing field would be smaller. Sure enough, by then, most of the young ladies my age were already married. A lot of my buddies in college had traded in their careers for marriage and a family. Most of the time, I walked around rather cocky, feeling proud of what I had accomplished in my life, but there were times when I envied the guys who were settled down now with nice families, and I wondered if that would ever happen for me. The young ladies I met at church who were still available were nice-looking, but I was still too busy with work to give them much attention. I wondered if I would ever meet someone who would cause me to want to toss everything aside and concentrate strictly on them enough to ever find myself a partner in life.

One day at the office, I was sitting in the conference room with many of the young lawyers who were all working on the same case together. During our break, we ate lunch that had been delivered by one of the cute young Black secretaries. After she left and we started eating, one of the guys began quizzing me about what I thought of her. I told him I didn't get involved in any office relationships. She and I were just friends, and that was all. There was much discussion after that about the pros and cons of office dating. One thought was that with how busy we all were, where in the world would we have time to ever meet a girl, if not at the office? But the opposite view was that if things didn't work out, you could end up in sticky situations that could interfere with policies around the office, even between you and your bosses. Both points of view had some merit to them.

I was not the only Black attorney at the firm. There were about four of us employed at Brighton & Wakefield. By then, we were now being called African-Americans even though we were not from Africa. I was happy that I fit in with all races at the office. I had been taught by my parents to be friendly, and that was how I acted toward everyone. However, I realized that I was considered as Brent Lake, an African-American attorney with the firm. Maybe it would always be that way.

Out of the blue, one of the young single lawyers at the table, Jay McAllister, spoke directly to me as I sat quietly enjoying my lunch and staying out of the dating conversation, and he asked, "Brent, have you ever dated a White girl?"

I was a little startled by the question as I sat there with a mouth full of food. After chewing my bite, I sat there quietly, thinking about how to answer his question. Finally, I said, "I have not actually dated a White girl before. I grew up in a segregated school and went to an all-Black college. In law school, I had many White lady friends, but I didn't really date much. I've always been too busy and too poor for much dating."

They laughed at my answer. Some probably understood my sentiment about struggling college students with little time or money. Then, Jay said, "What's the matter? Don't you like girls?"

"Yes, I like girls," I answered. "Some of the best people I know are girls."

Again, many around the room laughed at my answer. I knew Jay was trying to get into my personal business, and I wasn't sure I wanted to share my life with people I worked with. But Jay wasn't giving up so easily. In an attempt to poke fun at my lack of experience, he asked, "Have you ever loved a woman before, Brent?"

I put down my sub sandwich and wiped my mouth, giving me time to think about what to say. My mind wandered around in my memories, thinking about all the different girls I had known over the years. Of course, when it came to love, Astana immediately came to my mind, but I wasn't ready to reveal that history to anyone. Then, a smile came across my face, and I said, "Yes, Jay, I have loved a woman deeply before."

"Was she a pretty Black girl?" Jay continued with a smirk on his face.

"No, she was the most beautiful White woman I have ever seen." Everyone in the room perked up in disbelief at my mystery woman. Then, I added, "She was my grandmother." They laughed and began asking questions about her, surprised to know I had a White grandmother.

That seemed to satisfy Jay, and he stopped hitting me with questions. Soon, the conversation started up around the table about the merits of mixed marriages. I didn't get into any of it but sat quietly, eating the rest of my sandwich. I was struck by what one of the lawyers said in the conversation. "I think it is good to mix the races. Eventually, everyone will blend all together, and we will have no reason to be upset with each other when we are all stirred up like that."

I had mixed emotions about what he had said. I agreed that mixing with different people might help overcome our differences, but I wondered if he meant it as a means of eliminating the races he was opposed to. Was he referring to breeding out different races? I figured I would always be suspicious about how White people viewed me and my race.

"Hey, Brent, I heard you didn't watch the miniseries Roots that everyone is talking about. What's up with that?" another attorney friend asked. I explained I had already experienced my own roots stories and didn't want to go back and relive any of it. I just wanted to move forward and leave all that behind me.

After our meeting, Jay McAllister caught up with me and said, "Hey Brent, let's get together sometime and go out. I'll show you how to meet girls."

"Sure," I replied, with no intention of following up on his offer. I didn't want to let anyone in on my personal life. I guess I would forever be cautious and keep to myself. Not that I had any secrets. Well, maybe one.

Chapter 22

Once again, I found myself walking the streets of New York City. I was sent there by the firm to interview possible witnesses in a civil rights case that the firm was handling. It had been a long day of interviews and taking notes on what I had discovered. I was weary by the time I left the New York branch of our firm that evening and headed back to my hotel. I decided to walk the few blocks rather than try to catch a cab at that busy time of day. After sitting all day, I needed to stretch my legs anyway. I looked around in the store windows as I passed by and stopped at some and even went inside to pick up a souvenir for Momma when I spied something she might like.

Just as I was getting close to the hotel, I passed a bookstore. In the window were many new books on display. I was an avid reader, so I slowed down to browse a minute to see if any new titles caught my attention. I was in a hurry to get back to the hotel and rest up before supper, so I didn't want to spend much time. I just planned to scan the book covers quickly and then maybe come back later to purchase one if I saw something I liked. As I was about to pull myself away, I glanced at an interesting title. I can't say why it caught my attention, but it did. It was called *Precious Memories*. I directed my eyes back to the cover, noticing it had a picture of a southern-looking white porch swing on it. Something about it felt familiar. Then, I saw the author's name, *Astana La' Shore*. For a minute, I think my heart actually stopped. I felt a little weak but blamed it on being hungry after a long afternoon. A thought crossed my mind as I quickly peered through the display window of the store, cupping my hands around my eyes to block the glare, that maybe there was a book signing in the store, and I could surprise the author. I immediately turned toward the entrance of the bookstore with my heart racing and went inside. I started looking all around for any signs of a crowd that would indicate a book signing table, but there was no crowd, just people meandering around the shelves. I walked around the different displays until I finally found the table displaying the book I was interested in. I picked it up and felt nervous just touching it. I turned the book over to the back, and there was a photograph of the author. Staring back at me were those blazing aqua-colored eyes. They were penetrating me. I felt the book almost slip from my fingers, and I jerked a little to gain a tighter grip on it. I looked around to see if anyone had seen my awkward movement. Recognizing her name and photograph caused a funny reaction to come over me like I was caught with my hand in the cookie jar.

I didn't need to flip through the pages to decide if I wanted to purchase the book. I was already certain. I placed it under my arm while searching for my wallet as I quickly made my way to the counter. It was the same wallet the La' Shores got me that summer, and it felt strange to be holding both the wallet and their daughter's book in my hand at the same time. I had a sudden urge to share my close connection to the author with the store clerk, but I spared myself that embarrassment. When I was checking out, the clerk commented that I would love the book. She said she had read it and it was lovely. I nodded absentmindedly, feeling numb with my emotions all a flurry and with no words coming forth to speak. I was anxious to get to my hotel room and look over my purchase.

Once I got in my room, I was shaking as I took the book out of the bag. How could this book be causing such anxiety in me? It must have been the emotions that it brought to the surface, emotions I had tried to ignore for so long. Here I had faced competition in sports and remained strong. I had faced integration and survived and adapted. I had faced the competition of fellow students in college and ended up on top of the heap. Then, I faced the fierce competition of law school as we all feverishly fought for top spots in the best firms in the nation. But there, at that moment, I stood buckling in fear at the sight of a small book I held in my hands. I started to understand how my dad felt that day he succumbed to his emotions in front of the whole church.

Knowing I was starved, I ordered room service rather than wasting time going out to eat, and then I sat down at the desk in the room and started opening the book very slowly as if it were a priceless heirloom. To me, it was. I couldn't imagine what Astana would have written about. I started trying to figure out what had happened to her and where she had taken her life. Would the book reveal any information to me about her, or would it just be a fiction story with no clues? Here I was, a lawyer trained to get to the bottom of things, but I found myself almost too paralyzed to try to read her words. I slowly read over the title and then each word that followed on the back cover, like a detective investigating a case. Then, I started reading the story. It did not indicate that it was an autobiography. It read like a romantic fiction novel. Normally, that kind of book would probably not have caught my eye, but this time was entirely different.

I spent the rest of the night reading the book cover to cover, only stopping to eat my room service meal when it arrived. I couldn't put the book down. I noticed some of the racial conflicts in the book were not stories I had mentioned to Astana. I had tried to spare her most of what I had witnessed. It made me wonder if she had heard the stories from other farmworkers who may have come after me. I wondered if she had fallen for one of them. She seemed very detailed in the events she wrote about. I was, however, certain the love story was about me as there were too many similarities. I soaked up her words of description, hoping to learn the whole depth of what she felt for me. Her story ended with me leaving her that morning long ago. It left the rest up to the reader to decide what happened with the relationship. But the development of the love story was all there, and nothing was missing in what she wrote. It left you feeling that a sequel could someday be written about the couple, and that was a good selling point for future novels by the amazing author I had once loved. At that very minute in the middle of the night, I decided that the next day I was going to head to Echo Falls instead of going back to Dallas.

After my shower and breakfast the next morning, I called the office and scheduled a few days off before returning to work. I told my secretary I would be overnighting the materials I had gathered from my meetings in New York City, and she could pass them on to Mr. Jenkins, the lead attorney on the case, and explain to him my delay in returning to the office.

As soon as I packed up my bag, I made arrangements to over-night my files on the case and then called to change my flight arrangements. I planned to stop by and visit with Momma and Daddy in Horseshoe Junction before driving to Echo Falls.

From the moment I saw that book in the store window and still on my flight back home, I was a bundle of nerves. My emotions were rising and falling, and I was full of questions. Would I find Astana at her place, or would Cleon Jarvis be there? Would the farm be destroyed after he had his hands on it? Would she be married and have children by now? How would I take it if she was? It had been a little over ten years. What could I expect when I saw her? Would she be angry? I had promised to come back and let her know how I did in college. The thought of seeing her both scared me and excited me all at the same time. I had never experienced the kind of fear that was running wild all over my body as I made that flight back home.

I was glad I decided to go home first. The couple of days there helped me to settle down and gain back some control over my emotions. Momma and Daddy were happy to see me and spoiled me all they could in a short amount of time. I was overjoyed that they were getting around really well. They seemed to have finally adjusted to their empty nest and were enjoying a new freedom they had not experienced the majority of their lives.

Once I got in my rental car and headed on the long road trip to Echo Falls, the fears started creeping back again. I knew I would be a wreck if I didn't try to get them under control. Many times I almost turned around and headed back to Horseshoe Junction, but then I would think to myself that I would never know what happened to Astana if I didn't at least try to find her. I would never know for sure if she was married or if she hated me if I didn't keep moving forward. The only courage I could muster was the fact that I didn't think she would have written that book if she hated me. That thought motivated me to keep going.

When I finally arrived in Echo Falls, I drove slowly through town, looking in all directions seeing things that looked exactly the same but then seeing other new additions to the town. There had been some new construction, so that gave me the impression that the economy of the area had moved in a somewhat positive direction. My nerves turned to anxiety as I left town and headed toward the farm. I knew my past was about to stare me in the face. My heart was pounding in my chest, and it reminded me of the night when Astana sewed the buttons back on my shirt and how my body reacted to the closeness of her. I began to fear I was on the verge of a full-blown attack on my nerves. I had heard some of Momma's friends before talking about how they thought they were going to have a nervous breakdown. Now I wished I had listened more closely as to how they overcame their nerves.

I looked from side to side as I drove down the familiar country road. All the farmland laid out in perfect squares with perfect rows of their crops brought back memories of that summer when, for a short period of time, I worked as a farmer and had learned to appreciate that lifestyle. I reached the curve in the road right before the beginning of Astana's property, and tingles ran up and down my spine. It was a beautiful sight, but something was different. I think in my mind, I had pictured that by now, the farm would be rundown again like when I first saw it years ago, or maybe even worse than that if Astana had not had proper help to keep it up. But instead, everything was well-groomed, like an oasis in the middle of the desert. It stood out from all the other farms I had seen on my drive.

Finally, I arrived at the entrance of the farm where I had planted the cluster of plants around the crepe myrtle trees on each side of the road leading to the farmhouse. The irises and daffodils were no longer blooming, but the white lantana was full underneath the deep pink of the now tall, mature crepe myrtle trees. There was a new rock wall built behind the planted area, giving it the look of a grand entrance, and it was obvious that the area was well maintained. From the rock wall on the left side of the road rose a tall wrought iron arch that went up and over the road and ended on top of the rock wall on the right side of the road. In the middle of the arch were the words *Liberty Lake Resort*. Astana had finally named her place, and the words touched my heart in a special way.

As I started down the long road to her farmhouse, I noticed the road was now paved. Then, I noticed the line of Rose of Sharon trees Astana and I had planted on each side of the road. They were tall now and full of mauve-colored blooms. The tree branches stretched over the road on both sides, forming an arch that shaded the road. Between the trees, all down both sides of the road, was beautiful landscaping. It was a rustic design with large rocks placed here and there and grassy plants blowing in the breeze between the rocks. But every now and then, there were sections among the rocks that were bordered and filled with clusters of blooming flowers. It represented the open ruggedness of farm life right alongside well-defined borders, like the perfect lines in a farmer's crop. Down the middle ran sections of bordered low Mexican petunias with their purple blooms and lush green leaves. She remembered my warning about how invasive they could be and made sure they were contained. The borders were curved and looked like a creek twisting down each side of the road. I couldn't believe all I was seeing. It far surpassed what I had dreamed when I first thought of planting the section at the beginning of the road and then planting the Rose of Sharon trees. How could Astana have done this on her own? Surely she must have had help. She must be married by now and to a professional farmer from the looks of things.

As I got closer to the farmhouse, I noticed the garden and the orchard still standing with an abundant crop. They were weed-free and obviously well taken care of. I also saw in the different fields, row after row of a variety of flowers planted, like crops. I noticed a large parking lot to the side of Astana's house that was full of parked cars. I couldn't make out what was going on, but there were crowds of people meandering all around the place. Then, I noticed a new barnlike facility with people going in and out of it. I pulled up to a parking spot and sat there for a minute, looking around at all the changes and all the different people. With each passing face, I searched to see if it might be Astana. I wondered if I would recognize her if I found her. I had seen her photograph on the back of the book, but that could have been an old picture. Finally, I got out of the car and started walking around.

My eyes were open wide, looking in all directions in total surprise at what I was seeing. A thought crossed my mind that I might still run into Cleon Jarvis walking down one of the neat paths, and my concept of his farming ability would be destroyed.

Most of the people strolling around were dressed very casually, like they were camping or on a picnic. Suddenly my tan slacks with my white shirt neatly tucked in and my loosened necktie looked out of place. All I had with me were my office clothes, as I had not planned on this side trip when I left Dallas the week before.

I had been standing in one place with my hands on my hips while carefully examining the farm from every angle, turning slowly as I changed my view. I could see off in the distance a lake that was new to the property. I assumed it was the Liberty Lake. There were boats and people all around the lake, but from the spot where I was straining to see, they all looked like tiny specks. Finally, I pulled my long-distance focus back to my surroundings and turned to look at the farmhouse where long ago, I had been afraid to enter. It looked much the same. The main difference I noticed about the whole place was the abundance of color from all the blooming trees and the different flowerbeds all around. There was a window box with colorful flowers as well as hanging baskets on the porch. The colors made the dull rock farmhouse look beautiful and quaint, like in a storybook or a beautiful landscape painting.

I was startled by the sounds of two little girls running in the direction of a lady walking down one of the paths with some flowers in her arms. When they reached the lady, they hugged her tightly around her dress tail and giggled. She reached down to them with big hugs. Then, they turned, all three together, and headed in my direction toward the farmhouse. I could tell, even from that distance, that the lady was Astana, and my heart did a flip-flop in my chest. I wondered if the little girls belonged to her. They were talking and laughing together as they walked closer and closer to where I stood with my hands still on my hips, staring unapologetically. The summer breeze was swirling her sundress around her legs and blowing strands of hair in her face. I spotted right away the familiar pearls around her neck. I wondered if Astana would recognize me when she decided to look up. I waited and sweated with nerves on edge.

As she got closer, I heard the joyous sound of her laughter, and my heart melted. She was now within a few feet of me, and she finally looked up from the giggling girls and saw me standing there in front of her. As she continued on, she put her hand over her eyes to block out the sun as if she were trying to focus. Then, she came to a stop and slowly lowered her hand from her eyes and just stood there silently for a minute. Finally, she bent down to the little girls and said, "Will you two take these flowers over to Miss Opal so she can make an arrangement out of them?" The girls eagerly took the bundle of flowers and ran off toward the barn facility.

I had not said a word or moved an inch. I was just standing there like a statue. It felt like a moment that needed some reflection and time to soak it all in so I could remember every little detail later when I settled down and had time to think back on it. We were both standing and staring. Finally, I removed my hands from my hips and held out my arms on each side of my body as I swerved slowly from side to side, marveling at everything, and I said, "Wow! There must be some story to tell here."

Astana flashed a big smile, and that comforted my heart and calmed some fears. She took a few steps closer while nodding her head up and down and said, "Look what a handsome young man you turned out to be."

The sound of her voice was music to my ears, and I was happy to hear she thought I was handsome. I returned her smile and said, "Well, I was just a kid back when we first met. Remember?"

"Yes, I remember."

"It was a little intimidating back then to be infatuated with someone who had to wait for me to grow up. It didn't feel very manly. You seemed so much more mature than me."

Laughing, Astana said, "Oh, Brent, you were born mature. Who plans their whole future in first grade?"

Nodding my head as I wandered back in time, I finally said, "You were really something back then...you still are. I see you've made a lot of changes over the years. I would love to visit a while and hear about them if you are not too busy." Then, as an afterthought, I added, "Or if your husband doesn't mind you spending some time with me."

She looked at me with those eyes, and I wondered what was going on in her head or what she was feeling at the moment. Then, her words came out slowly and calmly, "I thought you were coming back. You promised...and I waited."

My heart hurt hearing her words and my hands automatically clutched my chest. How could I have broken my promise? I didn't know what to say next. I looked down at my feet, thinking of turning around and getting back in my car. I had grown up and had become successful, but I lacked any emotional courage. I had worked hard to protect my heart, but I never learned how to deal with my emotions. I realized I was still closed off from them, and it felt safe there. Finally, I drew up enough courage to open my mouth, and I said, "It has taken me a while. But I finally made it." I wasn't sure that was a good enough answer.

Astana broke eye contact with me and started looking around in different directions. I wondered if she was looking to see if anyone saw us together, maybe her husband. I didn't know quite what to think. When she returned her gaze in my direction, she said, "Why don't we go sit on the porch for a spell? This may take a while."

I walked slowly behind her with my hands shoved down in my pockets as we headed toward the farmhouse and up on the porch. She went directly to the porch swing I had made for her, and we sat side by side, just like we did that last night I was there. I recognized that the swing was the same one on the cover of her book. Once we adjusted ourselves into a comfortable position, Astana said, "I'll tell my story if you tell me yours."

I nodded in agreement to her request and said, "Sure."

"Well, let me see. Where shall I start?" Then, she pointed to the balcony of the garage apartment up the stairs in front of us. "I was rather lost after you left me standing there but also, in a way, more grounded than I had ever been. All I could think of was your promise to come back. My mind was suddenly flooded with plans of all that I could accomplish before you returned. I was truly motivated." She stopped and laughed a sad laugh and looked over at me. "My first line of action was to try to get your address from Mr. Turner, but he refused me any information other than the name of your hometown. He said that was the best he could do legally, or he could get in trouble. When fall came, I ordered the newspaper from there, hoping to read articles of your sporting events, and I thought I could feel a connection to you that way. But I discovered that the sporting events of the Black high school didn't make the local paper. That made me sad."

Again, she looked over at me, and I shrugged my shoulders, understanding her frustration, and said, "Yeah, that's how it was in my hometown."

"After that, I located the name of your church, or at least the one I thought was your church. Occasionally, I would see postings in their newsletters of your sports highlights offering congratulations on the seniors winning the team trophies. I read an announcement of you winning your scholarships, and I smiled when I read one was a track scholarship." She looked at me, and we both smiled, thinking about my world-famous race to find her that summer morning.

"You will not be happy about this, but Opal and I, along with her sweet husband, Earl, drove to your hometown, and I was at your graduation and saw your great speech. It blew me away."

"What?" I said, shocked. "I didn't see you there."

"I know. We were up in the balcony. You had made it clear that you didn't want me to come to your games, so I assumed you didn't want me to be at your graduation either."

"I probably would have passed out from nerves if I knew you were there. But I thought of you that whole night."

"I learned where you were going to college, and I tried my best to keep up on news from your college through any notices still from your church and also from different publications I subscribed to from the college, but there was not much news about you except for your track victories. I was so proud."

I laughed and said, "I guess having my nose stuck in my books was not very newsworthy."

"I decided that first fall after you left me that I would enter the junior college at the county seat over at Crayton's Corner. I took courses in business and landscaping. I was scared at first, but it was wonderful pushing myself like that." Turning to face me again, she said, "I have you to thank for helping me take that bold step. I learned so much about business, and it helped me with running the farm and handling my affairs. The landscaping courses, plus all your previous advice, started me piddling in transplanting plants. I was able to get a start on most of the plants by your suggestions of transplanting the saplings or buying potted plants and separating them and spreading them around. Can you believe it when you look at this place now?"

"No, I can't. I was sure you must have had help when I first drove down the lane and saw all the improvements. It's a paradise here."

Astana smiled at my compliment. "Brent, everyone started coming to me wanting to buy the Rose of Sharon saplings, and they all wanted me to paint signs on them for the loved ones they were buying them for. No one ever figured out they could get their own plants by pulling up the saplings of their own trees after they bought one from me. I guess that was good for me, right? You can imagine how many saplings I got from all the trees we planted in the lane on both sides of the road plus the ones I already had around the farm. Now, I have a whole field of Rose of Sharon trees, and I still have people coming to buy the potted plants from me. It's not much, but they keep on coming for more. Soon, this place was making a name for itself, and one day the pastor at the little church we attended in Echo Falls approached me with a question. He asked if he could bring the kids out to my farm for a camping trip. He said it would be so good for them because they were not allowed at just any camping facility. I was happy to provide them a safe place for a retreat. With my new business sense, I had all the families sign waivers to protect myself in case of any injuries that might occur on a working farm. It turned out to be a huge success. Word got around, and several different churches started coming out for religious retreats. They even paid me a fee for camping out here. Then, one day, several years ago, a developer was here on a retreat with his church, and he offered me a proposition. He told me a vision he had for this place where he would put in a lake and build small cabins all around, and that would draw an even larger crowd. He also wanted to put in a country store gift shop and a café right over there," she said, pointing in the direction of the barn-shaped building. "Opal works there now. It was far more than I could ever have imagined on my own. But his plan was to buy part of the farm and turn it into a resort but also allow me to keep my house and my own section of the farm, including all my crops, and I got a cut of the proceeds from the campers. It was a very difficult decision but one that I eventually saw the benefit of. I felt secure having my own place, and I was sure the resort part would be a success and also a ministry for families to come and enjoy time together. And the best part was that I got to live here and be a part of it all. I was no longer lonely. Yes, at times, it has been difficult having so many people running all over, but whenever it gets to me, I can take a vacation and get away. The price I received for the land he purchased for the resort will take care of me for the rest of my life."

"Wow, that's quite a story," I said, looking at her beaming with pride.

"Yes, it's been a wild ride. It helped me get over missing you so much, and in the meantime, I've become a pretty savvy businesswoman and also a darn good landscaper. I have contracts all the time now from people or companies asking me to landscape for them. Of course, now I have other people do the physical work for me. But when people see my place, they are willing to pay a high price for my consulting and landscape design services, hoping to transform their own property. Brent, I turned this dumpy little farm into a gold mine. Can you believe it?"

"Oh, yes. I always had faith in you. I'm so happy for you." Then, pausing, I added, "And what about Cleon Jarvis? Is he still bothering you?"

She rolled her eyes and then started that wonderful laugh of hers. "No, he finally left me alone, and so did Jackie."

I joined in her laughter, feeling relief. Then, there was silence, and I finally had to ask the scary question, "Did you ever get married? I saw you with those two little girls. I figured they were yours."

Astana looked at me, and her eyes gave me the same sensation they always did when I gazed at them. "No, Brent. I never got married. You might say I was pretty busy. I was meeting lots of men all the time in my work around here, but none of them had what I was looking for. None of them sent sparks down to my tiptoes."

I smiled and felt the tingles she was talking about inside my body.

"Oh," Astana said as if she had forgotten something, "did you happen to notice the sign at the entrance of the farm? I finally got around to naming this place?"

"Yes, I did notice. Kind of catchy," I said with a smile and raised eyebrows.

"Well, this was like your baby to me. Yours and mine. Liberty for your favorite word and Lake after your last name. You had already planted the seed of the masterpiece this farm could be, and I followed your lead and put in a lot of sweat to make it happen. And the name of the lake the developer put in is also called *Liberty Lake*."

We both sat there gently swinging a minute, staring at each other as we thought over what had been said. Then, Astana spoke and asked, "Why don't you tell me your story now and fill in the blanks that I missed out on?"

I laughed and said, "My story is not nearly as exciting as yours...and probably not nearly as successful. I guess you could say I was pretty miserable from the moment I grabbed that biscuit and that last kiss." We both chuckled, and then I began again, "I never got over the pain that had burrowed a hole in my heart. I was next to tears on my ride back to my hometown.

Being with my family didn't fill the hole in my heart. It eased it some, but the scab kept falling off. I told my momma about you and showed her the pictures I had. She liked you right away."

Astana smiled at that statement, and I started up again, "Then, I got busy with sports and school work. As you know, I was the top of my class, valedictorian speaker, and I received an academic scholarship and a track scholarship. That helped me with my college expenses. And I was on my way."

Astana interrupted and asked, "Didn't you meet anyone at college that you were interested in?"

I rolled my eyes in her direction as if to say, *Are you kidding?* Then, I clarified, "No, I never met anyone I was interested in. You got to know me well enough in those few months we were together to know I had no time for women and no money to spend on them. If you have no time or money, they don't seem to be as interested in you. Then, as I passed over all the available women, I discovered on the other end of the line when I started work that there were not many available women left to choose from. Also, I never developed the charming skills to lure women to me. Maybe they could tell my heart had already been stolen long ago."

Astana shook her head back and forth as if she wasn't buying my *lack of charm story.*

"I guess my good news is that all my hard work paid off, at least as far as a career goes. I landed a good position at a law firm in Dallas called Brighton & Wakefield. I've been there a couple of years, and they seem to be impressed with me." Then I laughed, shrugged my shoulders, and boastfully said, "What can I say?"

Astana laughed at my fake bragging attitude and said, "I knew you would make it."

I nodded my head with a forced smile on my face. Then, we both sat there in silence. Finally, I spoke again, "For the past ten years, I couldn't take a drive in the country without thinking of you. Every farmhouse I see or a field of corn growing, I think of you. Even the smells in the summer air are reminders of my time here. Every time I eat watermelon, homemade ice cream, or biscuits, I see your smiling face, and I hear your joyful laughter in my ears." Astana smiled and breathed in a big breath of air, filling her heart with pride from my words.

I began again, spreading my arms outwardly as if to embrace all the beauty around me. "This is nice. It brings back lots of memories." I pointed to a place on the porch and said, "I can picture you right now sitting on that ice cream freezer that night. How special you made my birthday for me. You will never know the feelings you stirred inside me that night."

Astana smiled broadly and clutched her hands to her heart. I thought I could see a trace of tears coming to her eyes.

"I would have totally lost it, Astana, if you had been the one to leave me, and I was stuck facing the memories of you all around me every single day."

"I did lose it, Brent," Astana exclaimed. "But I eventually chose a constructive way to channel my misery and ta-da," she said, pointing her arms in all directions towards all the blooming flowers, "this is what I came up with. I'm sorry, though, because it is a poor excuse for love."

"So you did love me?" I asked shyly.

"What? Do you even have to ask?"

"Yes. I was too young and so far removed from romance to know for sure what love was. I knew all kinds of things were going on inside me that I didn't know what to do with, but I didn't have an intelligent answer for it. I just thought it was a case of teenage hormones, but they're still here inside me, and I'm no longer a teenager."

"That was your problem, Brent. You always needed an intelligent answer. Love doesn't work that way. I think love has shown itself in a big way by the pain we've both suffered all these years. I think how we moved forward to make a success out of our pain was our way of channeling that love. I know when I worked around this place, I would think of you the whole time, and it felt so good. I would talk to you in my mind, and I would wonder what you would think of all that I was doing, never dreaming you would ever see it. I wanted you to be proud of me."

"I am proud of you. This is amazing. I also talked to you and thought of you in my hardest times. I could picture you cheering me on just like you said you would. You were what got me through those difficult years and those lonely times, and I also wanted you to be proud of me."

Astana patted me on the knee, and the same sparks flew through me with her touch. "I am very proud of you, and I never doubted for one minute that you would be a big success. I've never seen the kind of drive you have. I just wanted to be a part of it."

We both got our stories out, and I figured that was the end of our time together. I was wishing I had been slower and more detailed so the afternoon talk could have stretched out longer. I didn't know what to do next or what to say.

Astana gave me a break and spoke up first, "There's something I want to show you." She stood up and started walking down the path along the side of her house. I followed close behind her. When she stopped, we were at the tree we had planted for Robert. She invited me to sit on the bench I had made for her. I noticed the grass I planted there and how thick it was now, just like luxurious carpet. The tree had ten years' growth on it, and I noticed the different purple ribbons, one for each year. The first one she had tied on was far up at the top of the now tall tree. It had faded in the sun and rain. I followed the trail of purple ribbons for all ten years, with each newer ribbon being lower and brighter in color. Then, Astana asked, "Do you see the yellow ribbons?"

I looked closer to find the pretty yellow ribbon in the vicinity of where I remembered her tying it. "It doesn't show up as clearly," I remarked, "probably because that creamy yellow color blends with the branches."

"They are easy for me to spot. I added one each year on the anniversary of the day you left me."

I looked at her with a shocked expression on my face, then looked back at the tree, searching for more yellow ribbons. I stood up and walked over closer to the tree for a more thorough examination. Looking back at Astana, I said, "I can't believe you did that."

"Brent, I was grieving for you just as I was grieving for Robert."

"I'm so sorry I put you through that. I never wanted to cause you pain."

We were silent for a minute, and then Astana stood up and asked, "Do you want to look around the place?"

"Sure."

She took off walking, and I followed behind her again. "We're going to get the golf cart and drive around."

"You have a golf cart now?"

"Yes. You need one to get around this place. I'll let you drive. Now that you're a lawyer, I'm sure you're handy with a golf cart."

I laughed and said, "Not yet. They've kept me too busy to hit the golf course. Maybe when I make partner, if I'm allowed at their country clubs by then."

Before we got to the garage, Astana stopped and showed me her herb garden. The fragrance hit my nose before she said anything. She had some rosemary growing on the outside edge of the garden. They were full of tiny light blue blossoms. There was a trellis covered with sweet-smelling honeysuckle. Then, she showed me rows of lemon thyme, and she rubbed some leaves between her fingers and had me smell their wonderful lemon fragrance clinging to her skin. There were more rows of different kinds of thyme, then some oregano and basil. Further down were rows of mint and chocolate mint. Then, it ended with multiple rows of strawberries. I was quite impressed. Astana seemed especially proud of that spot in her yard and told me she had many recipes where she could use her own herbs.

We got in the golf cart, and I started it up and took off in the direction she told me to go. First, we went to a place nearby where there was a beautiful white gazebo with lavender wisteria blossoms on the vines that curved over the arches all around the gazebo. There were about six steps up to the gazebo floor. Astana said it served as a stage and was often used for weddings. I was impressed and could picture how beautiful of a setting it would be for a wedding.

Next, we drove by the orchard that I was quite familiar with, and then she showed me a big field of more strawberries, and she said that was where people came from all over at harvest time and paid her to let them pick strawberries for their families. Further out was a big field that would be a pumpkin patch in the fall. She said schools and churches came out to pick pumpkins and to go on field trips. They often had hayrides during that time of year. The path wound around in different directions and made for a nice hiking trail for the visitors there. You could get lost in the beauty of the farm with all the different fields. Closer to the barn were fields of flowers. She had one field that was full of lantana in all different colors. She said nurseries liked to come and get their pick to sell, and landscapers also came to her for choice plants. Finally, we came to a small section that looked like an orchard. It was full of Rose of Sharon trees of different colors. She said she decided to plant them since that was what got her started in the landscaping business in the first place.

I thought I was pretty good with landscaping terms and plants, but I saw some plants that day I had never seen before, and they were all looking healthy and thriving. She obviously had a real green thumb. She had sunny areas with plants that loved the sunshine, and then in the shady areas were plants that thrived in the shade. I could see how the visitors to the facility would love to walk all around and be close to nature and enjoy the tranquil surroundings.

Finally, we got down near the lake and the cabins, which were neatly laid out in rows like a motel. They were small and a little rustic but also with modern conveniences. We got out of the golf cart and started walking out on the dock. When we got to the end, we sat down and dangled our feet off and looked around at all the sights. From that vantage point, we could see her farmhouse off in the distance. The lake wasn't large enough for motorboats, but they had rowboats, paddle boats, canoes, and kayaks, and there were lots of people busy fishing and swimming.

"How do you like it, Brent?"

"I'm quite impressed. You've really been busy, haven't you?"

"Yes. It's been good therapy for me."

"I'm sorry if I drove you to therapy."

Astana laughed and assured me, "You can't blame yourself for all my problems. I probably needed therapy before you came along. If you remember, I was quite a mess."

"I guess that was arrogant of me to think I could do this much damage," I said as I pointed to all the beauty around me, and we both laughed.

"Well, you did do quite a number on me; that's for sure. But I like to think of it as motivational inspiration instead of therapy."

"Always with a good attitude," I said.

We spent the afternoon sitting in the shade of a tree nearby and caught up more with our thoughts. I was thrilled that she didn't send me off in a huff and was giving me some of her time. It was obvious that she must be a busy woman.

Finally, Astana asked, "How long can you stay? Are you in a hurry to get back home?"

"Well, I took off a few days. Actually, I'm supposed to be working on a case."

"What took you away from the case and brought you all the way out here?"

"You're not going to believe this...I saw your book. I read it all in one night."

"You're kidding. Really?"

Then, laughing, I said, "I'm here to collect my part of the royalties."

She laughed and slapped at my arm like she used to do. Then, I told her some of my thoughts about what I read. "I wasn't absolutely sure who the book was about. I mean, it seemed like me, but there were a lot of issues you brought up about race that I know I didn't tell you. I thought maybe you had developed those thoughts from others who worked on the farm after me, and that was where you got your information...and maybe your inspiration."

Astana looked a little hurt by my remarks but offered an answer, "When I was in college, I met many people from different walks of life. I got involved in peaceful protests and heard many stories from my friends there at college. I even attended one of Martin Luther King's rallies before he was killed."

"Really? That's wonderful. I can picture you now walking around with your braids and carrying a picket sign."

Astana laughed and said, "You had me pegged long ago. Remember telling me I would be marching for causes? What about you? Did you protest in college?"

I looked at her as if she should know the answer. "No. I didn't have time for such foolishness. Not that it wasn't a worthy cause, but I knew I had to finish college and not waste one minute or one dime, and then I could protest on the other end by working for equality through my civil rights practice."

"Leave it to Brent Lake to be practical."

We both smiled, knowing we had both fought for what was right in our own way. Astana stood up, and we headed back to the golf cart and took off again. "Can you stay for supper?" Astana asked.

"That would be nice. Kind of like old times."

When we got back to the farmhouse, we walked in the kitchen. It looked much the same, but Astana had modernized it some with new appliances and decorations. I noticed she still had the framed photo of us sitting on a shelf. She turned to me and asked, "Do you feel comfortable yet coming in a White lady's house?"

"I'm not sure I will ever be totally comfortable doing that, but I feel comfortable coming in your house. It feels like home."

She smiled and then went to the refrigerator and started pulling out leftovers to heat up. She had leftover roast beef with potatoes and carrots all around it. She got out some homemade bread and warmed it up, and the aroma of the yeast bread got my stomach rumbling. When we sat down to eat, Astana reached over for my hand and asked me to say the blessing. Touching her hand after so many years sent chills up and down my spine. I guess I had dreamed of her touch far too long to have it feel any other way. I took a deep breath to calm myself and then began, "Dear Father in heaven, how glorious is Your name. All I can say, Lord, is thank You. Thank You for all You have done in both of our lives. Thank You for giving us a path to success, as nothing comes without Your guidance, strength, and love. Lord, most of all, thank You for putting us together all those years ago so that this meal we are about to share today is all the more special to us. Lord, we beseech You to continue to guide us on the right path, always with You in our plans. In Jesus' name, amen."

Astana squeezed my hand, probably not knowing the power she had in her touch. Then, she put her napkin in her lap and smiled and complimented me on my prayer. While we got started filling our plates, I couldn't help but evaluate my feelings a little bit regarding Astana. When I first met her, I felt she was so much older than me and more mature. I felt we were far apart in most everything. That gap lessened during my time spent with her that summer. And now it felt like there was no gap at all. Yes, I was still in awe of her, but it was not an overpowering awe. More of a respectful awesomeness. I didn't feel like an adolescent anymore.

When we finished, we both stood up and started doing the dishes much like we had done before. I noticed Astana had a dishwasher now, but she said she hardly used it for just one person. It was just as easy to wash them the old-fashioned way. We laughed and continued talking while we stood side-by-side at the counter, both being flooded with so many memories.

I was nervous after we finished up the last of the dishes. I knew I should be heading back home soon, or it would be getting dark on me. But I didn't want to go. Finally, Astana asked, "Are you going back home, or can you stay a day or two?"

"I have some time, but I still doubt that they will allow me to stay at any of the motels in town."

"Sadly, that is probably true. Even after my protest marches, things are rather slow to change." Then, her mind started chasing thoughts, and she said, "You could stay in your old room upstairs...or at one of my cabins."

I smiled at the thought but wasn't sure what I should do. Then, she spoke up again and said, "Why don't you try one of the cabins, and then you can give a report back home in Dallas and maybe send some business my way?"

"That sounds nice. I would like that." She quickly made a phone call and arranged for me to have a cabin. She told the person on the other end of the phone that she would be by to pick up the key shortly. We drove the golf cart back to the lake, stopping first by my car to get my bag before going by the office to pick up the key. When we arrived at the cabin I had been assigned, Astana unlocked the door and showed me around like a realtor would show a potential buyer.

I placed my bag on the bureau. Then, I turned around to face Astana. We chatted for a few minutes, and then she suggested that I come back to her place in the morning for breakfast. I nodded and then walked behind her as she made her way to the door. I thought how funny the day had gone. We had spent the afternoon talking, laughing, and sitting close, but we had not hugged once. She turned around before leaving to get on the golf cart and finally reached up for that hug. It felt so natural but also set off fireworks, just like all the years before. Nothing had changed with my excitement when it came to her touch. I wrapped my arms completely around her and held on tight for as long as I thought was respectful. We had freely shared how we had felt about each other in the past, but I still wasn't sure how she felt about me in the present. I knew she had suffered because of me, and I had done my own share of suffering, so there were still a lot of unanswered questions. Maybe we would explore them tomorrow. I released my tight grip, and she slid out of my arms like a vapor, and off she went into the night.

I had trouble finding sleep that night. Just like so many nights that summer in the past, my mind was going over every little detail of our afternoon together, trying to figure out the nuances of her words and actions. My emotions were restless, and I tossed and turned, unable to find a comfortable position, not because of the discomfort of the bed but because of the discomfort of my raw emotions wrestling each other all night long. It reminded me of Jacob in the Bible wrestling with an angel all night. I figured I would be sore the next morning. One minute I was thrilled to have actually found Astana. Then, more thrilled that she didn't hate me, that she was still single, and that we were still able to have fun together. But then I tried to come to grips with what was next for us. What could be done with our different circumstances? We were still far apart geographically, and we both had our own successful lives. Maybe it was too late to make changes now. Maybe we missed our chance years ago. It was now the late seventies, but race issues were still on edge, especially with interracial marriage. Maybe it would always be that way. We had always tiptoed around that subject and had never really discussed it, probably because, to us, there were no differences to discuss. Astana was well aware of how prejudice followed me from her experiences with me at her church and at the farmer's market with Cleon Jarvis. But she had never really had to deal with what it would be like if the hate was directed at her if she were stuck with me. Judging from what all we had said during the afternoon and how we still reacted to each other's touch, I was almost certain that some discussion was going to happen when we were together the next day. I wasn't sure how I would handle it. Finally, I decided to give it to God. He was going to be up anyway. I ended up praying for guidance, asking God to provide me with the right words to say. Finally, I was able to close my eyes and fall asleep in complete peace.

The next morning, I woke up to a beautiful sunrise and remembered so many summer mornings when I saw that same sunrise at the same spot and at such a pivotal time in my life. I smiled, knowing I was back there in the moment, if only for a short while, and it brought me a joy I had not felt in a long time.

I dressed in similar clothes as the day before because those were all I brought with me on my trip to New York City. At least I ditched the tie and rolled up my shirtsleeves. I had no idea back when I left on my trip about the book or that I would be taking off on a detour.

I enjoyed the casual morning stroll back to Astana's house, observing all the different scenic areas along the path. I stopped at my car to drop off my bag. When I got to the farmhouse, I gently tapped on the same screen door from days gone by and smiled again as all those memories washed over me. I was living through some kind of time suspension where I was living in the present, but I was also consumed with ancient memories. It was a weird space to be occupying.

Astana came to the door all smiles, just as she used to do. Instead of inviting me inside, she came out on the porch and said, "We're going to have breakfast over at the little café down the path over there," and she pointed in the direction we would take. Then, she added, "Before, when you were here, we couldn't go to a restaurant or café together, but we can now. I always wanted to have that experience with you, and I'm not going to let it slip away." She smiled when she made her big announcement.

We headed off walking down the path, and I jokingly said, "I just figured in your old age you didn't cook anymore."

Astana slapped at my arm while laughing her great laugh and said, "How rude."

We entered the small café and found a seat. Everyone who worked there knew Astana, so I had to remark, "You eat here often, I gather?"

"No, not really. But I do know all the staff out here at the resort. They're sort of like family to me now."

We laughed, enjoying each other's company. I looked around the room and noticed people of different races sitting, and no one was staring. It felt good to have this opportunity to enjoy a normal social experience with Astana and to feel so comfortable about it. It was the late seventies, and I had been allowed in restaurants for quite some time. I often ate out with my co-workers in Dallas. But I had never had the pleasure of that experience with Astana. We ordered our breakfast, and it was out quickly. We ate and then sipped on our coffee and chatted for a while like this was a normal everyday occurrence, eating out together.

When we finished, I reached in my pocket to pay for the meal, but Astana assured me that there was no need. She told me she received her meals free of charge since it was on her property. She laughed and said, "Of course, if you ate with me all the time, they would probably revoke my privileges due to your huge appetite."

We strolled back to her farmhouse, looking at different flowers along the way. Once again, we sat out on the porch swing, enjoying the cool morning air and listening to the eager birds already busy with their chores. Even though I never considered myself a farmer type, I did enjoy nature. Any time I got to spend close to nature, I considered a treat.

Astana wanted to know all about my law firm and what I felt about the cases I was working on. It was hard to try to spin boring research into any kind of interesting story, but she found it all fascinating. I asked her about what she was doing with her life. She told me about her many activities and interests. She said she had enjoyed writing her book, so she was working on another one. She liked getting things out of her cluttered mind and organized on paper. Then, she laughed and said, "Living all these years alone, it feels like I finally have someone to talk to through my writing."

She changed the subject and said, "A year or so ago, I went to my ten-year class reunion at the high school. It was a lot of fun seeing everyone again. But it was also sad seeing that most of my classmates were married and had families. There I was, all alone with no kid stories to tell. Pretty pathetic, I guess."

"I doubt that anyone thought of you as pathetic. They probably envied you with your large farm, that you never gave up on, by the way, and all you have accomplished, including being an author. How many of your classmates have written a book? You've made this place into a showcase. I'm sure people know of this place from miles away, probably even many states away by now. I bet some were wishing they had your life. Heck, you could write another book—maybe a gardening book—describing all your plants and telling people how to grow them."

"That's sweet of you to say, Brent. You always had a way of rearranging my negative thoughts and turning them into positive ones with goals attached. That attitude helped me change my path years ago. I was your boss, but you ended up being my teacher. Strange when you think of it."

"I bet you were the youngest looking lady at your class reunion. You still look like a teenager."

She slapped at me again and said, "Hush your mouth. You know how I feel about teenagers." We both laughed again, enjoying our mutual humor, and I wondered if our behavior was normal for old friends getting reacquainted or if this was something special and different.

I lowered my head that was heavy with so many thoughts going around in circles. I was loving every minute with Astana and hated the thought that eventually, I had to get back to Dallas and back to work, or I would lose my job. I felt a closeness to her like no one I had ever known, but we had made such a practice of avoiding our real feelings because of our past situation, with me being her younger employee, and we were still in that rut. I felt like we were so comfortable in the rut that it was hard to take a leap of faith and step out of it to see where we might be headed. I finally felt I should make that move first.

I slowly looked up and saw her eyes staring back at me. She had a sweet, contented smile on her face. She looked exactly the same as she did ten years ago, but maybe more beautiful. I wondered what she thought of me. She had said I had grown into a handsome man, but what did that mean exactly?

Finally, I opened my mouth, and words came out. "Astana, what are you thinking about all this, you know, seeing each other again after so many years?"

She still had that big smile on her face as she rolled her eyes around as if looking for the right words to answer my question. "I guess the best words I could use to describe how I feel is that I feel somewhat complete. That probably doesn't make much sense to you, but before yesterday, I had this hole in my heart that I could never fill no matter what I did or how many successes I had in my life. There was always something missing. That something was you, and I knew it as soon as I laid eyes on you yesterday, standing there all tall and handsome. It was like glue had been dropped in that hole, and it was sealed. Now, I don't know how long it will remain sealed once you walk away from here. But right now, it feels really good."

I had been smiling the whole time she was talking about her feelings until she made that last statement. Then, I realized the pressure was turned back on me as to how this visit would turn out. All I could think for a minute was about the fear I had of disappointing her again. I remembered the look on her face that morning when I ran out on her and left her standing in her pretty nightgown with no hopes for any kind of future other than a vapor of a promise that I didn't really keep. I wanted to squirm from the discomfort I was feeling because of all that pressure, but I remained calm as if processing her words. I knew they needed a response.

"Seeing you has filled a hole in my heart too," I finally said. "I've stuffed my life as well as my emotions with my studies and my work. Now that things are starting to slow down, it has given me more time to think about all I've missed out on, and I definitely see a huge crater has been left in the wake of all my sacrifices. This whole time I knew you were the only one who could ever fill that empty space in my heart."

Astana responded back in a cautious tone, "How do you feel about me now that we've had this short time together? Have your feelings changed?"

Words were starting to come to the surface and spill out all over me, making a huge mess. "You don't know how thrilled I was to find that book of yours staring me in the face and, of all places in the world, in New York City, a place so far removed from either of us. After reading it, I didn't know if you would be here or if I would ever be able to find you. But I was prepared to search this whole area if I had to. I already planned to try to find Opal or other members from the church. Heck, I was even prepared to track down Cleon Jarvis if I had to."

That remark set off our laughter. "I was scared to turn down this lane to your house for fear of finding him running this place now. I certainly didn't expect to find you so easily, to find you walking down a path toward me looking as beautiful as I had remembered. But I was scared to death you were married, and your husband might come after me with a shotgun for approaching you."

We sat there, both soaking up our words that had been shared back and forth. Our minds were trying to process what we were hearing and compare it to our past emotions, along with new expectations, and then trying to comprehend where we stood in our own separate worlds now in present time. I still found Astana's veiled words hard to fully grasp and understand. I had never been a person who took hints easily. I had to have things spelled out for me. I was a little backward emotionally and wasn't sure how to navigate my feelings still to this day.

Astana finally said softly, "Now that you've found me, what are you thinking?"

"I guess it depends on what you're thinking," was my lame answer.

"I'm thinking," then she stopped abruptly and shook her head back and forth as if trying to edit her original thoughts.

"No, what are you thinking?" I asked again in a more urgent tone.

"I'm thinking I'm afraid to tell you what I'm thinking."

"What? You don't have to ever be afraid to tell me anything. Don't you think after all the pain we have both suffered all these years, we can take the truth for once? One thing we have both been exceptionally good at is holding back our feelings. Don't you think it's time we lay it all out on the table and let the cards fall where they may? If nothing else, at least we can live the rest of our lives knowing what we were both truly thinking. Don't we deserve that much?"

Astana nodded her head slowly up and down and then began again, "What I'm thinking is that I don't know if I can take you walking out on me again. I managed before, but I don't know if I can do it again. In reality, I know just because you found my book and just because you drove all this way to see me doesn't mean you are ready to permanently fill that hole you left behind all those years ago."

Tears were starting to trickle down Astana's cheeks. I reached for her hand, and we both sighed, knowing how hard our words were to spit out and how hard they were to swallow.

"Astana, I have wanted you for so long. Heck, I started wanting you that day I sat here on this porch and helped you shuck that corn, and I caught a glimpse of your pretty legs coming out of the bottom of those baggy overalls." Astana laughed at my remark and wiped away her tears. "That was the first day you actually carried on a conversation with me, and I think we clicked right then. That was the first time you flashed that big smile of yours that lit up your beautiful eyes. I saw an amazing joy in your face that day. It felt so genuine. Those pictures of you I've carried around with me all these years are about worn out. I see now they are no substitute for the real you. They definitely don't do you justice. Right now, my heart feels like I could easily call my law firm and tell them to shove my job that I have worked for all my life just so I could stay here with you."

I saw Astana now beaming and maybe feeling a little bolder with her own thoughts. She looked at me again and said, "I let you go once, Brent, but I don't think I can do it again. When you were here that summer, I had to watch my behavior. I knew my family and everyone in town were all watching my every move.

At first, I didn't think there would be a problem that I would have to keep in check since we came from two different worlds. I tried to think of us as aliens in some science fiction movie trying to function on the same planet temporarily. Remember my childhood story I heard that blue birds and red birds can't get married?" I nodded, and she continued, "In a way, I think that helped me relax around you, knowing there was no way we could be anything but friends. I finally let someone see the real me. And I think it was the same for you after a while. I imagine you thought of me as *off-limits*. You didn't have any plans about pursuing me, and therefore, there was no pressure. But what happened when we let our guard down was a true friendship."

Astana paused to regroup. "But then I think it grew into love. I wasn't prepared for missing you so much after you left. As the agony of missing you wore on, I tried to move forward without you. But there was always that tiny hope that maybe you would come back, and I couldn't completely let that go. I always held out a glimmer of hope that you might see my book, but it was a pipe dream. I tried to replace you by dating when I was in college, but nothing felt right. All my dates just made me think of you and miss you even more. Finally, I gave up and settled on being some old spinster for the rest of my life. I thought I had forgotten all about you, and I was positive you had forgotten about me. Then, I saw you standing there in front of me with your hands on your hips looking so handsome, and everything came crashing down all around me once again."

"Astana, I didn't want to walk out on you that day. I tried my best to think of my home as I rode on that truck to the bus station. What I discovered was this farm and my life with you had become my home. I certainly didn't want to hurt you. But I had the restraints of youth. I was living with my parents and still in high school. I had no control over what happened that day."

Astana jumped in and said, "I kind of hoped that you might seek me out once you graduated from high school. I pictured us struggling through college together but in total bliss."

I smiled, thinking of her dreams from the past. "I could have used you for sure. But I knew I didn't have anything to offer you. I could barely support myself. And you are so beautiful I figured you would have found a good husband by then and no longer remembered that young snot-nosed kid who worked for you one summer."

I paused to gather my thoughts before continuing on. We were both smiling, and I assumed it was from the thought of our many shared memories. I cleared my throat and then started up again, "All that is behind us. I don't know what your situation is now or how free you are. I am just getting started in my practice, so I have to stay where I am and get established."

"I understand your situation," Astana responded. "After all your hard work, you have to pursue the career you have worked for all your life. But do you have room for someone in your life?"

"Now, I've got room for you, and I have some sort of decent lifestyle to offer you. I never had that before." Then, laughing, I added, "But compared to what you have here, my lifestyle might not be all that inviting."

Astana laughed and said, "Maybe I could take care of you then."

Suddenly, I felt the full force of all my emotions that I had been holding back for so many years. They were charging me like a mighty army. My eyes began to moisten up, and my hands were shaking as I attempted to get out my words. "Astana, I love you so much. I always wondered if what I felt for you was love, but after all the years and then after seeing you again, I am positive that the word 'love' perfectly defines what I am feeling for you."

"Brent, I love you too and always have. It's not even debatable."

I could feel my practical brain cells trying to make their way to the surface to take over the conversation, and they kept screaming out, *But you will have this problem, and you will have that problem!* I decided they needed to be addressed and see where Astana stood on the subject. I closed my eyes so she couldn't see the pain I was seeing in our future if we were to be together. Then, I opened them to face her and started expressing my concerns, "My only fear is what we may face if we were to become a couple. I have known a few of my friends who have gone down that path, and I have seen their struggles. It's not easy."

"Brent, I'm not as sheltered as I appear. I found out a lot about those struggles when I was in college. I don't want trouble. I would be crazy to say that I was looking for trouble because that is not who I am. All I know is that I love the Black part of you; I love the Indian blood that runs through your veins and the White blood. I love all of you. When I look at you, I just see who you are, Reginald Brent Lake, a beautiful soul and a great-looking man. I couldn't tell you how much I loved your handsome looks when you were here. I didn't think it was appropriate back then in that moment. Besides, there were so many other qualities I loved about you besides your physical appearance. I loved that you loved the Lord. I loved that you were so disciplined and you worked so hard. I admired so many qualities about you. I looked up to you. Then, there was our chemistry. Your touch or our closeness brought pure excitement all over my body like I'd never felt before. Now, I want to be your helpmate, and together, we can get through whatever struggles we have to face. Remember the Bible verse that says, 'If God is for you, who can be against you?' I want to show the world our love and how normal we are together. With God's help, I want to be that future that Opal saw in us all those years ago."

"You make it sound so easy."

"No, I don't think it will be easy. But I refuse to back down from a fight."

"What about our children? Do you want to put all that burden on them?" I didn't give Astana a chance to respond to that question. I suddenly stood straight up, startling her and causing the swing to sway back and forth. That long-awaited panic attack started creeping boldly to the forefront of my emotions. It was quickly out of control and taking over my body, making me feel like I couldn't breathe. I didn't want Astana to see me that way. I wasn't experienced in how to handle the flurry of emotions that had overtaken me so quickly. I suddenly blurted out the words, "I'm sorry, but I have to leave."

Astana stood up from the swaying swing as I turned to leave, and she shouted, "Brent, you can't do this to me again."

I stopped in my tracks with my back to her, and she continued, "I understand your concerns, but you're not giving me any credit here, and you're not including me in the discussion. Something happened to me that day at the Friendship Holy

Church when you were treated badly. I swore when we drove away from that building that I would never allow someone to treat me badly again or anyone that I love. I will not stand for it. That is why I marched in protests in college and I used my artistic talents in making picket signs expressing the needs of our movement."

I answered back in between my waves of panic and said, "That's not the same as living daily in the prejudiced world that I live in."

"You don't realize that White people fighting for Black causes are treated with hatred too. I've already experienced that. Sometimes both sides hate you. But I made my choice long ago on that issue. I guess all your years with your nose in the books caused you to bypass what was going on all around you. You missed the movement I was fighting for. How can you fight for the civil rights for other people when you won't even fight for them in your own life? If that's your attitude, then I fear you will not be a successful attorney."

I stood there with no words to respond. All I could do was try to focus on calming my breathing and the out-of-control panic racing through my body. I had never experienced anything like what was happening to me before, and I was scared.

In my silence, Astana started up again, "Brent, if you're not willing to fight for us, then what we had was not love. When you truly love someone, you will do whatever it takes to be together. It is *impossible* to be apart. I know we have both managed to survive without each other and have even managed to become quite successful. But if you walk away again, I will know for sure that what we had that summer was not love. It was just a teenage fantasy all along. You say, 'What if we have problems? What if our children have problems?' What kind of argument is that for a lawyer? You are supposed to fight, not give up without a struggle. If we were together, I would walk proudly, showing the whole world our love. Who knows, maybe we could be a part of changing the world. Or maybe our children will change the world. But you can't go around saying *what if* about everything. What if we're conquerors? You will never make a great attorney if you can't even sum up the case for your own happiness and for your future. Think about that."

My panic still wouldn't budge. It would not let me think about anything but the panic and how I was losing the battle of its control over my body. I pressed my hand to my forehead and started to leave, but Astana stopped me with her words once more. "I waited for you for ten years. I began to think waiting was the one thing I was really good at. After all, in my mind, I felt like I had been waiting for Robert to return from the war, and then I was waiting for you to return like you promised. But if you walk away from me again, I won't be sitting here waiting another ten years."

My heart was breaking. I finally realized the mistake I had made by avoiding emotions and relationships all my life. That must be why I couldn't deal with them now. Most people experienced little skirmishes with relationships from puberty to adulthood, but I missed out on all that. I'm sure some fancy therapist could have a hay day analyzing this mess for me. All I could do was sigh softly and then step off the porch and walk away. I tried to get away as fast as I could, but my legs felt numb. I kept pushing them forward, trying to walk swiftly down the path to try to find my car.

In my confusion, I didn't even remember where I had parked my car. I suddenly felt like I was in a race to get to it. Finally, I saw it on the last row of cars, and I quickly fumbled for my keys in my pocket and unlocked the door to crawl into the hot car that had been shut up in the heat of the day. I immediately turned the key and cranked up the air conditioner. I tried deep breathing to calm myself down. It wasn't working. I put the car in reverse and backed out of my parking space. Then, I headed down the long lane I had traveled so many times before. The same lane that had been in my memories for the past ten years. I tried to analyze my panic attack, and I blamed it on how I had worked so hard all my years of schooling since first grade through law school as an excuse to avoid my real life. Studying had been like a drug, masking my emotions and my fears. In the process of accomplishing my goal, I sacrificed everything, including my chance for happiness and love. Why had I chosen such a complicated relationship for my one true love? Obviously, when I was faced with the freedom to seek love and grab hold of my life, the panic slipped in through a crack right when I let my guard down.

I rolled down the window to get some fresh air as I attempted again to calm myself down. Sweat was beading up on my face. My hands, which were gripping the steering wheel, were shaking. I started looking at the trees I had planted in the lane there at the farm. Memories of that more relaxed summer started coming to the surface. The summer air hit my nostrils, and it was so familiar. I began to get some relief from the pure panic that had struck me. Suddenly, the tension started to ease.

When I got to the end of the lane and looked again at the landscaping I had done to the entrance of the farm, I smiled, and that brought about a wave of peace, thinking how my work had gotten me through hard times that summer and healed my loneliness. I closed my eyes for a minute and placed my head on the backs of my hands that were holding the steering wheel. Then, memories of that day when I sat in the back of the truck as I was leaving the farm hit me. Suddenly, I could feel those same feelings once again. How something other than panic took over my body that morning. It was pure desperation to not lose the love I had found that summer. I could picture getting up and banging on the truck for Mr. Turner to stop and let me out. I remembered the sprint back to my apartment and bursting through the door to see Astana. Suddenly, my body began to change from panic to exhilaration. Those memories were so fresh now, and they replaced the dread and trepidation that I was feeling just a few minutes ago. I still had my head down on my hands, and I continued my deep breathing. Suddenly, a horn honked from behind me. When I raised my head and looked in the rearview mirror, I saw a car had been sitting behind me and was getting frustrated. I raised my hand and then took off, only to make a big sweeping U-turn, stirring up some dust, as I spun my car around and headed back down the lane.

Panic tried to work itself back up to the surface, as I worried that Astana would not welcome me back when I so gallantly returned. She may not find it gallant at all this time. She had told me she would not wait for me. Then, I began to panic that I would be overcome with nerves again if I tried to be convincing. How many times would she allow me to let her down?

After I pulled up in the parking lot and parked, I took out a handkerchief and wiped the sweat from my face, and once again took a deep breath. I also said a quick prayer because I definitely needed more to lean on than my own understanding and strength. Finally, I opened the door and got out of the car. I hurried back to the farmhouse, but Astana was not there on the porch where I had left her. I tapped on the screen door, but she didn't come to let me inside. Finally, I started walking around the grounds. As I strolled around the yard, I came upon Astana sitting on the bench I had made for her long ago. She had her head down and her hands folded in her lap as if in prayer. Astana looked up with a shocked look on her face when I approached. I didn't know what to expect at this point. She might be prepared to slap me across the face after all I had put her through and how little I had fought for us just a few minutes earlier. I cracked a halfhearted smile and asked, "What are you doing?"

She quickly replied, "I've been sitting here praying about how I'm going to get all of those yellow ribbons out of that tree. What you are you doing back here?"

With a wink and a quick smile, I said, "I had a sudden urge for a biscuit."

It took a minute, and I could see Astana mentally processing my words. Then, she slowly allowed her lips to spread across her face and light up her eyes, remembering that I had grabbed a biscuit that morning long ago. I could sense she understood my message. She stood up and walked closer to me, and we slid together like we had always been meant for each other. Our lips touched with the same passionate explosion as our last kiss, and we didn't want to let go. Immediately, all my stress and all my worries about a future together faded away as quickly as they had attacked me in the first place.

I took hold of Astana's hands and held them in front of us. By then, we were both smiling. "Astana, I promise I will stay as long as necessary to claim my life, my love. I will never leave you again. But please be patient with me and realize that loving someone is so new to me. I am not sure I know how. But I am positive I want to try, and I know you are the one who can teach me. I want to practice it and put as much drive and determination in loving you as I have put in reaching my other goals. Will you help me with that?"

Astana smiled even broader and nodded, trying to hold back her tears. I looked at her with such love. Here we were, finally talking about life as an interracial married couple, blue birds and red birds. I think we were both remembering the kiss from the past that had carried us through our memories for all those years we had been apart. I scooted even closer to Astana and wrapped my arms around her tightly. The warmth of her body set off the same kind of electrical charge that had always gone all over me since her first touch. Looking into her amazing eyes, I asked, "Would you like to come home with me and meet my family? We can see how that goes. Then, we can see how life is in Dallas. If it is too difficult there, I can transfer to a California law firm and see how we fit in out there. If we are still not happy, then I guess we can always come back here and make the most of our talents in the little community of Echo Falls."

"Brent, we are going to be just fine no matter where we go. Eventually, we were accepted here in Echo Falls, so we will fit in anywhere. And the answer is yes to going home with you. I can't wait to meet your family."

Astana reached her hand up to my face and stroked it softly. I could see her eyes dancing with excitement. I stroked her hair and pushed it behind her ears before leaning closer and taking another kiss, just like I had longed for and dreamed of for so many years. Like that summer morning when I took off running down the road after jumping off Mr. Turner's truck, this kiss was just as wonderful, even more so, knowing it was the beginning of a lifetime of kisses.

That day Astana packed some bags, and we took off for Horseshoe Junction. Momma was thrilled when she saw us come through the door. Immediately, Astana fit right in with my family and around town just like she did when she walked into Whispering Hope Chapel years earlier. I am sure there were some who had negative thoughts about us as a couple. That was just the way it was back in those days. Some may have accused me of being uppity. That was a common accusation, and they thought it anyway because of my successful career. I was not in control of their thoughts. I finally had a life to live. I had waited long enough for it. I had sacrificed enough for it. I was grabbing it and never letting it get away from me again, no matter who approved of us. We both decided that night that we were going to listen to our hearts from now on. We didn't want to miss out on the blessings God had in store for the two of us any longer.

From there, we caught a flight to Dallas. I was much more concerned about how Brighton & Wakefield would accept my future wife and me because it could be a game-changer for them if they felt it was a problem for the firm. I was prepared to turn in my resignation if they were not accepting. When we started walking down the streets of downtown Dallas that morning to go to the office, Astana reached over and took hold of my hand. She looked at me with a smile and raised eyebrows as if to say, *We've got this, Brent.* Her bravery surprised me but also encouraged me. At first, I was nervous and shy about holding the hand of a White woman, making it obvious that she was not a client or just a friend. But with each step we took, the more confidence I felt racing through my body. In the beginning of that long walk, I felt my head lower a bit, and I didn't make eye contact with anyone. As we continued on, I began to raise my head higher and became more empowered. I started looking everyone in the eye, giving my traditional nods of hello and good morning. Astana clutched my arm tighter and chatted joyfully as we walked, showing everyone that she was one happy lady and she had won the prize she had been waiting for.

When we arrived at the office, I knew Astana would sell herself when everyone met her. She had that kind of personality. Just like I described to my momma years before, when Astana walked in the office, she lit up the room, and everyone gravitated toward her. She put us all at ease with her professional but cheerful conversation. She had a way of making us all feel equal, and before the meeting was over, she had sold the two of us like we were a matching set of luggage in their eyes. When questions arose, Astana posed a question or two of her own. *Were any other employees at Brighton & Wakefield investigated about who they chose to marry? Why would a law firm that specializes in civil rights only investigate the private life of one of their few Black employ-*

ees? By the end of the discussion, my boss suggested that maybe the firm should look into hiring Astana if she ever decided to go into law.

We didn't feel the need to tell our whole story of how we met. It was obvious that we knew each other very well, and we had put our relationship on hold in order for me to finish my education. The firm seemed to like the discipline we had displayed in our lives and how we had arranged our long-range goals. After a few meetings with the top attorneys in the firm, it was agreed that my personal life was not a problem to the firm. They even suggested that it could be an asset since we were both actively involved in civil rights. Everyone that met us remarked that we were a very handsome couple and made a great team.

I took some time off, and we were married on Astana's farm under the white gazebo surrounded by color, the color of people and beautiful blooming plants. It was a day to remember with both families mingling in harmony. Many of my attorney friends were also there, as well as some close classmates I had met over the years and members of the Whispering Hope congregation. The only sad note that day was when we both shared our thoughts, saying how sad we were that we had wasted ten years waiting to finally be together, but we felt there must be a reason our love took the long twisted journey it did. We were just thankful that I found Astana's book sitting in the display window that day in New York City, and it led me back to Echo Falls, and I finally found my love. We planned to make up for those wasted years, and I think it helped us to never take each other or our love for granted. All we had to do was to think back to our time apart, and that caused us to hold on even tighter to what we had finally found in each other.

Life was not always rosy. There were times when we faced hardships. Not financial hardships but hurt feelings due to ignorant people. It hurt me to be the source of that kind of pain for my family, and I struggled with guilt, but Astana always laughed it off and kept moving forward. I would often re-hash all my old worries, and Astana would set me straight. She would say, "What I want is for you, me, and our future children to change the world. Let's be happy and make others envy what we have between us. We will raise our children to be happy and to love everyone. When people see us walking down the street, they will be thinking, *What a lovely, brave family they are.*"

"Are you sure you're not an artist?" I would ask. "You paint everything so rosy. There will be those who try to spoil our pretty picture."

"Of course, there will. So are we supposed to live apart and give up a great love because there *might* be some problems? That's not how I roll. Just ask Cleon Jarvis."

I couldn't help but laugh, remembering Astana hitting Cleon in the chest with both fists flying so fast they were a blur. "I believe you."

Astana would question me, asking, "Are you going to walk out on me again?"

"Frankly, I would be afraid to try that move ever again," I would answer with a big smile on my face. But then a worried look would cross my face, and I would repeat my old line, "You don't know how hurt I will be, though, if you or our future children ever have to suffer because of me. It will break my heart if I ever see you attacked because of me when I know you could have easily walked away."

Astana would assure me that walking away was never an option for her, and she would add, "Brent, I understand how you feel. But we have to stand up for our love. We have to stand up for what's right. You know some people will hate us for being Christians, but you're not going to give up on the Lord, are you?"

"No, of course not," I would say. Then I would begin again with possible negative aspects to our situation, "We will have to get used to being stared at and hearing whispers behind our backs."

Astana would speak up abruptly, "I won't be able to hear them because of all our laughter, and I will be too busy looking into your eyes to see them staring at us."

Things did change over the years, but some things remained the same. We decided not to allow ourselves to be shackled by folks who would not accept the changes. Just like in Echo Falls, people in Dallas quit noticing us as different. We were just two people who loved each other. We had a variety of friends, and through their friendship with us, we bridged a lot of gaps. People from both sides were finding new connections with each other through their association with us and discovering similarities they never dreamed of. We always remembered Opal telling us that we were the future, and we hoped we made her proud.

Through our contacts in Dallas, we sent a lot of business to our Liberty Lake Resort, and that helped us with our business there in Echo Falls. It was also a very nice vacation spot for us and also a great place to gather for our family reunions over the years. It continued to be an oasis in the south that literally represented all colors with all the beautiful flowers everywhere on the farm and with all the different races of people freely running around enjoying visits there.

Astana finally had her chance at motherhood. We had our first child, a baby girl, and we named her Liberty La' Shore Lake. She was as beautiful as her name. She was a beacon to the future. Liberty brought us great joy. She loved both sides of her family equally. To her, there were no differences. We were all just family. She had her mother's beautiful aqua eyes with the same sparkle. She also had Astana's bold, uninhibited personality and her great laugh. From me, she got her drive and determination. The love we all shared together dispelled the myth about blue birds and red birds mingling. For the first time in my life, I felt as though people began to see me as Reginald Brent Lake, loving husband to Astana and devoted father to Liberty, a darn good attorney, and a good Christian man. Every day was a blessing, and I always gave the good Lord all the praise and glory for the blessings in my life. I felt liberated, always moving forward and never looking back to dredge up old wounds or to dwell on hatred. There was no room for that in my life, and I wasn't going to let anything rob me of my joy.

Looking back on our lives, we realize we were trailblazers. We now see interracial couples of all colors and mixed children everywhere, and there are no longer lingering stares or shocked facial expressions. We remember when that was not the case. Astana helped me overcome my early fears for my family. She wouldn't let us hide away, hoping no one would notice us. She was always out front and center, getting involved in Dallas' society, and she made being different seem vogue. With her help, I learned to really live my life, unabashedly proud of my beautiful mixed-up family.

Everyone has their own story. This is mine. We all play the cards we're dealt. Back then, some were deeply scarred by their experiences in the Vietnam war. Others never got over the struggles and cruelties of the civil rights movement and the pain they suffered. As a Christian, I made the decision to live each day as a child of God, letting the beauty of Jesus be seen in me through my actions. That's how I let go of my anger, along with the help of my Lord.

I could have chosen hate. It was there for the taking, and some may say I earned it. But when I think about the life my Father has planned for me, I have to choose love.

Chapter 23: Astana's Reflection

I slowly closed the journal with a sigh, feeling so lucky to have found it. I would have it from now on whenever I needed to be reminded of our love. It was more special to me to have our story in his own words.

I was so proud of him for his determination from such an early age. He lived the life he had planned. He was a successful attorney and had a very fulfilling career helping others. We did a lot of volunteer work together and contributed to many charities over the years. We saw a lot of changes in society but realized that there would always be work left to do. He was a loving father and raised Liberty in the ways of the Lord. That, too, made me proud. He was a shining example for us to look up to.

He promised he would never leave me again. He knew how much time I had spent waiting. It was just not in our plan. I was two years older than him, so we never considered he would check out first. Then, just as we were relaxing in our retirement back on the farm, he left. This time, he did not leave me alone. I had our daughter and our grandkids. That made a big difference, but it still never soothed the ache I had from missing him.

I missed the two of us sitting on the porch swing talking about old times from when we first met. Sitting out there that morning, I could see visions of us in our beginning stages when we were first falling in love.

When the grandchildren arrived that afternoon, they immediately climbed up on the porch swing with me as they always did. Tears were trickling down my face over the beaming smile I had plastered there. They were startled and confused when they saw me. Liberty started asking questions right away, wondering what was wrong. I simply replied, "I received a surprise visit from Gramps today."

They were excited about the journal when I showed it to them. Liberty wanted to read it immediately, but I reminded her that I had plans with her and the grandchildren first. I went inside the house for a few minutes and returned with a bright red ribbon in my hand. "We're going to put a new ribbon on the tree for Gramps. I put a red ribbon on last year when he left me, and it's time to add another one."

We left the journal resting on the porch swing and took off for the famous ribbon tree, as the kids called it. It created lots of shade now, and they often liked to ask me questions about the different colored ribbons and have me tell stories about the people they represented. They loved to roll around on the plush grass there, not realizing their Gramps started that grass years ago. When I finished tying the red ribbon on the tree and backed away so we could look at it, my youngest granddaughter tugged at my skirt tail and asked, "Grammy, what color of ribbon do you want us to put on the tree for you?"

In my mind, I could hear Brent rolling with laughter at her question. It made me smile, knowing we were still so connected that way with our forever humor. I smiled and told her they could pick some bright color that would remind them of me, and that would make me happy.

Soon, I was asked to tell them stories about the ribbons. When they heard again about their grandpa, they said they felt sad for me. It wasn't long before I broke into the story from *The King and I* and reminded the grandchildren that not long ago I had a love of my own, and I started singing the lyrics loudly of "Hello Young Lovers Wherever You Are." They laughed and held their ears, acting embarrassed that their grandparents were ever young and in love.

About the Author

Janis Crockett lives in Round Rock, Texas, with her husband, Willie. She enjoys time with her family and especially with her grandchildren. She is also active in her church activities and different ministries.

CPSIA information can be obtained
at www.ICGtesting.com
Printed in the USA
LVHW080024110422
715852LV00007B/188